I0822660

ECHOES OF A CRIMSON STORM

VOLUMES OF ELEMENTUM
VOLUME III

Echoes of a Crimson Storm
Volumes of Elementum
Volume III
by Megan L. Adams

Published by Golden Tome Press

Editing by Shelley Lopez

ISBN:)Hardback) 979-8-9899327-2-6
ISBN: (Paperback) 9798294177621
ASIN: (ebook) B0G32WG46Z

Volumes of Elementum

Shadows Within the Fire

Bound by Earth and Ice

Echoes of a Crimson Storm

In loving memory of my Papa,
Ronald Wesley Weber
April 10, 1928 to November 17, 2024

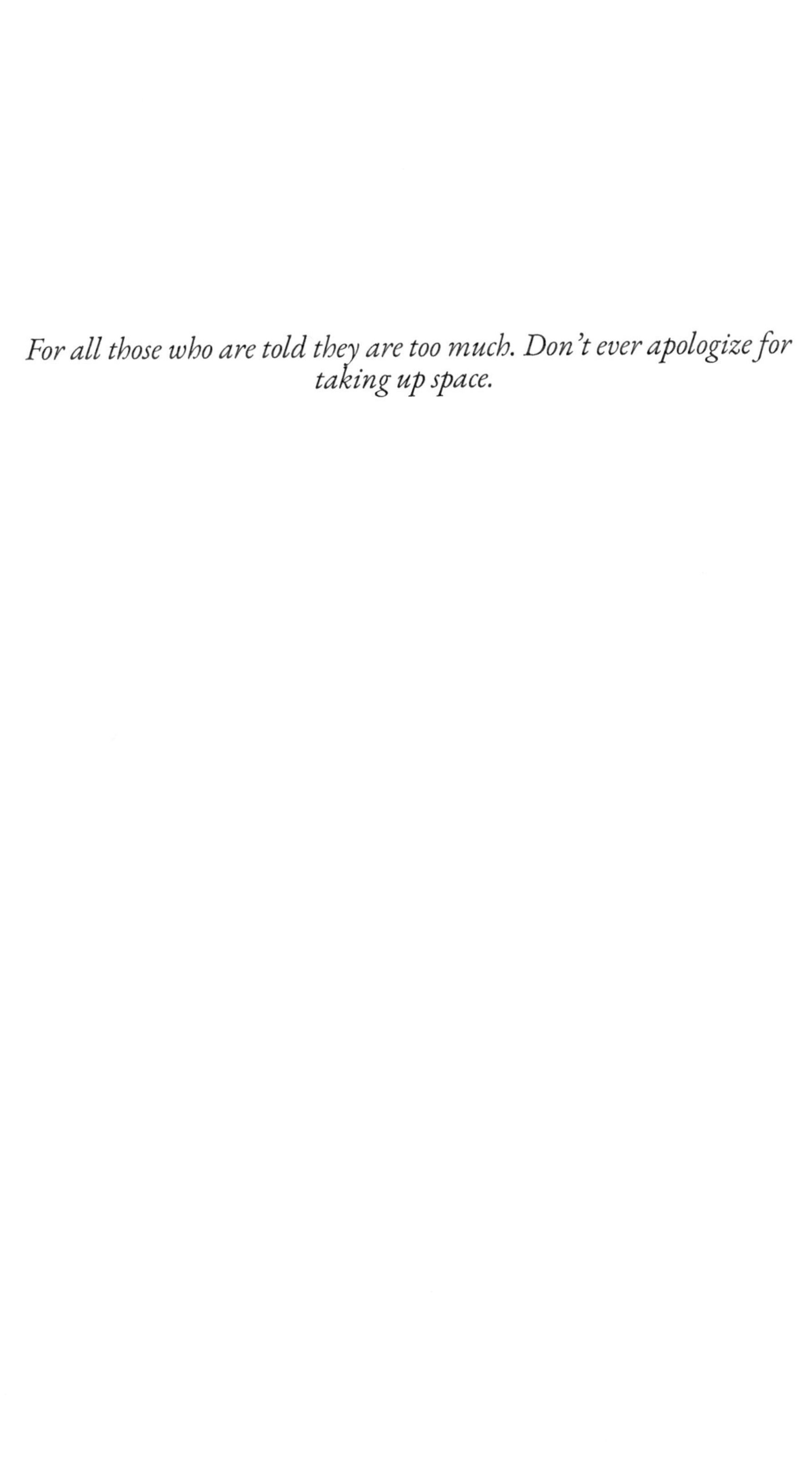

For all those who are told they are too much. Don't ever apologize for taking up space.

QUINTERRE
AGNI
ANRUIN TEMPLE
BAXMAR RANGE
FIRE FAE KINGDOM
AIR FAE KINGDOM
LAETO SELVA
FOREST FAE KINGDOM
MALLA RIVER
GEYSA
TASKUN TERRITORY
GLISSDEN
MOUNT LENDORR
NOIRDAN LUMIR
WATER FAE KINGDOM
RAVEN FAE KINGDOM
KOSMIMA
THE MORTAL RE
Cassandra Lynn 2025

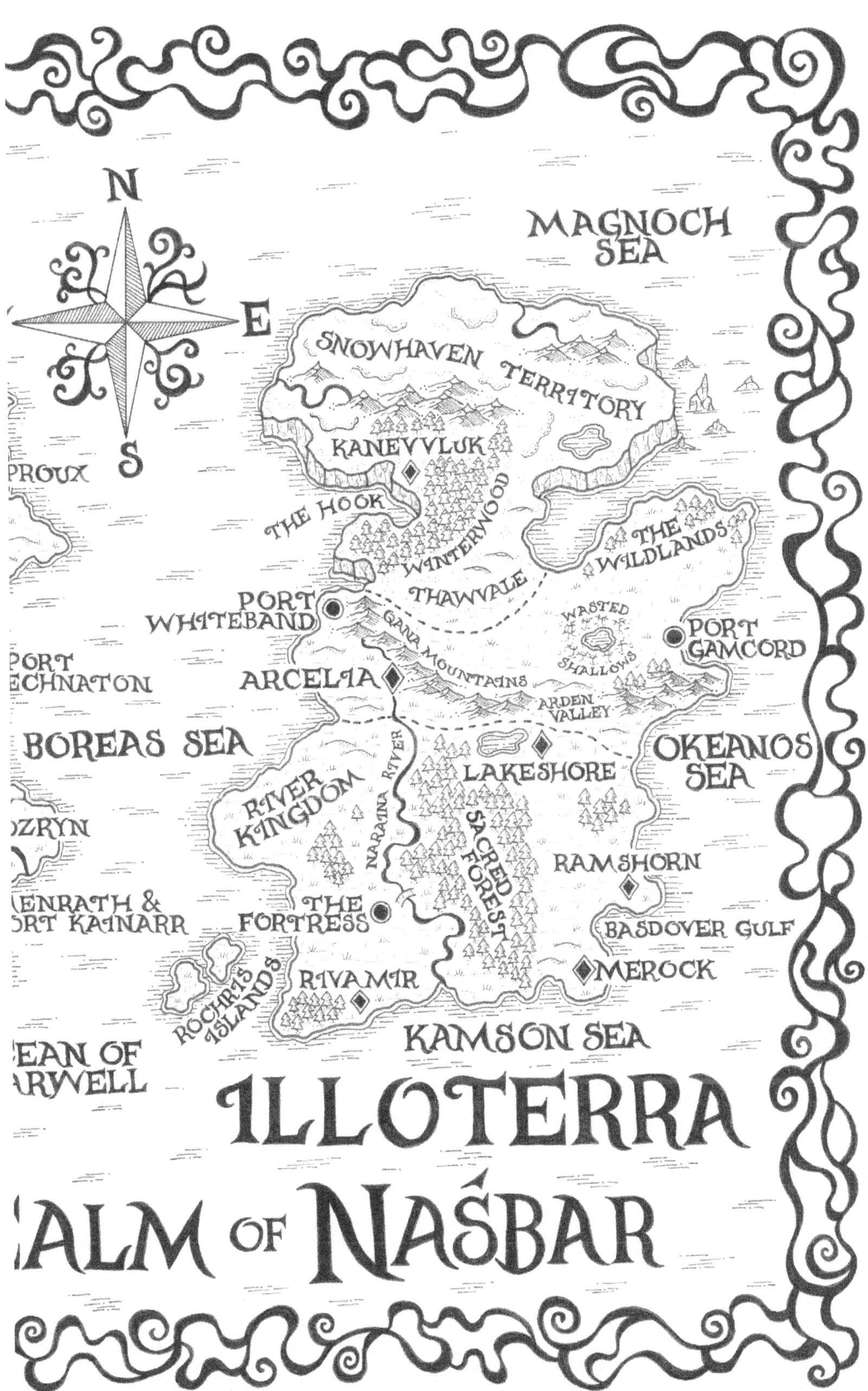

N
E
S
MAGNOCH SEA
SNOWHAVEN TERRITORY
KANEVVLUK
THE HOOK
WINTERWOOD
THE WILDLANDS
THAWVALE
PORT WHITEBAND
QANA MOUNTAINS
WASTED SHALLOWS
PORT GAMCORD
ARCELIA
ARDEN VALLEY
OKEANOS SEA
LAKESHORE
RIVER KINGDOM
NARAINA RIVER
SACRED FOREST
RAMSHORN
THE FORTRESS
BASDOVER GULF
MEROCK
RIVAMIR
ROCHRIS ISLANDS
KAMSON SEA
PROUX
PORT ECHNATON
BOREAS SEA
OZRYN
ENRATH &
ORT KAINARR
EAN OF
ARYWELL
ILLOTERRA
ALM OF NAŚBAR

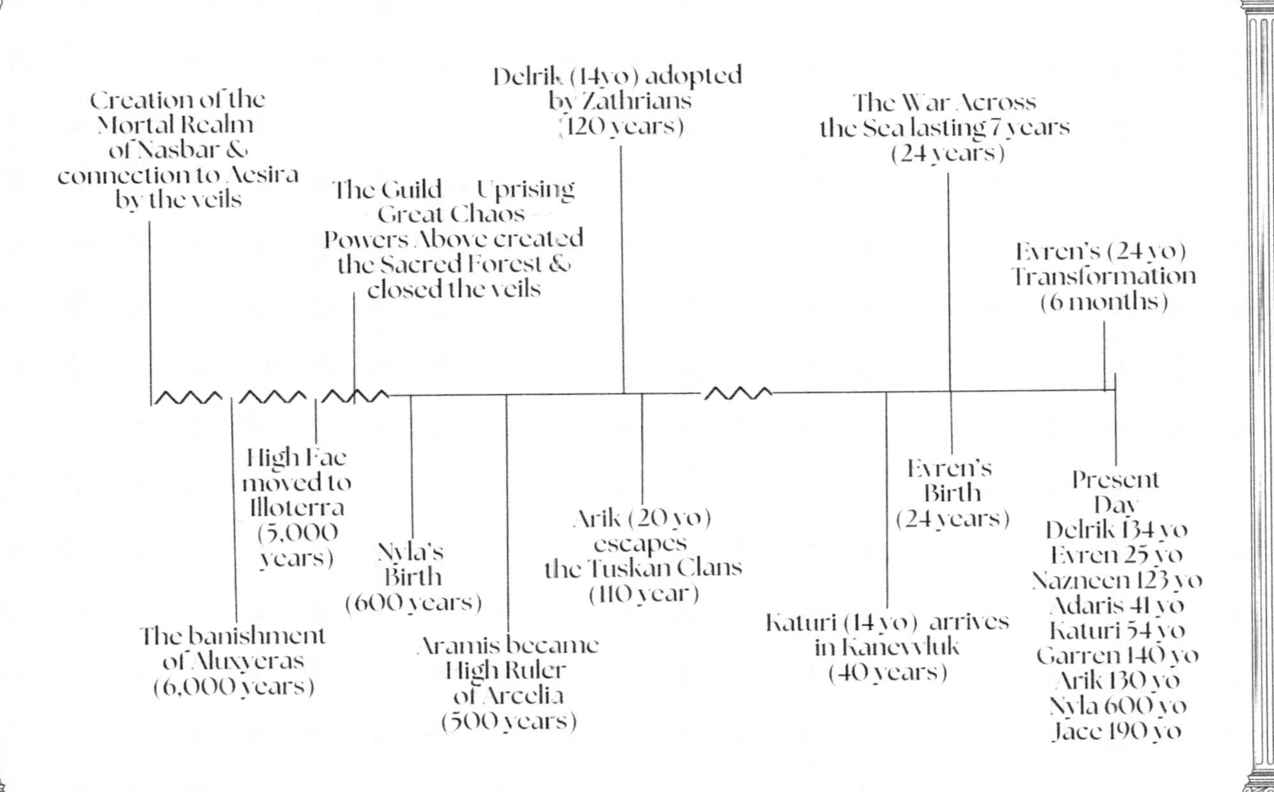

Creation of the Mortal Realm of Nasbar & connection to Aesira by the veils
The banishment of Aluxyeras (6,000 years)
High Fae moved to Illoterra (5,000 years)
The Guild Uprising Great Chaos Powers Above created the Sacred Forest & closed the veils
Nyla's Birth (600 years)
Aramis became High Ruler of Arcelia (500 years)
Delrik (14yo) adopted by Zathrians (120 years)
Arik (20 yo) escapes the Tuskan Clans (110 year)
Katuri (14 yo) arrives in Kanevvluk (40 years)
The War Across the Sea lasting 7 years (24 years)
Evren's Birth (24 years)
Evren's (24 yo) Transformation (6 months)
Present Day
Delrik 134 yo
Evren 25 yo
Nazneen 123 yo
Adaris 41 yo
Katuri 54 yo
Garren 140 yo
Arik 130 yo
Nyla 600 yo
Jace 190 yo

CONTENT WARNING

This story contains cursing, violence, sexual content, death, and torture.

For those readers who do not want to read explicit romantic scenes, including dominance and bondage, skip the following chapters. Skipping these chapters will not affect the plot in any way.

Chapter 17
Chapter 22
Chapter 26
Chapter 43

PRONUNCIATION GUIDE

Adaris Byrnes (a-dar-us)
Alekxander
Aluxyeras (Alux) - (al-ux-ee-air-us) (al-ux)
Anders
Aramis Zathrian (air-a-mis zath-ree-an)
Arabelle Halloran Byrnes (ara-bell hal-oh-ran)
Arik Hanover
Aura
Cadoc Byrnes (kaa-dahk)
Calia Zathrian (cal-ee-ah zath-ree-an)
Captain Tage Lark (tay-j)
Carpus Musmar
Corynne (kuh-rin)
Davi del Mar (da-vee del mar)
Delrik Valhar (del-rik val-har)
Desmund Allerick
Drake
Dusan (doo-shan), god of earth
Eleni
Elliot Valhar (val-har)
Elenora Allerick (el-a-nora all-er-ick)
Eryx (ee-rix), god of fire
Evren Byrnes (Ev-ren)
Garren Eckhardt
Genevieve Hanover Eckhardt
Hadeon Allerick (had-ee-on all-er-ick)
Haizea (hi-zay-uh), goddess of air
Healer Uzin
Holden Eckhardt

Jace Eckhardt
Jae
Kairos (kai-rus) Julian Harland
Katuri Harland (kat-or-ee)
King Ziven
Knox
Larissa
Liam Winfield
Lilliana Hanover
Logan Dimitri
Luiz
Marselina Moriko
Master Rikard Farren
Master Endri Salcido (end-ree sal-see-do)
Miranda
Morgan Valhar (val-har)
Nazneen Zathrian (naz-neen zath-ree-an)
Nyla (nye-la)
Oliver Hanover
Ondine (on-deen), goddess of water
Rhea (ray-uh)
Renwick Ashewood (ren-wick ash-wood)
Rylis
Rishley Boldnaire
Salina
Sundance
Tage Lark
Thane Verena
Vidarr Fanenos (vee-dar fan-ee-nose)
Wren Fanenos (fan-ee-nose)
Yara
Zji'ndar Abril (zen-dar ab-ril)
Cities, Landmarks, and More
Aesira (ee-zi-ra) Sanctum
Affinity Celebration
Amplifying Stone
Animum Fae (ah-ni-mum)
Arcelia (are-sell-ee-a)
Ashlyra (ash-lie-ra)
Basdover Gulf (bas-dover)

Battle of Glissden
Baxmar Range
Bloodthorn
Boreas Sea
Boto Encantado
Brigadeiro (bri-guh-dee-row)
Cataleya's Key
Cessan Void
Circle of Dark Hells
City of Agni (ah-g-nee)
City of Gyors (gee-or-s)
City of Laeto Selva (lay-toe sell-va)
City of Lumir (loom-eer)
City of Proux (pru)
Darkwood
Di-gara (die-gar-a) neve (nee-v) roth (raw-th) var (var). Consors (con-sore-s) par par) rikni (rik-nye). Kaj-far (ka-j-far) ato (ah-tow) un isla (oon-is-la)
Doloryum (Dolor) (doe-lor-ee-um)
Elementum (el-e-men-tum)
Essence Scrolls
Evermere (ev-er-mirror)
Fiend
Forest Fae
The Fortress
Geysa
The Great Chaos
The Great River
The Guild
The Hook
Illoterra (i-lo-terra)
Kanevvluk (kane-vluck)
Kilnard (kil-nard)
Kiscarine Pass (kis-kaa-reen)
Kítani (key-ta-nee)
Koshmara (ka-osh-mar-a)
Kosmima
Lakeshore
Lilura Steel (lil-er-a)
Magnoch Sea

Medina
Menrath (men-wrath)
Merock (mer-ock)
Milla River (me-la)
Mortal Realm of Naśbar (naz-bar)
Mount Lendorr (len-door)
Mountain Fae
Noirdan (nu-ar-dan)
Ocean of Warwell
Okeanos Sea (oh-kee-on-os)
Orb of Sfar
Osomal (os-oh-mal)
Ozryn (oz-ren)
Port Echnaton
Port Gamcord
Port Kainarr (kay-nar)
Qana Mountains (kaa-nuh)
Quinterre (queen-tare), also known as the Western Continent
Ramshorn
Raven Fae
Relika Stone
Ring of Teris (ter-is)
Rivamir (riv-a-mirror)
River of Naraina (na-rain-a)
Rochris Islands (row-kris)
Sacred Forest
sana conso lenire
Satyr
Snow Sprite
Snowhaven
Snowhaven Fae
Taskun Territory (task-un)
Temples of Anruin (an-ru-in)
Thawvale
The Uprising
Visola River
Warblade of Silverlight
Wasted Shallows
Water Fae
Whiteband Port

Winterwood
Wood Nymphs
The Wildlands

ECHOES OF A CRIMSON STORM

Volumes of Elementum
Volume III

Part One

ONE
NYLA

Northern Baxmar Mountains

A twisted, leathery hand held me to the ground by my throat. The claws of the fiend sank into the ground, caging me. My chest screamed in pain where it had sliced into my skin when it pinned me down. I'd managed to evade the advances until I tripped over the rocky terrain. My palms burned as they bit into the sharp ground from my attempt to catch my fall. My head smacked against a stone. My ears were still ringing loud enough to temporarily drown out the mayhem around me. The fiend stared down at me, its face splitting into a toothy grin. Its mouth was full of elongated, needle-sharp fangs with canine teeth that resembled the Koshmara horses of the Void. I'd read about them and seen drawings in ancient texts. Those teeth could rip out your throat with one bite. Its skin was twisted with wretched swirling scars from deep cuts that hadn't healed correctly, and then it was set on fire. The skin was pulled so tightly over the bones that you could see it stretching over the bones at each joint, as if it might finally break with every moment. Its limbs looked like they had been stretched beyond what should normally be acceptable for a living being, leaving them lengthy and awkward. Crimson eyes with slits for pupils racked up and down my body as if it was deciding if I would be a snack worth having. Its nose, or at least what should be a nose, had the appearance of being bashed in. The only feature that still resembled the fae it had once been was the ears. The elongated ears that were now small were black at the tips, but otherwise intact.

Fiends, horrid creations from the dark, twisted mind of Elenora Allerick. Once Fae, they were transformed with dark magic to serve an even darker purpose. They were warped and disabled; some winged, others moved on all fours. Hadeon had been breeding them to build an expendable army to fulfill his goal of devouring the whole continent.

The weight of its hand lifted from my throat, and I sucked in a needed breath of air. The fiend's forked tongue darted out to taste the air around us. Then, to my absolute disgust, he drew that tongue up my cheek.

A keening whine, followed by clicking sounds, came from the back of its throat—a way of communicating. Large looming wings with talons at the peaks were stretched wide, blocking my view of the rest of the ravine we'd been traveling through. While it was distracted, I tried to roll over and scramble away. I made it a few feet. The earth trembled beneath me as it jumped, its feet landing on either side of my legs. It brought its clawed hand down, grabbing me again and slicing open my arm. A pointed tail swished back and forth. It reminded me of the adders in the Taskun Territory before they struck out at their prey.

I reached for my elemental air magic. It was like a faint wind, barely strong enough to send ripples over a lake. I breathed in the terror. It gripped me. What was going on? Why couldn't I summon my power? I was going to die. Right here. Right now.

I looked around for Knox. My familiar had disappeared, leaving me alone. He'd been traveling ahead of us to scout out our course and look out for potential threats. I hadn't seen him since this morning. I reached for him, but couldn't find him anywhere.

My blood was soaking into my clothes. My veins burned like hot lava being poured into my wounds. I'd never foreseen my death in my many years of receiving visions, but that didn't mean it wouldn't happen. I didn't dare take my eyes off the fiend.

Suddenly, warm blood sprayed across my face and into my eyes. I opened my mouth to scream, and thick liquid splattered across my tongue. The distinct taste and smell pierced my senses, making my stomach flip. An arrow poked clean through the chest of the fiend. Someone had shot it from behind. The fiend looked down at the wound but didn't release its grip on my arm.

How in the circle of dark hells did the arrow not slow it down? I only had a few more moments before he'd squeeze the breath right out of me. My power was on its last dregs, whether it be from the prolonged fight or having the wind knocked out of me, I wasn't sure. And my fighting skills were practically nil. I should have paid closer attention to Nazneen, Katuri, and Evren during their daily training.

I'd relied too heavily on my elemental magic. Nazneen had insisted I at least learn to defend myself, but I always brushed her worries off as paranoid.

If I survived this, I'd never hear the end of it from her.

I fumbled at my waistband for the small knife Nazneen gave me when we left the City of Proux. The edges of my vision started to darken, and dizziness made me feel as if I were swaying back and forth. I tried to suck in a lungful of air to no avail. It felt like something was sitting on my chest. No oxygen was getting to my body. Finally, my fingers gripped the leather-wrapped handle. I brought up the deadly blade of a small knife, driving it deep into the fiend's throat. It stuck out from the side of its neck. The beastly demon's horrible eyes went wide when my dagger sank into its withered flesh. A piercing scream ripped through the air. I'd never been particularly gifted at wielding weapons. I'd certainly never stabbed anybody. Being a priestess in the ancient Temple of Anruin, serving the Powers Above was a quiet life of prayers and peace. But I was no longer living a life of service. At this point, I was just trying to survive.

Brilliant, red eyes turned flat and lifeless. The fiend's clawed hand released me, reaching for the embedded blade. Acrid breath puffed across my face in its struggle not to leave this realm. It hissed a final, gargled sound as it collapsed on top of me. I summoned my dwindling elemental air power from deep within me and let out a current of air. It was enough to push the majority of its weight off my chest. I could breathe, but I was still trapped beneath the weight of its arm. One of its too heavy arms flopped across my waist. For a moment, all I could hear was high-pitched ringing and muffled chaos around me.

Blood—warm, metallic, slimy—soaked into my already damp clothes. I wanted to scream, but my lungs were leaden. The stench surrounded me. I wanted the creature off me, but it was too heavy. The burning pain was secondary to the sucking sensation of my incoming vision. I forced myself to focus on all my training and techniques as my world shifted into the future in a shimmering haze. I reigned in the plunging drop of my stomach and centered myself around my vision. If I fought against it, it would swallow me whole. They were all-consuming.

The world around me faded in and out of focus. My heartbeat slowed, and the flash of a vision crossed my mind.

Crimson eyes flashed with sinister wrath. There was fire, choking smoke, and destruction. Pleas of mercy filled my ears. I felt concentrated betrayal, but then those eyes took up my entire field of view. Almost the same color eyes as the fiend's had been. Villainous rage held me captive. The slitted pupils widened with recognition, and then mournfulness replaced the rage. I couldn't pull my attention from those eyes. They saw deep into my soul, and in return, my soul welcomed the intrusion.

Then, as quick as the vision had come, the present all came back—metal on metal and the cries of death. Now was not the time for visions, but I'd never been able to control when they came. The vision had been brief, but an overwhelming feeling of heaviness hung like a lasting fog over the mountains. Or was that my consciousness seeping from me?

I strained to stay awake. I couldn't just give in. I'd surely be killed. I need to get to safety.

I surveyed my surroundings to regulate my breathing. One by one, my senses returned. I sucked in a breath, counting in for four seconds, holding, and then out for four. Finally, I regained my control, noticing the wild mountainous peaks looming above. The setting sun painted the skies of northern Quinterre in stunning streaks of color. The last of the day's light was ebbing, and shadows raked over the gray stones. I heard nothing but the rushing of blood in my ears.

I tried to turn to my side. I managed to move a few inches, pushing the dead fiend's limb off me. I finally dislodged my lower body. I grunted painfully as I rolled to my hands and knees. My muscles trembled with the effort. My chest burned something fierce. I peered down. The shredded fabric of my dress left me almost completely exposed to the elements, and deep gouges were striped above my breasts. Each lungful of air was agony.

I drew in a shaky breath. I'd never been good with the sight of blood. I smothered a sob that threatened to take over.

Why had I left the temple? I'd been safe and happy inside the marble walls. All I'd wanted was freedom to make my own choices. I've been told I was too intense, too much, too adventurous all my life. Now I was on this bloodied battlefield, fighting to survive.

I pushed myself up to standing on shaky legs.

We, my new companions and I, had been on our way to the fire fae kingdom's capital, the City of Agni, in search of another relic. It was the closest to the air fae kingdom. Delrik, the infamous bounty hunter, led us along the Baxmar Range north to the border. His bondmate, Evren, was with us, as well as his sister and future ruler of the Mountain Fae in Illoterra, Nazneen Zathrian. Princess Katuri Harland and Garren Eckhardt, second son of the Snowhaven Fae and technically a prince, were also traveling with us. No wonder the fiends were able to spot our entourage. We were a walking bullseye.

We'd searched for the air relic all over the air kingdom and the City of Proux. I'd known it wasn't there. I'd lived there my whole life. I'd been through every part of the temple and the grounds. And after holding the relic we'd found in Noirdan, the Relika Stone, as Haizea had called it, I knew that I would've been able to sense the air relic if it were there. I wasn't surprised the relic wasn't in Proux. Nothing was that easy. The relics had been lost for so long, forgotten by most until now. Only the leaders of each kingdom knew they still existed.

Once, long ago, the High Fae had access to the gods through the veils with the Temples of Anruin. Each leader of the High Fae kingdoms was given a relic to open the veils and speak directly to the gods. The relics—five in total—were each imbued with powers from the gods. They were keys to open the veil between Illoterra and the realm of the gods, Aesira. But when the Uprising happened, the gods permanently closed the veils to protect Aesira from the evil that had been brought into the Mortal Realm of Naśbar. There was no written history of what happened to the relics after the veils were closed. They seemed to have just disappeared. Over time, they were forgotten completely.

"Nyla," Nazneen cried out from across the ravine, breaking me from my thoughts.

My eyes darted around, searching for her, feeling deep unease at something looming nearby. Something was wrong. Knox was gone, and the usual heaviness of my magic was absent. The wounds throbbed at the same pace as my heart's frantic beating. Prickles crawled up my spine as if someone was watching me.

Her voice was full of alarm, running at a full sprint toward me. My eyes locked on hers. A fresh surge of panic hit me. She leapt over a fallen fiend and fell another with a blind swing of her sword. Her eyes spread wide, and I saw her open her mouth to scream something else, a warning maybe. It was like she was moving in slow motion. A footstep sounded behind me. The last thing I remembered was pain lancing the back of my head before everything went dark.

TWO
NYLA

"You are a priestess of the temple. You do not belong traipsing across the realm looking for these so-called relics."

Salina's voice was growing louder with each word. Her voice bounced around the circular dome of the temple. The stamped copper reflected the light against the pearly-white columns—an exact replica of the Sanctum in Aesira. We had just wrapped up morning prayers, and I'd pulled Salina aside. She's always been my teacher and, as I grew older, my sounding board. She was the closest thing to a friend I had. The other priestesses made themselves scarce at Salina's growing outrage. Their eyes darted back and forth between us.

I ignored them. The only time they'd shown interest in me was if they needed something. Otherwise, they ignored me, which was fine. I was used to it.

It was a deceptively bright day outside the temple. It looked like spring, but the air had a harsh bite to it. Winter was coming fast. Here in the mountains, winter could be unforgiving if we weren't prepared. Which is why we needed to leave now if we wanted to find the other relics. We needed to make it to Laeto Selva. If we waited much longer, the snow in the Baxmar Mountains would make it impassable by foot until spring. Flying was obviously an option, but making such a long journey would drain us of our powers. With only Garren, Evren, and I able to fly, we'd have to carry the others and our supplies. We needed to be ready for anything, which meant reserving our powers and hiking most of the way. I was not particularly looking forward to camping every night in the snow. I'd never slept outside a day in my life. But we couldn't delay. We had to leave now.

I'd never seen Salina so frustrated. Even when I'd kept bringing up the discrepancies in Essence Scrolls. Eryx, the god of fire, had altered the Essence Scrolls to hide the banishment of Aluxyeras, the goddess of spirit, and the fact that there was a fifth relic. The continued discussion of the relics had pushed her over the edge.

Salina had seen the ancient relic when we'd returned from Noirdan. She'd held the Relika Stone and sensed its power. I couldn't understand why she was so adamant about ignoring what was right in front of her. Sensing my distress, Knox appeared along the edge of the temple circle. He only entered the temple when we were alone, otherwise his massive wings risked bumping into others. He wasn't one to enjoy being touched.

I opened my mouth, but my mentor interrupted me.

"You don't even know if they all still exist. For all you know, they were destroyed."

I placed my hands on my hips. "Why would Haizea, the goddess of air herself, bother to tell us about them if we couldn't find them. Are you going to go against a goddess?" Haizea had come to me over six weeks ago, confirming the relics to be real and very much still in existence. "I would trust a goddess to know whether one of them had somehow been destroyed. Plus, we already have the Relika Stone."

"Your duty is to this temple and to serving the gods." She slammed her walking stick into the ground like a petulant child.

"I am *serving the gods by finding the relics and preventing them from falling into the wrong hands."*

"That is not for you to do!"

I turned away from my mentor. I'd always looked up to Salina. She's been my teacher and friend for so long, but I needed to do this. Ever since we returned from Noirdan just over a month ago with the spirit relic, the Relika Stone that had been set inside of Elenora Allerick's circlet, my future had been unclear. Not only in my decision to go with Evren to find the remaining relic, but also in my visions. I'd spent countless hours a day meditating, but my future remained a mystery for the first time ever. I could only see glimpses of the others in Laeto Selva—flashes of green and light. My future was covered in haze. Did it mean I would die? I didn't think it was time to enter Evermere, the land of the mortal afterlife.

"You can't leave," Salina said again. For the thousandth time.

Salina crossed her arms over her chest, and her cane was balanced precariously against her hip. She'd been young when I first came under her instruction. But after 500 years, her age was showing. She wasn't like the High Fae. Most didn't know she was half-human and half-dryad. She once had dark green hair, but it has since turned white.

I straightened my spine. I was already taller than Salina, but I steeled myself anyway. "I am. We are leaving tomorrow morning."

We hadn't truly decided on when we were leaving. We were waiting for my visions to guide us, but I was angry and frustrated. Also, I didn't trust that my gumption would stick if Salina kept demanding I stay behind.

"If you go, you aren't welcome back."

Stunned by her ultimatum, I shouted the first thing that came to mind.

I lifted the necklace from around my neck, the one with the symbol of the gods, and handed it to her. "Fine!"

Salina's eyes went wide like I'd smacked her across the face. Was she serious? Was I serious? If I left, I'd never be allowed to return? Salina straightened her robes and gripped her cane tightly in her bony hand. With her other hand, she took the necklace from my fingers.

"Goodbye, Nyla." With a look of resignation, she turned and hobbled away.

How quickly I'd fallen from her grace.

I studied the retreating back of my elderly teacher and friend. I'd never see her again. Not with her age. I always thought she'd held on to her mortal life so that I wouldn't be alone. With me gone, would she pass over to Evermere without hesitation?

Nazneen appeared in the main doorway of the temple. The look of melancholy on her face and her slumped shoulders told me everything.

"How much did you hear?" I asked.

"All of it. It was hard not to hear you," she said.

She leaned against the wall with her arms crossed over her chest. She didn't move any closer.

She indicated the temple with a swirl of her finger in the air. "It echoes."

Nazneen had grown on me. She was funny, feisty, kind, and brave. She didn't mind my awkward silences like others. She never tried to fill the quiet, and I appreciated it.

I'd grown accustomed to the little quintet, even Garren.

If I truly left Proux and the temple, where would I belong? Would I be accepted into their friend group? They were practically a family. I'd never had friends before. And after 600 years, I didn't remember much about having a family. The temple had always been my home.

I'd never known any difference. I'd traveled far and wide across Quinterre many times in my life, visiting the other ancient temples and learning more about our realm—teaching the essence scrolls, studying the original scrolls, and setting up smaller temples across the realm. Salina traveled with me on occasion to help establish new temples or repair ones damaged after the war. Every time I traveled to new parts of the continent, I'd always return. This time would be different.

But what it all came down to was trust. I needed to go. Haizea wouldn't have told us to find the relics if she didn't want us to. The fates had set my future on a specific path, and even though I couldn't see it, I needed to do this. I didn't belong in Proux anymore. And if my future meant death, then I'd see Haizea in the afterlife and gladly enter Evermere.

I believed in the possibility of peace in our realm. I'd seen too much hatred and destruction in my five hundred-plus years in this world. I wanted to do something to right the wrong. It was unlikely I'd be able to make a difference, but I had to try.

Nazneen quietly studied me for a beat before she pushed off the wall. "What time are we leaving?"

I took a deep breath, burning all the bridges to my past with two words. "At sunrise."

THREE
DESMUND

I sat perched on a rock that jutted out over the valley. The space was a narrow basin carved through the Baxmar Mountains, which separated the Air Fae and Fire Fae Kingdoms. A natural border built right into the continent. I'd been traveling on my own over the last few weeks on foot, slowly making my way north before cutting west.

My father had ordered me to go to the Forest Fae Kingdom, to the City of Laeto Selva, as part of a "diplomatic mission" as he called it. It was just busy work, a way to keep me out of the way. I'd been sent on these excursions before. I'd travel to the smallest villages and the largest cities all throughout Quinterre. It wasn't something new. However, I'd decided to take my time on this journey. If I were honest, I'd much rather face the elements solo than be twiddling my thumbs in mindless meetings.

What was the point of rushing when I'd rather not be home anyway? I welcomed the quiet and solitude of a cross-country excursion. At home, there are always men traipsing in and out at all hours of the day, so loud and angry. My father's voice booming and commanding, bossing people around. I was required to sit there and show my face in solidarity.

Traveling always brought me the peace I searched for. There was nothing better than the fresh air and wind against my face.

Just outside the City of Proux, I stumbled upon a group of High Fae—four females and two males. I hadn't bothered passing through the city itself. I'd had enough supplies and was familiar enough with the continent to know where to restock.

However, my curiosity was piqued. It was odd to find such a large group this deep within the mountains, much less High Fae. High Fae were typically associated with royalty or nobility in Quinterre. To travel far north this time of the year, and without any kind of guard, was an interesting choice. One of the males was brutish-looking.

Maybe he was a guard for the females. They also had a red wolf and some type of bird of prey traveling with them. Winter was harsh in the Baxmar Mountains, and conditions could shift faster than a snap of your fingers. However, they didn't seem bothered by the bitter cold.

I maintained my distance but followed out of boredom. I wasn't one who needed the company of others, but after weeks of speaking to no one, I'd grown tired of my own thoughts. I knew I shouldn't let myself get distracted. I wanted to make it to Laeto Selva within the next new moons, but something had drawn me in. I was just defiant enough to follow that curiosity rather than the directions from my father. I'd eventually do his bidding. Eventually. And he wouldn't know the difference several weeks made.

I'd nestled myself high up on a cliff's edge above their temporary camp. The sun was about to slip below the horizon, painting the sky in an array of pastels. I'd just settled in to eat dinner. I'd actually taken the time to set up camp, tent and all. I could smell a storm coming. The air felt heavy. I'd need protection from the wind tonight.

The group was all sitting around a fire. One female had massive, black wings. The soft feathers rippled in the bitter wind. She wasn't dressed for the weather, but didn't seem bothered in the slightest at the cold. The red wolf was curled around the feet of a red-headed female who was facing away from me. I studied the wolf. It was the exact shade of the female's hair, an uncommon color for wolf breeds, and strange markings across its face. The tip of its nose was tucked in a thick tail. I couldn't hear what was being said over the whistling wind, but they seemed merry about their journey.

Suddenly, the wolf perked up and made eye contact with me. I froze. There was no way it could see me this far away. Its ears twitched, and the fur along its back stood on end. I'd encountered my fair share of wolves on my wanderings. I had no problem defending myself if required. Bright green eyes focused south with too much understanding for a mere creature.

Then the solitude of the mountain was broken by a keening howl. I instantly recognized the sound—fiends.

Before I could get to my feet, at least a dozen gnarled, black beasts swooped down from above and dove into the valley. One nearly took off my head with its long tail, given how low it was flying. It brushed the top of my head. Clearly, I was not the object of its focus because it didn't even turn around. It had its victims locked in its view.

The fiends somehow knew exactly where to attack, despite the ground being partially concealed behind the rocks. They must have been tracking them. I hadn't seen any other people nearby, so they couldn't have been tipped off. It was the only explanation. They weren't smart enough to blindly stumble upon prey.

The two males bolted to their feet. Weapons were drawn. The hooded one drew a bow, reaching for a quiver of arrows I hadn't seen at his feet. The other unsheathed a longsword. As the sword hissed against the leather, a sea dragon appeared seemingly from nowhere alongside the glistening steel. A female with shoulder-length hair also held a sword. The two smaller females froze but didn't stand. Rather, they waited and listened. I realized their assessment of the situation wasn't based on fear. No. It was a calculation.

Twelve fiends circled and then dove downward. The second one from the front swooped lower first, but an arrow was released by the surly one, hitting his target with precision. The fiend fell from the sky, a trail of blood in its wake, and crashed into the ground with a sickening crunch on a boulder. If the arrow hadn't been a killing blow, the snap of bone against the rock was an indication.

In a whirlwind of light and power, the whole passage was ablaze with fire. I ducked behind the rock and shielded my head. The intense heat dissipated as quickly as it appeared. In its place was a fiend, smoking and dead. What in the circle of dark hells was that? I counted the remaining fiends. Ten.

There was no doubt in my mind that these Fae were expert fighters. I watched as their powers were wielded as skillfully as their swords.

The female with the red wolf was whipping thorned vines from all directions as if they were extensions of her body. Their barbs scratched and tore at their enemies' flesh. It couldn't be? An earth elemental?

Another female, petite and blonde, moved with the artful—yet destructive—grace of a typhoon, swirling her arms in a circular motion. The fiend closest to her couldn't withstand the wind, forcing them to land within reach of the deadly vines. She must be an air elemental. Two elemental fae in one group was rare.

I'd never seen High Fae with elemental powers before. Of course, I'd heard stories about elemental High Fae from nannies growing up. I'd seen a lot of fighting in my short one hundred and fifty years. Between being caught during the war and the legacy of my family, blood and gore were a daily part of life. I'd been too young to fight. At least, not on the front lines, much to my father's dismay. My power of astral projection was considered passive magic, but was still in high demand when it came to delivering missives and participating in treaties. With diligent practice, I'd learned to project myself in various degrees, from being nearly invisible to a full corporeal body that was indistinguishable from my true form.

Truthfully, I didn't have the stomach for useless bloodshed, so I made myself useful in other ways. I assisted the healers as much as I could. While I wasn't allowed in active battle, my home was located so close to the war that I kept plenty busy tending to injuries. Alchemists and healers taught me how to mix healing potions or a death draft when injuries were too bad.

Another stream of fire shot from above, taking me completely by surprise. The inferno chased after another fiend. It swept out of the way of the flames and turned a hissing sneer at the fire elemental. It dove again for one of her friends. She reached toward the fiend, her hand splayed as if she could grab it. A red ruby ring shone in the firelight. When she made a fist and drew it to her chest, the fiend was pulled forward like it was being drawn by a string. With her opposite hand, she pushed a pin prick of fire to the fiend. It moved fast and went straight to its bony chest. Its leathery wings twisted and fractured. As its skin cracked, it started to glow from flowing embers. It plummeted to the ground, clawing at its own body and screaming. The elemental fire was consuming it alive from the inside. By the time the charred body hit the ground, the remains crumbled into ash.

Nine.

Light glinting off a sword caught my attention, and I watched as another of the females beheaded another fiend.

Eight.

She turned on her heel and skewered two more to the hilt. Impressive.

Seven. Six.

She planted her booted foot into its chest and shoved the pair from her blade. Thick, black ichor dripped to the ground. Carelessly, she stepped over their tangled limbs to continue her attack.

The Earth elemental and one of the males stood back-to-back, ice and earth striking out at fiends. Ropes of earth sprang from the ground, ensnaring one fiend before it could get too close. The ropes squeezed until its body was severed in half, spurting black blood everywhere. The sea dragon snapped its head from the body. The sound of shattering bone echoed up to me. Gross.

Five.

A fiend came from nowhere and grabbed the female by the throat. It yanked her and spun until she landed against its chest. The fiend's mouth opened, and right before it sank its teeth into her neck, spouts of water invaded its mouth, drowning it.

Four.

The fire Fae sprouted wings of fire and soared into the group of incoming fiends.

"What. The. Fuck!" I couldn't stop the words spilling from my lips. She separated fiends on the ground, keeping them from attacking in groups, and cutting them off with balls of fire before they closed in. The large fae male on the ground watched her back. If any fiend got too close, arrows blocked their path. Though they missed often, none of the High Fae had been taken down yet.

I'd never seen such coordinated fighting. Not just the power they each possessed, but their trust in one another. I would never offer anyone such trust, especially on the battlefield.

The air elemental caught my attention. Even in the heat of battle, she looked beautiful, ethereal. A charge of energy buzzed around her. Her muddied and blood-soaked long blonde hair was plastered across her face. She moved with a casual calm, a wild cat on the hunt. A fiend stalked toward her. She reached forward, fingers spread wide. Then she clenched her fist and pulled it to her chest. The fiend's chest caved in on itself, literally pulling life from it.

Fuck.

Three.

She turned on the fiend before that one hit the ground. It tried to take flight, spreading its massive wings. With a flick of her wrist, a gust of wind twisted a nearby tree from the ground and skewered it through the fiend's back.

Two.

Keening cries. Scratch that. More fiends appeared over the ridge on foot.

I didn't bother counting this time. There were too many. This was clearly a well-planned ambush. Before I knew it, a fiend had the blonde cornered. It slashed out its clawed hand. She jumped back, but not fast enough. Talons scraped across her chest, leaving behind streaks on sliced skin and blood. Strips of her flesh hung down as she stumbled back and fell.

My stomach plummeted to my feet. No.

It pinned her down.

"Knox!" I heard her call out.

I looked around but no one else was there. No one came to her aid. When she struggled to get out of its grasp, it dug its claws into the skin of her arm. As she drove the knife into its throat, the one with the bow shot at the fiend. It went down and collapsed on top of her.

Not her. Of all of them, not her. I couldn't understand why I had such a reaction to her death. I'd seen death before. A lot of it. It was a hazard of working with healers.

There was a soft glow surrounding her. The setting sun must have been playing tricks with the light. One heartbeat. Two. Three. Then she sucked in a sharp breath, and her eyes shot open. Slow to recover, she struggled with the weight of the fiend but managed to make it to her feet. She was a bloody mess, covered in grime and gore. Then time lagged. My heartbeat sped up as I saw what would, without a doubt, be her end.

I stood from my crouched position. She couldn't see one of the remaining fiends that had snuck up behind her. The world around me slowed, unable to do anything to stop the inevitable. Though my magic was useless to protect her from this distance, it flooded my veins. I wouldn't be able to project myself in time to block the blow I knew was coming.

The female with the sword called out, and the blonde whipped her head around in the direction of a name that was swallowed by the winter wind. That name. I wanted it. Needed it.

"No!" I cried out, but no one could hear me.

My cry was snuffed out by the chaos and the mountains. By the time I'd made up my mind to sacrifice my hiding spot and astral project to her side, it was done.

The monstrous creature lifted its wooden club and swung. It contacted the back of the female's head with a sickening smash that seemed to echo off the mountains and inside my head.

Her body dropped to the ground. The offending creature bent and grabbed her by the foot to drag her away.

The one with ice magic grabbed the earth elemental and pulled her away. They ducked in time as a lance swung over their heads. Her body landed hard on top of his, and he rolled them both.

Sparks reigned down as the steel met stone. He lifted her from the ground—one arm beneath her knees and the other around her back—and ran toward the large one with the bow. Arrows flew in rapid succession, covering the others as they disappeared into the mouth of a cave. Once the fire-winged one was safe, the big one followed.

A wall of fire pushed the fiend's back. I shielded my eyes from the searing blaze. The pair of fiends retreated, their angry clicks of communication echoed off the rocks. When the fire finally went out, the High Fae were gone.

The fiends were lost in their own frenzy. They searched for the High Fae but didn't discover them. It was as if the mouth of the cave had disappeared. Did one of them have the ability to blink on top of their elemental magic?

In the confusion of the fire, I'd lost track of everything. I scanned the ravine, my eyes zeroing in on the fallen High Fae. I could see her. She had been dropped behind a large boulder. Maybe they hid her for later. One of the fiends' leaders landed heavily amid the chaos. Bigger than the others, the ground quivered when he touched down. The surrounding fiends all bowed.

The biggest fiend made his way to the entrance of the cave, guided by a lesser soldier. It sent out a signal, and another appeared beside him. They hadn't bothered checking on the female who was lying on the ground beneath my perch. My magic tingled in my fingers and spread upward toward my chest. My astral projection glittered beside me. It nodded at me, then disappeared and reappeared several feet away. In its invisible form, only I could see where it was hovering close to her fallen form.

After a stilted conversation, the fiends took off into the sky. Any injured fiends were finished off and left behind. I'd watched as one of the remaining fiends had not-so-gently nudged her with a foot before losing interest and taking back to the sky, following his leader back to wherever in the circles of dark hell they called home.

FOUR

KATURI

I felt a sharp tug on my arm, and my body was yanked to the side, slamming into Garren. Garren grabbed my arm and pulled me away right as a fiend swooped down from above, its talons stretched toward me, just out of reach. Thank the Powers he'd caught me; his strength prevented us from toppling over. Even in the midst of the mayhem, the bond between us flared in its unique harmony. I took a moment to press my face into his chest. Three fiends lay dead on the ground at my bondmate's feet, and it made me love him even more. Eleni grabbed the edge of a wing and tugged at it, growling low.

With my elemental earth power, I summoned sharpened shards from the rocky, mountain ground to sever the heads from their deformed bodies. We would burn the bodies, too, once all this was over. I wanted no remnants of the hellish beasts to remain behind.

"We need to get out of here." Garren looked around for a safe place to retreat.

While we had taken down several fiends with minimal effort, we were clearly outnumbered. It would only be a matter of time before one of us was injured, or worse.

A sharp yip came from Eleni. She'd found a place to hide. I spotted the narrow cut in the mountainside. I would've missed it if it hadn't been for Eleni.

"There," I said, pointing across the pass. "We can take cover there."

Garren scooped me up from the ground effortlessly. He shielded me with his body as we ran for cover. He erected a wall of ice as a shield between us and fiends. Sharp talons scraped and clawed at the ice like rabid animals as the fiends fought against the shield and Drake. Delrik was by my side in an instant, hurling shadows against the ice as the talons cracked it into thick chunks.

Evren shot fire over our heads at the airborne fiends to give cover to Nazneen. Delrik scooped her up and ran past us to the opening in the mountainside. The heat of the elemental fire instantly melted the ice shield, but we were already far away. We made it to the safety of a carved inlet, followed by Evren, panting and covered in blood. Thank the Powers, the cave was large enough for all of us.

We were all panting heavily. I pressed my hand into the stone, thanking the earth for the protection.

"Where the fuck did they come from?" Delrik asked.

His eyes were solid black, and the shadows danced on his fingers. The silky, black tendrils reached out to his bondmate protectively, as they leeched the small amount of light from the cramped space that came from the setting sun. The tendrils wove together and disguised our hiding spot, preventing any light or prying eyes from entering the cave. To anyone passing by, all they would see was the shadow of rocks. The ice shield melted away with a wave of Garren's hand once the shadows were in place.

"From the circle of dark hells," Garren replied as he wiped the viscous gore from his front.

"Evren, where did that come from? Moving the fiend with just your hand?" Nazneen asked with stunned curiosity.

Evren lifted her right hand and wiggled her fingers in front of her. The Ring of Teris, a deep ruby set in lilura steel, winked in the dim light.

"That is the ring that the gods created to strip Alux of her powers and contain her. When someone uses their powers against you while you are wearing the ring, the ring steals the power. I knew you had the ring, I've never seen you use it before." Katuri answered, looking over at Evren.

Evren looked from Katuri to Nazneen. "Somehow Renwick ended up with it. During our last encounter I stole it from him. I used Renwick's power of telekinesis against the fiend. I didn't even realize I was doing it. I just knew that the fiend was flying at your back, Naz."

My heart pounded loudly in my chest. Garren brushed his fingers across the back of my hand. I wasn't sure how long we had until the fiends came after us again. Would the shadows hold them back? Through the hazy shroud, I spotted the silhouette of a fiend at the entrance of the cave. It made a clicking sound, and a second one appeared. They seemed to be having a conversation. The breath in my lungs froze. I didn't dare breathe or move an inch. The last thing we needed was for them to come through the shadows. Fighting in such a confined space would be nearly impossible. We all waited with bated breath.

After what felt like hours, they flew off and disappeared into the ever-darkening sky. My legs gave out from underneath me, and I sank to the cave floor.

My head snapped up at a sudden realization. "Wait. Where's Nyla?" I asked.

"A fiend took her down," Nazneen said. "It attacked her from behind. I couldn't get to her fast enough." She shook her head, then dropped down on the ground next to me with her legs stretched out in front of her. "I saw it dragging her off."

No. She had to be wrong. My heart sank. Nyla couldn't be dead. Just because she went down, didn't mean it had killed her, right?

"It's not your fault," Delrik said. He hugged his sister with one arm, the other still holding fast to Evren's hand.

"We'll go find her," Garren affirmed.

Garren leaned out of the mouth of the cave, through Delrik's shadows, to see if all the fiends had departed or if any remained behind for another ambush. He turned and nodded to Delrik. Determination flowed down our bond to me. He pressed a kiss to my forehead. "I'll be back."

"You can't be serious?" I squeaked.

My bondmate is insane.

He was not allowed to leave. Certain death waited out there, but also...Nyla. I couldn't just leave her alone to fend off all those fiends.

"I'll be right back. We just want to make sure the coast is clear before we all search for Nyla," he said. "Drake, can you fly out and see if you can spot Knox? They may be together."

Drake swept from the cave soundlessly.

"We will gather our packs and come back for you," Delrik said. "Aura?"

Evren's familiar, Aura, clicked her beak and then flew through the shadows and into the ravine. Her sleek, black feathers blended seamlessly into the night sky.

"She fell over there," Nazneen said, pointing toward a piece of rock that jutted out over the valley, high above our heads.

"That's where we'll start," Delrik said. Then they ducked into the night.

The three of us sat quietly together, waiting for Delrik and Garren to return. If it weren't for Evren's comforting arm wrapped around my shoulders, I'd be pacing like a madwoman. Nazneen was too preoccupied with her thoughts. A trained warrior and spy, her mind worked faster than I could even imagine. She sat cross-legged in front of me, her tongue in her cheek as she mumbled to herself each idea that popped into her mind.

"There isn't another way. We will have to either go back down the mountain the way we came or continue through the valley to the Agni. We could fly, but we'd risk the fiends spotting us until we can see higher than the mountains. Right now, they have the high ground." Nazneen nodded at her own plan. "Yes. It's better to stay on foot for now and travel at night. At least until we have higher ground or trees for coverage."

Between Nazneen's spy expertise, Delrik's bounty hunting abilities, and our combined powers, we should be safe until we reach Agni. Especially now that we knew we were being watched. We'd be more careful concealing our tracks and watching our backs. The goddess Haizea had set us on this path. I trusted she wouldn't lead us wrong.

FIVE
DESMUND

My boots skidded down the sheer slope into the open basin below. Rocks tumbled down the near-vertical drop as I picked my way down to the valley floor. It couldn't be wider than a hundred feet. It was pitch black. The double moons that usually graced the sky were hidden behind thick clouds, mirroring the devastation of the last few hours. I strained my eyes as I scanned the valley. Through the darkness, I could barely see the female's body lying still on the ground. I wondered if her stillness was due to being unconscious or possibly even dead. And if she were dead...

Why did it bother me so much that she'd been killed?

The moment the sun dropped behind the high peaks, darkness swept across the mountains. I hadn't seen where the High Fae had gone. One minute, they were there near the mouth of the cave. A cloud passed overhead, casting the valley in a dark shadow, and then they disappeared. I watched what I believed to be the entrance until darkness fell. That had been about an hour ago. It was a rough estimate. It was hard to tell without the movement of the stars how much time had passed.

I walked past the female's body, giving it a wide berth. The fiends hadn't bothered to take her as a prisoner, presumably because her skull had been bashed in. I stood, leaning against the boulder, and summoned my power. My astral projection appeared several hundred feet before me near the entrance to the cave. It was completely invisible to anyone looking in its direction. I could only see the shimmering outline of it myself. Projecting myself a hundred feet away took barely an ounce of power. I'd honed my gift beyond what anyone ever expected of me.

When my magic first developed at fifteen, my parents weren't happy about its passive nature. I think they'd hoped I'd be given an active power. Alas, just one more way I'd failed as a son.

I pressed my non-corporeal hand into the stone. I could only see darkness, but I heard muffled voices. I'd been right in assuming they'd taken shelter in the mountain. I strained to listen.

"Where the fuck did they come from?" one of the males asked.

"From the circle of dark hells," the other replied.

That was the truth.

My heart pounded in my chest. I wasn't sure if more fiends were on their way. I didn't want to stick around and find out. I'd break down camp and walk through the night. Following the High Fae group had been a way to pass the time. I wouldn't let my curiosity be my downfall.

I recalled my projection before turning to make my way back to the steep side of the mountain. I looked over to the motionless blonde one last time. I turned to leave, but I couldn't stop the nagging feeling in my gut that I should check for sure that she was indeed dead. It was the healer in me, I suppose.

The petite female was prone on the ground, lifeless. I looked over my shoulder, then sighed at myself before walking over to her.

I don't know why I was so intrigued with the female. I approached with caution. She was even smaller than I'd imagined. She couldn't be taller than five feet. I watched her chest for proof of breath and saw none.

When I moved closer, I noticed faded marks all over her body. They weren't raised and rough like scars. They were smooth, more like tattoos. Her body was like a canvas of art stained by dirt, blood, and bruises. The sheer panels of her dress were ripped to shreds, exposing her stomach, chest, and shoulders. The leggings were torn, too. Every inch I could see was marked with runes—pale ancient marks, as if the Powers Above had carved the Essence Scrolls into her very skin. They shimmered faintly despite the diminished sunlight. There was magic within the eerily, strange runes. The wounds the fiend sliced into her chest were still bleeding and oozing something putrid. Such a beautiful creature shouldn't have died in such a horrible way.

I knelt beside her and brushed her matted hair away from her face. At the touch of my fingers, I saw her chest take in a shallow breath, and an almost-inaudible groan came from her dry, cracked lips.

I jerked my hand away.

Fuck. She's alive.

I reached out and let my fingertips hover over her delicate wrist. Even though our skin didn't touch, her hand twitched in response to my presence. Her head rolled over, and her face contorted in pain. Her eyes cracked open, looking up at me. Two different colored eyes—one eye as blue as sapphire, the other a kaleidoscope of blue and brown—stared blankly up at me. I couldn't help but be hypnotized by them. I found myself leaning closer. When she blinked, breaking the connections, I pulled back.

This had been a mistake. I shouldn't have sought her out. She was clearly in misery. I should kill her and let her carry on to Evermere. I knew nothing of this female and the potential danger she brought across my path. It felt so natural to defend myself from risk.

I withdrew the sword that hung at my hip. With both hands gripping the hilt, I raised it above her, but at the last second, stopped. I didn't know who she was. I didn't know where she came from. But...

I couldn't do it. I couldn't take her life.

There weren't many options. I could bring her to Laeto Selva with me. She would slow me down. I wasn't in a hurry to do my father's bidding anyway. There would be healers in the city who could give her the treatment she needed. The king was expecting me. I could drop her off at a healer before going to the castle. The king knew who I was, but I didn't know if anyone else did. She'd be able to find her friends once she was healed. That would be a diplomatic move my father would approve of.

Yet, Laeto Selva was a far trek. I had mending skills, but I wasn't sure if I would be able to patch her up enough to make it all the way to the Forest Fae healers. I should put her out of her misery. No one deserved to die slowly from a wound like that.

My head tilted to the side, sword still raised, as I studied the delicate High Fae. I wasn't a healer, but I'd been trained to use what I had at my disposal to tend to wounds. I always carried a healer's kit in my travel pack with assorted herbs, and I'd been taught basic healing. That, combined with her High Fae healing powers, meant she'd be good as new in no time. Then I could carry on with my mission. A short detour. At least I hoped that would be the case. I wasn't sure if my skill set would be enough to save her, but I needed to try. Or at least that's what my gut was telling me. I'd learned over the years to trust my gut. It kept me out of trouble...for the most part.

I re-sheathed my sword. I bent and snaked my arms around her limp body and lifted her into my arms. She was lighter than a feather. She didn't regain consciousness when I moved her. It was probably for the best. I carried her battered body back up the steep embankment to my camp, doing my best to avoid slipping. Though the valley offered protection from the winter wind, it did nothing to protect against the cold temperature. As I felt the frigid air seep into my bones, snow began to fall. I picked up my pace. If I were freezing fully clothed, then she wouldn't last much longer.

I ducked into my tent, kicking off my boots to prevent dragging dirt inside, and lay her on my bedroll. She shifted away from me and mumbled something. I carefully cast protective wards around the campsite to block out our noise and deter anyone or anything from wandering our way. I knew several of the High Fae had elemental powers, but I wasn't sure what other magic they possessed or if she was a bondmated pair.

Once I was satisfied with the layers of wards, I stood and rifled through my bag for my healer's kit. Finding it, I set to work cleaning her wounds. The three long gashes open across her chest were the worst. One of them was so deep I could see her actual collarbone. I could smell the poison; its tangy scent hung in the air, and I tasted metal on my tongue. Thank the Powers I wasn't squeamish.

The blood had dried, and I had to pull the tattered fabric of her dress away from the deep wound. It tugged at the jagged edges. It was a blessing she was unconscious since I had only a small vial of dolor—a herb with sedative properties—in my kit.

It wasn't common in my homeland. In fact, not much grew where I was from. Those who lived there relied mostly on fishing, hunting, and trade. Even the forest in the southern mountains was a day's trip on foot. Everything else was imported, and many couldn't afford the steep prices. Luckily, I'd learned how to identify the precious herbs and flowers, so as I trekked further north, I was able to replenish my supplies. It was one of the benefits of having a healer as my teacher. The Air Fae Kingdom had an abundance of foliage to choose from.

I spread my pack on the ground, surveying my inventory. The more I inspected the inflicted damage, the more my uncertainty grew. Even the master healers wouldn't give her a high likelihood of survival. Deep blue and purple bruises had already formed on her abdomen and lower body from the fiend falling on her. Just by looking at her, I would guess she had at least four broken ribs. She also had a considerable cut on her upper arm.

I carefully cut her dress apart and removed it from her in pieces, draping a thin blanket over her mostly naked body. Only a thin shift remained, although it too was soaked in fiend blood. I debated for a few minutes. I'd seen nudity in my line of work with the healers. It didn't bother me in the slightest, but there weren't many females who'd appreciate being stripped down without their consent. She did have a breast band and underwear beneath the shift, though.

Despite my initial hesitation, I cut the shift off and discarded it. I didn't dare to remove anything else, even if it made my job harder. If she somehow survived, I'm sure she wouldn't be happy to wake up completely naked.

I held my hands over a wound, fingers spread wide. I focused on the energy flowing through my body and recited the incantation to share that energy and restore hers—*sana conso lenire*. With a simple turn of my wrists and a touch of my fourth finger on my left hand, her rune-covered skin knit itself back together before my eyes. The edges lined up perfectly, leaving the runes uninterrupted. Healer Uzin would have been proud. I wasn't skilled enough to handle larger injuries with spells alone, but shallow cuts and scrapes were easy. The mastery came from making the scars invisible. Sadly, that wouldn't be a probability for the ones on her chest and arm. I sterilized a needle in my candle's flame and began the tedious task of suturing her up. I started with a deeper layer and thread spelled to dissolve over time. I took great care in making sure the muscles lined up properly before the top layers of skin were closed.

When I finished dressing the wounds and casting the healing spells on the lesser injuries and stitching up the deeper lacerations, I rinsed the blood—both the female's and fiend's—from my hands . I'd need to fetch some more water tomorrow. I saw a small stream a short way back the way I came.

I watched her for a long moment. She looked so close to death. The thought made my chest hurt.

I leaned down close to her, my mouth hovering close to her ear. "Rest. You're safe," I whispered before getting up and settling by the fire just outside the tent for the night.

SIX

KATURI

My breaths were ragged. I was running out of oxygen. This mountain was going to cave him and crush me. I was going to be crushed by my own elemental. I was losing it. Delrik's shadows had sealed us in this blasted cave, protecting us from the fiends if they chose to return, but I needed fresh air. As in, if I didn't get out of this enclosed mountain, I'd risk my life diving through the shadows. Seriously, I had about five more minutes. Delrik's inky shadows writhed as if taunting me. Eleni rested her head on my knee, knowing my anxiety of being trapped beneath the ground.

I couldn't take it. I wiped my sweaty palms on my pants and quickly stood.

It wasn't until the immediate threat had passed that I noticed Nyla wasn't with us. How could we have left her behind? How had I not noticed? A pang of guilt stabbed me. I was too focused on Garren that I'd literally left her behind. If—no, *when*—we found her alive, I'd beg for her forgiveness. I couldn't sit still. I paced back and forth. Each time I made a pass across the small space, the walls got closer and closer together. Okay, that wasn't true. The walls weren't moving. Was I walking faster? I tried to shake the tension from my body, but nothing was working. I needed Garren. I needed to get out of this cave.

Garren and Delrik reentered the cave, followed by Aura, after what seemed like an eternity. I held my breath, waiting for Nyla to follow. But she wasn't there.

Delrik was to Evren in seconds. He lifted her from the ground and pressed his forehead against hers. The shadows wrapped around her in an embrace.

Coming to my side, Garren brushed the back of his fingers across my cheek, and Eleni whimpered at my feet. I pressed my hand into his chest and let his beating heart steady mine. His ice magic reached into my palm and calmed me.

"She's gone. Delrik and I looked everywhere," he said. "Drake is still out. He's flying north and is going to meet us in Agni. He's hoping to spot Knox and also lead any straggling fiends away from us."

I sucked in a breath.

Nazneen said, "Maybe she got up and walked away? She was only momentarily unconscious."

"She probably realized she got separated and made it somewhere safe. She's a seer, she'll know that we are going to head to Laeto Selva after Agni, and she'll meet us there." My bondmate seemed confident she was safe, so I leaned into his assurances.

Aura hopped from Delrik's shoulder to Nazneen's and gently nibbled at her ear. Nazneen absentmindedly ruffled the sleek feathers on top of her head.

Evren reached out and grabbed my free hand. She agreed with a nod.

"She may be tiny, but she's a badass," Nazneen said.

They were right. I'd seen Nyla fight in Noirdan. She was a force to be reckoned with. She may have been knocked down, but she was too strong to stay down. At least I prayed to the gods that it was the case. And with Knox, her getting to Laeto Selva wouldn't be a problem. Eleni curled herself around my legs to comfort me.

"If she doesn't show up in Laeto Selva, we'll send out a search party. But it isn't safe to stay here," Garren said.

"Agreed. We need to get moving," Delrik said.

Delrik stroked a finger down the delicate feathers of one of Evren's wings. She was hardly ever in a partial-shifted form anymore.

"Now that we know we were being watched, we need to be more careful concealing our tracks and watching our backs," Delrik stated.

"I'm already ahead of you, brother. Once we get clear of the mountains and back to the forest, we can fly the rest of the way," Nazneen chirped.

Evren and Nazneen gathered the last of the water skins, and I double-checked the packs Garren and Delrik had salvaged from where they'd been abandoned when we were first attacked. Nothing appeared to be missing, thankfully.

We walked back through the valley the way we'd come to a stream. We refreshed our water supply and cleaned ourselves up. The water downstream ran murky and polluted with the grime of the fiends.

I followed behind everyone, lost in thought. Hadeon clearly knew where we were if the fiends had found us. I think he was enjoying taunting us. Hadeon Allerick. The bastard. The one trying to find all the relics to open the veils between realms to release the Great Chaos, just as his father had done during the Uprising. Hadeon's father was the one responsible for establishing The Guild.

I'd heard of the Sacred Forest, the result of the god of earth trapping the evil within the gnarled trees. The gods left the forest stretching across our realm as a reminder of the Chaos and what happens when those revolt against the gods.

I stepped up next to Evren. "You've been to the Scared Forest, right?"

Her steps faltered a moment. "Yes. It isn't really a place I'd visit again if I could help it."

"Most wouldn't voluntarily step into the Sacred Forest," Nazneen said. "Well, I say most. Delrik loved the Sacred Forest. It's like his happy place."

"It isn't my happy place. I just don't see why everyone is terrified of a bunch of trees," he said from in front of us.

Him and Garren were leading us. We'd decided to travel at night and stay off the well-known path for safety. Delrik was on high alert, as were his shadows. They clung close to our group, ready to shield us from prying eyes.

"What do the trees look like?" I asked. I'd read about them and seen drawings.

"I had to pass through the Sacred Forest when I ran away from home. And Delrik and I had walked through it again on our way to Arcelia. The Darkwood Trees had bark black as midnight. Branches spread low and wide, some even sweeping so close to the ground I could perch on them. They intertwined and stretched to the sky. The trunks were thicker than the stone pillars holding up the bridge leading to the River Kingdom and they reached well over fifty feet. The canopies of the Darkwood trees were all dark green and brown leaves as large as my hand. Deep veins ran through the leaves like veins in an arm. If you held it up to the sun, they almost appear to be pulsing."

Delrik took over for his Ashlyra. He spoke as if he'd memorized the text from a book, his voice monotone and flat. "Each tree was said to be an evil being trapped forever by the God of Earth. It's why the black bark was twisted and gnarled as if it were reaching to escape something. The gods left the forest stretching across our realm as a reminder of the Chaos and what happens when those revolt against the gods. The forest was a whole new creature itself. It is said to breathe with the wind that whispers throughout its canopy, like a pulsing presence. Eerie noises coming from deep within it like a foreign language no one could understand, beckoning visitors to go deeper."

I'd wanted to visit when I'd first arrived in Illoterra, but Holden, Garren's father, had forbidden it. He kept Kanevvluk locked up tight. All of Illoterra was so different from Quinterre.

Now, here I am. Heading home to Laeto Selva in search of a long-lost relic in an attempt to save our realm. What could go wrong?

SEVEN
NYLA

I blinked and was met by blinding light. I snapped my eyes closed against the pain and barely managed to roll to my side away from the brightness. My head felt fuzzy, and everything began to spin. Vomit came up before I could stop it. My stomach clenched as it emptied completely.

I sucked in a painful breath once the retching stopped. The cool fabric of the bedroll pressed against my cheek. It felt wonderful against my clammy skin. I was hot, yet freezing at the same time. I groaned as my stomach heaved again.

Okay. The light wasn't blinding, but it was brighter than the back of my eyelids.

What happened? I strained to remember.

There were fiends. A lot of them. I remembered killing one...or had I? I recall the taste of its blood in my mouth. I squeezed the bridge of my nose, begging my head to cease its pounding. Evren, flying with her onyx wings stretched wide. Nazneen calling out to me and...

Fear gripped me as everything came back in stark clarity, and my hand flew to my chest. I howled as pain sliced through me. My raw throat made my scream come out in just a rasp.

All of it had been real. It hadn't been a dream or a vision.

"You're awake."

I went rigid, not daring to breathe.

I wasn't alone.

Where was I? And who in the circle of dark hells is here with me? Everything hurt, but the back of my head and my chest most of all. I felt so weak. The stench of blood and antiseptic herbs filled the air.

Buttery sunlight filtered in through the flap of the tent I was in as it was pulled back, casting the stranger in shadow.

"You're awake."

I reached for my air magic, for Knox, for anything, but my power wasn't there. Nothing. The panic that had begun to creep in at the memory of the fiend atop me was about to explode at the deep, baritone voice. I couldn't let my weakness show. I didn't know who this male was, but I was clearly in a very vulnerable position. I couldn't even protect myself. Was I still dreaming? This definitely wasn't a dream. I was in too much pain for it to be a dream. I sucked in an agonizing breath and almost passed out again at a spasm as my chest expanded.

This is not good. Salina was right. I shouldn't have left the temple.

"Sorry about that," the low voice with a thick accent said. "I didn't mean to startle you."

Dark hells. That voice was terrifying...and as smooth as silk.

My head was swimming. I couldn't place it. The accent. I'd heard it before, but I couldn't remember where. Somewhere in the southern part of Quinterre, maybe? My head was swimming, and I couldn't focus. I blinked several times to get my eyes to focus.

He stepped into the tent, and the flap closed. Although I was thankful for the lessened light, the feeling of being trapped had dread ratcheting higher and higher. I swallowed painfully against my raw throat.

"It took you long enough. I thought you were taking a turn for the worse, but last night your fever broke."

Was that a touch of irritation in his voice? I tried to call upon my elemental air yet again. Nothing. Powers Above, now was not the time to be helpless. I looked everywhere but at him. But as if he were a flame and I was a moth, my eyes were drawn to him, starting at his feet and traveling up, up, up to his face. Fuck, he was massive.

The male cleared his throat. I was staring. I couldn't help it. The male before me, standing with a predatory stillness, had a hysterical laugh slip from my lips. My muscles ached as I pushed myself up to a sitting position. I felt exposed under his scrutinizing gaze. The way he was looking at me was like I was an unwanted thorn in his side. How long had I been out of it? How long have I been alone with him? He said last night, so that means I'd at least been out a day. I guess since I was alive and breathing, that was a plus. He hadn't killed me. Yet.

"Where am I?" My tongue was heavy in my mouth.

He shrugged. "Somewhere in the Baxmar Mountains, just outside the border of the Fire Fae Kingdom, I believe."

Okay, so in the same place I'd been with the others. Maybe they were still nearby.

"And my friends?"

"Friends?"

I had been alone when he found me?

"Who are you?"

"Who are *you*?" he countered.

I pressed my lips together in irritation. What was with repeating my questions?

He took a step forward, and I sprang to my feet. Well, I tried to. My knees buckled beneath me, and the edges of my vision went black. Everything tilted as I fell back to the bedroll. Even through the layers of bedding, I felt the bite of the stone on my knees. My hands caught me, so at least I remained somewhat upright. The knotted mess of my hair swung into my face, blinding me monetarily. He didn't try to catch me. He also didn't retreat. He only let out an irritated sigh.

"Powers Above," he muttered and rolled his eyes.

Three long strides and he was standing over me. He squatted down so that we were almost eye level. Almost. Even squatting, he was taller than me, and I had to tilt my chin up to look at his face. The skin on my chest pulled tight, and I winced. I was completely at his mercy. His pants pulled tight over defined, powerful muscles.

He was so close. Maybe only a foot away. I could reach out and touch him, which I definitely did *not* want to do...

His eyes, a vortex of color, took me in. There was something so familiar about him, but I couldn't place it. I squinted. His face came in and out of focus. Haunting, dark eyes. Straight nose. Squared jaw. Then a shimmer of the light, like I was peering at him through water. For a fractured moment, the male I was looking at morphed into something scary. A ripple. It was either the dim light playing tricks on me or I'd had my head bashed in harder than I'd thought.

Lines formed between his brows as he scowled at my assessment of him. I wanted to trace the lines with my fingers. No one was ever this close to me. Most stayed a healthy distance from the most powerful seer and elemental in the Air Fae Kingdom. My heart was fluttering faster than the wings of a hummingbird trapped in a cage, just like I was trapped within his gaze, and I couldn't slow it down. Something that wasn't fae nor human. Something different and unknown.

"You're staring." His voice was pleasant, smooth, almost hypnotic.

My eyes dragged down the column of his throat to his chest. His shirt clung tightly over muscles cut with precision. The V of the neck was open, showing off the rich, smooth skin of warm chestnut. His shirt hugged his muscular arms. Strength and power radiated from him. His elbows were resting on his knees, hands casually relaxed. Powerful thighs and...bare feet. He wasn't wearing shoes. Why did I find that charming?

I shifted backwards away from him. He reached out toward my upper arm and pulled me closer still.

"Don't touch me," I snapped.

The moment the harsh words left my mouth, I felt guilty. Embarrassed maybe? Why? He hadn't moved quickly or in a threatening way, and yet I acted like he was about to attack me.

Something flashed momentarily when he leaned in a touch closer. Something terrifying gripped me. A flash of something. And then it was gone.

I wasn't used to being touched. Sometimes, people touching my bare skin would cause visions. But mostly, I wasn't ever close enough to others, physically or emotionally, to be touched without permission. Hazard of the job, I guess. Physical contact was always on my terms. Except for Nazneen. She was allowed. She wouldn't know what a personal boundary was, even if it smacked her in the face.

I quickly cast my face down to my hands, clenching tight to the blanket. His other hand shot out, this time not bothering to move slowly, and caught my jaw. He forced me to look into his eyes again. Darkness rippled across his face. That underwater feeling again. His fingers felt rough against my skin, but his grip wasn't painful, just firm. He drew in a deep breath. Something about his dark eyes felt out of place, like they didn't belong to him. As he exhaled, his pupils expanded.

He was fucking smelling me. Powers Above. Males were so gross.

I had been frightened when he first came so close, but now I was annoyed. Who did he think he was, touching me like that? I narrowed my eyes at him and jerked my face free from his grasp.

"I need to check your injuries. I've spent the last three days keeping you from dying. And I'm not going to let your stubbornness be the thing that kills you." He reached behind him to grab what looked like a healer's pack. "I'm no healer, but I've been keeping your wounds clean. Now hold still and stop fighting me."

I hadn't had a chance to survey the scrapes, cuts, and bruises that covered me. Now that I was focused on something other than the stranger, I could feel my whole body throbbing again. Everything felt woozy as I took in the blood and stitches and...

Powers Above I'm going to faint.

"You alright?" he asked.

He must have noticed the color draining from my face. Or maybe I was flushed? I couldn't tell. I hated blood. The smell of it. The sight of it.

"Fine." I swallowed the metallic taste in my mouth.

Each injury pulsed at the same rate as my quickening heart. I sat back on the bedroll. He didn't release my arm. Was he steadying me so I didn't topple over? He wasn't being a brute, but didn't let my guard down. Once I was settled, he released me.

I suddenly realized most of my clothes had been removed. Had he removed my clothes? My breast band was all that was covering me. A thin blanket was pooled in my lap. I lifted the blanket to cover more of myself. He ignored my shyness and carried on laying out his supplies and studying each abrasion thoroughly. His hands were nothing but professional as they examined me. I wondered how long he had been a healer. Wait, he said he wasn't a healer? How did he learn such skills?

Why hadn't my High Fae healing powers healed me yet?

Like he could read my mind, he answered my unasked question. "I'm not sure why you are taking so long to heal. You have a nasty wound here." He placed a finger over my heart. Energy danced across my skin at the contact. Darkness was veining out from three stitched cuts that ran from my collarbone to my sternum. "If it was from the talon of the fiends, they like to dip their talons in poison. I assumed that's what was preventing you from healing. I've been using a salve to draw out the poison. It's working, but slowly. You may still have side effects for a few days. I'm not sure how long your magic will be dampened."

How does he know about poison? And how does he know about my magic?

"How do you know I have powers?"

He arched an elegant eyebrow. He traced his eyes along the arch of my high-pointed Fae ears. "I assumed."

I absentmindedly touched my ear.

He shifted so that he was kneeling next to me rather than crouching, and confidently reached for my arm again. His eyes asked silent permission before his long fingers curled around my bicep.

He unwound the bloody fabric bandage that was wrapped around my upper arm. Carefully, he lifted my arm for closer inspection before dabbing salve on the stitches. It too had black veins streaking from the jagged edges, but they were much more faded than those on my chest. His touch didn't hurt really, just itched as he layered on the pungent goo that smelled heavily of herbs. Then he muttered a healing spell under his breath.

"Sana conso lenire."

I recognized it as one similar to those the healers of the temple had used when working with the refugees from the war and again with those we'd rescued from Noirdan. I'd enjoyed watching the healers work over the years at the temple. They had such kind eyes and soft hands. Even the most terrified child could be calmed by their gentle voices.

He moved on to a few smaller scrapes that appeared mostly healed after he'd rewrapped my bicep. As he focused, his hands were gentle. The corner of his mouth tipped up slightly. He seemed pleased with his work.

He sat back on his heels and wiped his hands on the clean scrap of fabric. He studied me.

"The last one will be easier if you lie back."

I looked at him in question. His eyes dipped to my chest. His brows were tense and his jaw tight.

I couldn't stop the blush that crept across my throat. "Oh."

This wasn't the first time I'd been nearly naked in front of a male. Priestesses weren't *required* to remain celibate. It was only a recommendation. After 600 years, I knew my way around my own body and that of a male. So why was I blushing like a young girl?

EIGHT
DESMUND

Color continued to spread down her neck and across her chest, making her ivory runes stand out, but she lay back on the bedroll without a fuss. The thin blanket that she'd had a death grip on while she was sitting was now draped across her flat stomach. I peeled back the layer of bandage that I'd secured around her chest, leaving only a breastband.

She kept her eyes focused on the tent ceiling while I worked. Her breaths were controlled and even. Practiced. It was obvious she was doing her best to hide her fluster. I could hear her wildly pounding heart. Even her fists were clenched tight.

I took the opportunity to study her face as she clenched her jaw. She looked peaceful while sleeping. Now, she was a completely different creature. There were dark smudges under her eyes like she hadn't slept in days, which was the exact opposite. All she'd done was sleep. I couldn't even rouse her to eat. I squeezed drops of water from a clean shirt onto her parched lips. It was proof that the poison was truly taxing her body and magic.

"My name is Desmund," I finally said in an attempt to break the unease.

She blinked twice and then looked at me. Those eyes—heterochrome mahogany and blue. They made mine feel dull in comparison. They held so much wisdom.

She hesitated a moment. "Nyla."

"Nyla." It flowed off my tongue in an elegant, smooth way.

Like the way a bird glides through the sky on a breeze. My mouth tipped at the corner in what I hoped was a friendly smile. I wasn't one to smile, so I wasn't sure if it looked more like a grimace than anything.

She swallowed, then quickly returned her gaze to the ceiling.

I worked quietly, too busy in my own thoughts for idle chit chat. She'd asked about her friends, and I'd evaded the question. I wasn't planning on telling her that I'd watched her fight with the fiends. I saw the blow that had knocked her out. I didn't tell her that after I'd brought her to my camp and handled her wounds, that the two males she'd been traveling with had climbed up the steep mountainside to where I'd been camped in search of her, or that I'd overheard them discussing their plans at the stream.

I placed a heavy ward around the campsite to prevent detection. I'd stood just outside the tent, Nyla hanging onto the last thread of life only three feet from me. The two males stood talking, their voices low and muffled from the thick enchantments. They stood with their backs to me, so I couldn't see their faces.

"Kat isn't going to be happy with leaving Nyla behind," one of them had said.

"We don't have a choice. If we stay, we will surely be attacked again," the other replied.

I'd watched from my perch above the pass as the males returned to the cave. When the sun peeked over the horizon the next morning, they'd made their way to the stream, and I sent my astral projection to follow.

They trekked south, back down the mountain, no more than half a mile, not knowing their friend was so close, and I didn't dare inform them. The water's edge of the small stream I'd passed just yesterday. I was invisible, hanging back in the sparse treeline. The winged one stretched out her ebony wings. The morning sun was swallowed up by their darkness. They were so different from the fiends' wings.

I'd watched as they packed all their belongings and started off north to the Fire Kingdom. If the fiends being so close were any prediction, I'd say they weren't going to be happy with what they found when they arrived in Agni.

I dipped another clean scrap of fabric into an herbal tea I'd brewed and began to clean around the stitches. The wild yarrow and calendula were widespread near Proux. The aloe and lavender came from my healer's kit. Nyla hissed when it touched her skin. I hated being the cause of her pain, but didn't withdraw. It had to be done; there was no point in prolonging the process. Another tip I'd learned from the healers.

The wound was raw and angry, but the black drawing salve made of ground charcoal, lavender, and rosemary was doing its job. The poison was already receding. The black veining had been creeping up her neck by the time I'd finished stitching her back together. Now it was only an inch or so from the original wounds.

After I cleaned it thoroughly, I pulled out the jar of salve and applied a thick layer.

"I'll be able to remove the stitches in a few days."

These would not heal as nicely as the other runes, unfortunately. The thought of having anything marring her skin made my heart ache.

Nyla nodded but kept her eyes focused on a point above her. She was strong. There were few who laid completely still while being tended to.

Nyla was quiet while I redressed the wound. I'd studied the runes on her body while she'd been unconscious. They were the ancient languages. I'd never been taught to read or speak the ancient language, but it was easy to recognize them.

I gathered the ends of the binding and secured them over her chest. I was done caring for her wounds, but I didn't want to take my hands off her. Not yet. Just one more minute of her softness under my rough fingers.

The moment I was done, she rolled away from me and sat up with her back to me. She clutched the thin blanket to her chest. She wasn't revealing anything scandalous, yet my imagination was running wild. I breathed in her scent again. A crisp, fresh breeze mixed with potent herbs. I knew what her skin felt like beneath my fingers. I relished it.

I stood to give her privacy before I did something stupid like give in to my carnal thoughts. I pulled the tent flap back to leave.

A demure voice followed me like a gentle current. "Thank you."

I faltered upon hearing her words. It was an odd feeling. I wasn't used to receiving gratitude for anything or from anyone.

Part Two

NINE
GARREN

The City of Agni

We headed north, away from Proux and closer to the unknown City of Agni. The capital of the Fire Fae Kingdom was isolated by the volcanic mountains of the Baxmar Range. Not even Delrik had ventured this far north before. Due to the wealth of nutrients in the volcanic soil, they didn't have to rely on imported food to sustain their kingdom. They were almost as isolated as the Snowhaven Fae were in Illoterra. Though, the king of Fire Fae traveled more than my father, High Ruler Holden Eckhardt of the Snowhaven Fae. The moment we crossed into the Fire Fae Kingdom, the climate changed. Glistening, white winter land became arid and dry.

The city was quiet. No insects hummed. No birds or scurrying animals. A gentle wind tossed a shredded banner to and fro. The Fire Fae Kingdom was in the northernmost part of Quinterre. Mountains on the eastern side separated it from the Air Fae Kingdom. The Fire Fae had always had some kind of tension with the rest of the High Fae Kingdoms and kept mostly to themselves. However, since the war and King Ziven, the new king of the Fire Fae, coming into power, the establishment of strict rules across the kingdom lessened the tension.

"There should be a shield, but I don't feel it," I said.

"Me either," Delrik agreed.

"Maybe they knew we were coming?" Katuri said from my side.

"No. It isn't like the Snowhaven shield that keeps people out. It just alerts the kingdom of larger groups to prepare them for potential attacks," I explained.

Though I'd never experienced the various wards around the kingdoms of Quinterre, I'd studied each of them in preparation for the war. The War Across the Sea or The Great War as it was called here in Quinterre.

When we stepped over the border, Evren stopped dead in her tracks. As if energy flowed from the ground directly into her, a ripple of power rushed up her body, flaring her sleek wings wide. Fire erupted at their tips and her eyes blared brighter than embers.

"What was that?" she asked, concerned.

"That, Ashlyra, is you connecting with your elemental fire. It must be heightened since we are in the Fire Fae Kingdom," Delrik explained.

It took us only a few days to reach the lower elevation of the mountains where the trees began to grow again. They were different from the Baxmar Range. They had sparse leaves with thorns along their trunks. Off in the distance, volcanoes lined the horizon. The earth changed in color the closer it got to the volcanoes.

"The volcanic ash and lava fields look burned and black, but they are rich in minerals. Perfect for growth. It's only the surrounding area that looks dead," Evren said.

Evren spent so much time with her nose in a book in Kanevvluk, she probably knew every part of the histories in Quinterre.

"You're like a walking library aren't you, Ev?" I poked her in the side.

She rolled her eyes and Aura, who'd been flying back and forth above us, swooped down and gave me a gentle peck on the top of the head.

"Aura, love! You know I'm right?"

She replied with a sharp screech.

I'd seen drawings in books of the City of Agni. A thriving city of agriculture and technology. Rolling fields of rich, dark soil and brightly colored crops of all shapes and sizes. The technology here was far beyond that of the rest of the continent. They thrived on engineering and the sciences. What was considered modern to the rest of the realm was far in the past in Agni.

However, that was not the city we found.

I could smell the smoke—thick, unpleasant sulfur—before we saw the smoldering remains of the city. The sky was a hazy amber. Katuri covered her mouth against the ashy air. We picked our way through the deserted, demolished city. Swirling mist hung low over the mountains. No. That wasn't mist. It was hissing steam and ash. I swallowed in an attempt to wet my parched throat. The air was too dry. My water magic was not a fan of the lack of moisture in the air.

The keep that had once surrounded the city had crumbled to the ground as if it was smashed by giant boulders. The city was also in ruins. Not too far in the distance sat two steaming volcanoes, which now towered above us. According to historical references, they were a representation of the god of fire and his consort. The Temple of Anruin stood out at the base of the two slumbering giants.

"What happened here?" said Evren. She clutched her chest.

The once grand city has been reduced to rubble.

"That must be the temple," Katuri said.

"Or what's left of it," I sighed.

"It's the best place to start," Katuri replied.

We picked our way through the charred city toward the temple. A dull clanging from a bell near the keep walls moved in the arid wind. It only added to the eeriness. Small fires burned. Evren, on instinct, reached out toward a nearby fire and it jumped from its source to her hand, essentially smothering it out. The fire absorbed into her skin.

"Whoa! That's never happened before. It's like my elemental power summoned the flames and they obeyed."

"Let's search for survivors," Delrik suggested.

We split up. Delrik and Evren moved off in the direction of the still-smoldering fires. Evren snuffed them out one by one. Not going to lie, that was a pretty nifty trick. Katuri and I made our way through the center of the city and the opposite side of the keep. The city was nowhere near as large as other cities I've visited as far as land. Rather, their buildings stretched into the sky.

"I don't understand how this could happen," my bondmate said.

I took her hand and soothed her through our bond.

"The fiends must have attacked the same way they had in Proux," I said.

"They seem to be moving quickly."

Were the fiends going city to city? I felt worry through the bond and studied Katuri's face as her eyes swept over the destruction. Was Katuri's home and family safe? I knew she was nervous about returning to Laeto Selva and reuniting with her family. The last thing she needed was the threat of fiends torching the forest before we arrived.

"Over there," Nazneen called, pulling Kat and I both from thoughts.

I turned to see her pointing in the direction of a circular structure. The temple. We climbed our way over debris toward the temple. It was barely standing. Once we reached the top, we all stood shoulder to shoulder in shock.

Suddenly, there was a snap and a column came crashing to the ground. Shit. We were too close. I threw myself toward my bondmate and formed a shield of ice around us. I pulled at my power with all my strength. There was no moisture in the air and the heat coming from the volcanoes was melting my shield faster than I could replenish it. The marble column nearly smashed us. It landed only a few feet away.

"Kat!" Nazneen yelled and rushed over to check we were alright.

"I'm fine. We're fine," Katuri called back.

Debris and ash plumed in the air, making me sputter and cough. When the air cleared, I spotted someone buried in the rubble.

"There's someone over here!" I said.

Katuri and Nazneen scrambled forward, pulling large chunks of crumbled marble off the priestess. I was right behind them.

A woman lay beneath the rubble. Chocolate brown hair was a tangled mess and most of her skin was covered in a layer of ash. Her eyes were dull but widened slightly when she saw us. She wore the same symbol as Nyla—a pentagon with two circles. A priestess of the temple. Or at least, she had been. Her lips and around her mouth were a pale shade of blue. She took short, gasping breaths. A massive beam lay across her chest, slowly crushing her to death. Katuri tried to lift it, but it was too heavy. I tapped her shoulder so that Delrik and I could grab an end. We began to lift. It budged, but the priestess cried out in pain, causing us to stop.

"Don't," she wheezed painfully. "It's over. It's my time for Evermere."

Nazneen lifted stones larger than my fist off her arms. Each stone revealed more damage. The bone of the priestess' forearm jabbed through the skin. I cringed. How could she not feel that? I guess when you're being crushed slowly to death, a small broken bone was the least of your worries. Nazneen knelt beside the dying priestess. She reached for her swollen hand and clasped it, offering the only comfort she could in the last moments.

"What happened?" I asked.

"Hadeon Allerick," she gasped painfully. "He did this."

"He was here?"

What the fuck? Hadeon himself. I could see him sending out his fiends to do his dirty work, but to show up himself. He must be more desperate for the relics than we initially believed. Evren and Delrik stepped up behind me.

"He took it," the priestess shuddered out roughly.

"Took what?" Nazneen asked.

"The Orb of Sfar. The fire relic."

"Shit," Delrik cursed.

How had she known that's what we were looking for?

"The relic was here?" Katuri asked, now kneeling beside Nazneen.

The priestess swallowed and feebly nodded her head. "Yes. We've been keeping it safely hidden for centuries."

"But how?"

"Only the most trusted priestesses of the temple knew. We passed down the unwritten words to keep the truth hidden from those who may use the relic for evil. Even King Ziven didn't know where it was. The gods wanted the relics to be kept safe after the Uprising so that's what we did."

She let out a weak cough. Had she not trusted the king? Nyla had told us that only the highest-ranking High Fae knew about the relics originally. It seemed odd that the king of the Fire Fae didn't know where the Orb of Sfar was located.

"But it was all for nothing." The priestess coughed, a trail of blood leaking from the corner of her mouth. "He has it now."

"Where is the king?"

"Hadeon killed him before setting the city on fire with his pyre. King Ziven refused to ally with him and give the names of the priestesses. He killed almost all of us. One by one. It didn't matter. He found the relic anyway."

Mad props to the fire king for staying strong and not giving up the priestesses.

She coughed again and then with one last, quivering breath, went still.

Nazneen leaned forward and brushed a hand over her face. "May you rest peacefully in Evermere."

A lone tear slipped down Katuri's soot stained cheek. I hadn't known this priestess, but the weight of her death hung over us.

"What now? Obviously, there is nothing for us here."

Katuri stood and slowly surveyed our surroundings. The city was not only demolished but also abandoned. Either the people were all killed, or they ran for their lives. Hadeon hadn't been here that long ago. Hours maybe. Most of the rubble was fresh, still hot to the touch. How had we missed him? How had we not heard the commotion?

"We need to get to Laeto Selva as soon as possible," Katuri stated, almost in a whisper.

My head snapped to my bondmate.

Laeto Selva was our next planned stop, but the fact that Kat was now in a hurry to get there was a new development. While I knew she missed her childhood home, facing her father again was nerve wracking.

"We can take our time," I began.

"No. We don't know where Hadeon is going next. He's been one step ahead of us and laughing at us all along the way. I can't delay the inevitable."

"I'll be by your side the whole time," I said as I laced my fingers with hers. I sent a comforting wave down our bond.

"I'm pretty sure my father knows where the relic is that had been given to the Forest Fae. I remember a special room that was guarded around the clock and warded against entry. I peeked in once. I'd been maybe nine years old. The door had been cracked open, and I'd heard my father's voice inside. When I spied through the opening, I'd seen him in a heated whispered argument with another male whose back was turned to me. The room had been empty, except for a pedestal and a glass case. A firm hand had pulled me away before I could see any more."

I shifted into my sea dragon form to scan the area and check for any survivors. There were none. I used my elemental water to douse the remaining fires alongside Evren. She'd done most of the work while we'd been with the priestess. The dry air left me feeling parched. Thankfully, we wouldn't be here long. I dipped into a small lake. Its water tasted like sulfur and was warmer than bath water, but it was water, so I wasn't going to complain.

By the time we'd made our way out of the city and discovered a safe place to rest, it was night. A small stable on the outskirts of the city keep's walls. It was one of the only buildings still standing.

It was a rickety thing. Thankfully, we were no longer in the mountains with the piercing cold so that sparse walls wouldn't be a problem.

"This will do," Evren said.

She was always so positive.

"Agreed. I don't think the fiends will be returning. They've clearly completed the task they were sent here for," Delrik agreed as he kissed his bondmate's head.

Evren had no issue starting a fire for us to cook a meager meal of quail and potatoes. Nazneen, with all her spy and warrior training, was a pro at cooking over an open fire.

"Do you remember when we first met?" Nazneen asked Evren. She was squatting next to a pile of brush and twigs we'd gathered.

"And you were terrified I was going to burn down Arcelia with my fire curse?"

With a twist of her wrist, Evren sent a spark from her fingertip to a stick Nazneen was holding out for her to light.

"Look how far we've come! Trusting you to light the fire while I'm sitting right here," Nazneen said, twirling a small twig that was lit at the end. "You can even control that grump of a brother of mine."

Delrik, with his enhanced speed, knocked Nazneen over on her butt, but she just laughed it off. "I'm just playing, brother. You know you are my favorite person ever!"

Eleni's head snapped up. "Second to you of course my gorgeous canine."

Satisfied, Eleni relaxed her head on her crossed paws.

"Evren, did you really try to burn down their house?" Garren asked.

"No! I simply burst into flames. Well controlled, I assure you," she replied.

"There was nothing controlled about that night," Delrik said.

"You're just mad I dragged you all over the continent after that and got you cursed by Alux. But we'd never be here today if I hadn't."

"True my Ashlyra. Very true."

We were all quiet and retrospective the remainder of the evening. Not much was said. No jokes were cracked. We'd seen the growing darkness in Noirdan, and now, the City of Agni was decimated. It was heavy on all our shoulders.

We rose with the sun the following morning. The sun's rays cast a golden glow, making the city appear to be alright again.

Just as we were preparing to leave, I spotted movement across a vast open field. Several horses were running free. Clearly their owner had released them in hopes of saving them from the invasion. The poor beasts were scared and confused.

"They're thoroughbreds," Evren said with a broad smile. "My father loved to collect expensive things from all parts of the realm. We had several of them in our stables growing up. I loved visiting them, but I wasn't allowed to ride them. They were one of his prized possessions."

"They're beautiful," Katuri said in awe.

Katuri walked over to the fence that separated the open field and the barn. She stepped over the charred remains of a fence and out into the field. I felt her earth elemental power blossom like a spring flower and then surround her. She stretched it outward and toward the confused animals. I could see the moment her magic contacted them. I could feel it too. Through our bond, their fear was a bitter taste in my mouth. But then they calmed, eased by the comfort of my bondmate's power. I'd never seen her use her power with animals before and it was a sight to behold. The horses willingly trotted over to her. They nudged their noses against her open palms. She scratched their noses and then pressed her forehead to a dark copper one whose face was almost completely white and dusted with soot and ash. Seven horses. I send a quick prayer of thanks to the Powers Above for providing us with transportation.

Eleni jumped and played through the legs of the stallion. It snorted at her and bumped his nose at her.

"Sundance," Katuri said with a smile. Her smile was the most beautiful view in the whole realm.It'd been days since I'd seen it.

"What?" I asked.

"His name is Sundance," she turned to me. The horse knickered. "It's like he's telling me his name. I can feel it in my heart."

I joined her at the fence. "That's a fancy trick."

"I wasn't sure if it would work to be honest."

I pressed my lips to hers. "You surprise me more and more each day."

There would be no restocking of our supplies as we'd planned. We'd have to make due with what we had. Thankfully, the stable had tack for the horses. Katuri refused to leave them behind. We strapped our ever-lightening packs to the two extra horses. At least the horses would make our trip easier.

Katuri stopped and squatted to the earth. "I want to try one more thing before we leave." She dug her fingers into the volcanic soil and closed her eyes.

"I can feel the earth. It's sad. But there is hope there too," she said.

She squeezed her eyes tighter. I felt my water magic being drawn into her, combining with her earth magic. Where her fingers touched, green grass sprouted. My water and the minerals in the earth spread quickly, turning the charred pasture green again. We all watched in amazement.

I bent down next to my bondmate, and ran my hands through the new grass. I gripped her chin tightly and kissed her with my everything.

"Now, when people return, they'll have healed land to regrow their crops."

TEN
NYLA

Somewhere in the Baxmar Range of Northern Quinterre

We stayed at the camp above the narrow valley for two more days. Two days for my mind to run wild with all the insane potential reasons my powers were gone. Desmund had said it was poison, but I didn't know if I trusted him. I was too weak to fend him off if he decided to attack or take advantage of me. But he tended to me with gentle hands and very few words. At this point, I had no choice but to trust him.

I still hadn't healed completely, but it was the first morning I hadn't felt dizzy upon sitting up, so I figured I'd try to stand. Desmund only spoke to me to clean my wounds and offer meals. He was usually gone when I woke up, but I knew he slept in the tent each night. There was a tidy pile of blankets on the ground next to the tent entrance and his scent, woody and sweet, hung in the air. I wasn't sure where he was when he wasn't tending to me; I didn't ask, and he didn't offer the information.

I shivered in the chilly morning air. Desmund had given me one of his shirts. Not only was it loose fitting but it buttoned up the front so that I didn't have to lift my arms to put it on. It made changing my bandages easier.

I tentatively stretched my arms over my head. The stitches in my arm pulled but they weren't painful. My legs were wobbly, but I managed to make it across the tent. Desmund had had to duck his head each time he was inside the tent, but I was short enough to stand to my full height. I pushed aside the tent flap and stepped into the morning air, shielding my eyes from the bright daylight. I shivered.

Desmund was sitting on a fallen tree trunk. A fire was burning in front of him. I looked around, taking in my surroundings. We were still in the mountains. To my left, I could see the valley where I'd fought the fiends. Where I had been left behind. I took a breath in, trying not to think about the abandonment. It wasn't the first time in my life I'd been left behind.

My mother and father had left me at the temple. I don't even remember what their reasoning was. It was so long ago. I'd been born there, raised there, trained there. Priestesshood was all I knew. And even though it was my choice to stay behind when my parents moved on, it still left the sting of being left behind. I could have chosen to go against my fate of being a priestess, but it didn't seem worth it. I'd eventually end up back here one way or another.

I'd always belonged to the temple. From my very first breath, I knew I would never have another life besides this one. Or so I thought. That was until the other elementals came into my life and turned it on end.

Desmund cleared his throat.

Well, I wasn't completely alone, I guess. Had he watched the fight? Had he seen me be ambushed by the fiend? Was that how I'd ended up in his care?

Desmund rolled up some articles of clothing and stuffed them into a pack. "There is some oatmeal for breakfast if you're hungry."

I looked in his direction. He hadn't lifted his head, just continued packing.

Why was he helping me? What was his motive? Did he believe he could use my seeing powers in some way? He said he knew I had magic, but I didn't know what exactly he knew. I was used to people asking me to read their futures. I never did. It was too unpredictable. Yes, some things came to be, but for minor life things, one small decision could send one's future in a completely different direction. I also found it tiresome to dig through other's minds and futures just because. I had more important things to do. I'd leave the future telling to the fortune tellers. Parlor tricks. Using cues from people's reactions to make educated guesses.

"Are you going somewhere?" I asked.

"We are going to Laeto Selva," he spoke without turning to me.

"We?"

"I mean, I guess I could leave you to fend for yourself. But considering how weak you are, I think it's in your best interest to come with me. I'm not going to sit on top of this mountain and freeze my ass off. It's only going to get colder."

I had to give him that. I wouldn't survive a day out here alone. Especially without my powers. They still hadn't returned. Knox, my familiar who'd been by my side for 600 years, wasn't here to protect me. My best guess was he'd return when my elemental air power did. Hopefully, that would be sooner rather than later. I was truly at the mercy of the gods and Desmund at this point.

It was convenient that Desmund was going to Laeto Selva. Almost too convenient. That's where everyone was headed after Agni. I could follow him there. It was better than traveling by myself in my weakened state. We had been banking on Evren's fire elemental keeping us warm during our hike over the mountains. He must have some magic or spell over the tent to hold in the heat because I hadn't noticed the bitter cold at night once my fever had lifted.

"If we want to make it before the next new moons, we need to get moving," he said.

He stood and disappeared inside the tent. I took his seat on the fallen tree trunk and leaned over the fire. I extended my fingers toward the flames and let the warmth seep into them. My clothes had been ruined during the fight. All I had was Desmund's shirt and a pair of old pants. I wasn't dressed for this climate in the slightest.

There was indeed a bowl with oatmeal in it. My stomach growled loudly at the smell of cinnamon and vanilla. I glanced quickly over my shoulder. How unladylike. Hopefully, Desmund didn't hear that. There was a fabric napkin and spoon sitting on the tree trunk. I lifted the bowl into my hands and breathed in the steam.

When Desmund exited the tent again, the bedroll and blankets I'd been sleeping on were rolled neatly and held together with a knotted tie. Then he methodically began taking the tent apart. I watched him work while I scarfed down breakfast. He probably could've set up and taken down that tent with his eyes closed. I watched his corded muscles methodically untied the stakes and wound the ropes neatly around his forearm, tying the ends in a slip knot. The fact that those brutish hands were so tender in their healing was a wonder.

Once he finalized packing the tent, Desmund dropped the overstuffed pack at his feet. He began to walk my way. I couldn't move. I sat there on the fallen tree, immobilized by the male coming toward me. As he grew closer, I tipped my chin up to keep my eyes on his. He stopped before me for a beat. One. Two. Then he draped a heavy cloak over my shoulders. It smelled just like him and it took everything I had not to bury my nose in the fabric.

"We should get going."

ELEVEN
KATURI

The City of Laeto Selva

I had mixed feelings about going home, but I knew we needed to. We needed the earth relic; I needed to put my feelings about my father aside. I had to keep the relic out of Hadeon's grasp and the best way to do that was to ensure its safety. It was time to finally face my father after forty years. He was the only other leader of the High Fae that may have information about where the relics could be. I only hoped we could make it to Laeto Selva before Hadeon. He might be heading this direction, or maybe already here. Although I was angry at my father, I didn't want the rest of my family to suffer the same fate as those in the Fire Fae city.

For the last few miles, I could feel the earth growing stronger. Now that we have crossed into the Forest Fae Kingdom, my elemental earth power stretched and awoke, but it wasn't until we reached the edge of the dense rainforest that I finally felt like I was home again. Unlike the separation between the Fire and Air Fae Kingdom, the Forest Fae had a dazzling barrier that surrounded the entire kingdom. A moss-green, transparent wall delineated the territory. It glittered in the sun. When we stepped through the barrier, it brushed along my skin like a hanging vine, gentle and soft. My magic welcomed the barrier of my home.

In response to my heightened magic, Sundance took off into a full gallop. I felt Garren on his horse at our heels. The anticipation of being in the rainforest was growing. I threw my arms aside and tossed my head back with a laugh. I let the wind sweep through my air.

I stopped Sundance before entering the dense trees. I turned my face to the sky and shut my eyes. I felt the wealth of life all around me. I took a deep breath. Rich air filled my lungs, my soul, fueling my magic. I swung my leg off my horse, and landed with a soft thump on the ground. Eleni was by my side, leaning into me the moment my feet hit the ground. Garren, who'd been just behind me, stopped and stood up in his saddle. I patted Sundance's neck and grinned at my bondmate. Evren, Delrik, and Nazneen weren't too far behind us.

I bent and removed my shoes and stockings. I wiggled my toes into the moist earth. I squatted to the ground, needing to press my fingers into the ground. It was calling me. I stretched my fingers out and greenery flowed from me. Rapid tendrils of all shades of green swirled out and around me. Flowers bloomed and the trees fruited as they reached towards me in return. Eleni grew before my eyes from the size of a large fox to an adult Kanevvluk wolf, who were closer to a small pony than dog-like. The first time I'd seen one of the legendary wolves in the Snowhaven Territory, I almost wet myself. Eleni's fur rippled with reds and bronzes as she shook herself out and arched her back in a stretch.

"I'm guessing even Eleni can feel the earth's power," Nazneen said as she and the others stopped their horses beside us.

The scent of the soil, leaves, and fragrant flowers filled my nose. The scent of an impending thunderstorm hung in the air. I'd missed the rolling sound of thunder.

I'd been homesick, but being back now, I couldn't hold back the tears. My vision blurred as they flooded down my face straight from the depths of my soul.

Garren appeared at my side. He kneeled next to me and my vines coiled around him the same as they had me. He pressed against me and wove his fingers into the hair at the nape of my neck. I welcomed his steady presence.

"Welcome home, Little Flower."

He twisted my hair around his fist, gave it a slight tug, and draped it over my shoulder. Then he pressed his lips to the side of my neck. When I looked up at my bondmate, my heart swelled with love. How had I ever looked at him with disdain?

I closed my eyes at the feeling of his mouth on my skin. He reached over my shoulder and pulled the strings that held the top v of my shirt loose enough so it slipped off one of my shoulders. His lips trailed from my neck down to my shoulder. He rumbled a sound of utter satisfaction and then gently bit into the shoulder.

"You are mouthwatering, Little Flower," he said in a husky voice.

"Did you eat enough at breakfast?" I teased.

"I haven't had a taste of you in days. I'm desperate. Desperate for anything."

I tipped my head back and laughed. I wasn't expecting him to pull me backwards. I collapsed into his chest. He rolled us through the grass in a tangle of hands and kisses and teeth. Garren pinned me to the ground, stomach down, and my hands tucked behind my back held down by his body weight.

"Are you laughing at my pain, Little Flower?"

"No," I replied, breathless.

"It sure sounded like you were laughing at my pain. Because that's it. Pain. It's painful not being able to touch you the way I want. Not being able to bury myself inside you."

One hand snaked forward and under my chin. He tilted my head back and to the side so his teeth could graze my jaw.

"Maybe I should give you a little taste of what I'm feeling," he whispered into my ear. He rolled his hips into my ass.

I moaned and arched back into him.

"Later, Little Flower. Later."

Then his body weight was gone and my hands were free. I rested my forehead on the cool dirt. My bondmate was infuriating. He wasn't the only one a needy mess. I, too, have been suffering without our daily trysts, but it is what it is. We'd have to wait until we had privacy. And that was at least another day or two.

Garren stood and offered me his hand. I smiled up at him. Winking, he pulled me to my feet and wrapped his arms around me. Eleni bound over to nuzzle between me and Garren. The top of her head fit perfectly under my arm. She dropped down into the grass and began to roll around on her back. I couldn't help myself. I flung myself down next to her, stretched my arms over the head, and rolled around. Every part of my skin that touched the earth sung with praise for the god of earth.

Suddenly, Nazneen dropped down beside me. "I could totally go for a nap."

I barked out a laugh.

"Or at least a snack. I'm famished," she said.

"When are you not famished?" Evren asked as she joined us, the pack with food in her lap.

I swear she ate more than anyone I knew.

Garren stood above me, hands on his hips, shaking his head.

"I think I spotted a mango tree," I said, sitting up and looking back to the forest.

Sure enough, there was a mango tree a few feet away. I reached toward the tree and answering my call, the tree leaned toward me. A vine from a neighboring tree plucked the fruit and deposited it into my waiting palm. I withdrew my knife from my boot and sliced into the thick peel. Bright juice dripped down my fingers. I handed a slice to Nazneen first, then Evren.

The moan that came from Nazneen was indecent. "Powers Above this is the most delicious thing I've ever tasted!"

Aura swooped down and took the next piece from my fingers as I reached from my seated position to give some to Delrik.

"Even the bird gets some before me?" Garren laughed. Aura landed heavily on his shoulder, and he grunted under her weight. She held the slice of fruit out as if to share.

Eleni wasn't the only familiar affected by the surge of magic. Aura had grown several inches as well since we'd left the Fire Fae Kingdom. She couldn't even perch on Evren's shoulder without knocking her over anymore. Evren's power had surged and with it, so had Aura's.

We all lounged in the field, gorging ourselves on fresh mangoes until we couldn't stand it anymore. The horses grazed peacefully not too far away. I wasn't worried about them wandering. They seemed to understand we could offer them protection from the fire dangers of the world. I had a feeling Sundance wouldn't leave Eleni's side. They seemed attached at the hip.

I didn't want to break our relaxation, but I knew I couldn't put it off any longer.

I drew in a shaky breath. "Okay. Let's go. It should only be a half a day's walk from here."

We stood sluggishly and stretched to bring blood back to our tired limbs. Days of hiking and riding had taken its toll. Sundance's head popped up when he noticed our movement. He walked over, his head bobbing with each step.

"Hey boy. Are you fully rested?" I asked, nuzzling against him.

He let out a snort and tossed his mane.

I laughed. "Alright. Then let's go home."

I secured his saddle and then mounted it. We slowly made our way to the heart of Laeto Selva. The dense forest wasn't the best for riding horses. We dismounted after about an hour and instead, led our mounts through the underbrush. I knew the way by heart, even with being away for the last forty years.

The city itself wasn't surrounded by a battlement like Kanevvluk or Agni. Quite the opposite. The city was open to all that wanted to visit. The forest thinned as we approached homes and stores. Instead of cobbled stone streets lined with brick houses, the roads were made from thick slabs of stone. Some of the smaller side roads were just the forest floor smoothed by foot traffic. Many of the homes were built into the trees themselves, carved hollow with curling staircases that opened into platforms above the ground. Others were built from fallen trees that had been sawed down and smooth into panels. Small streams wove throughout the city, providing water to everyone that lives here. Every part of the forest was written into the city.

It had begun to rain, and we'd all donned our hoods. Drake, Garren's familiar, who'd made an appearance once we'd entered the forest, was dancing in the rain above our heads. He hadn't been a fan of the Fire Fae Kingdom. It was too dry. I felt Garren's elemental water struggle with the arid climate of Agni. Drake had kept close to the lake rather than camp out with us at the dilapidated barn. However, he seemed to be enjoying the rainforest as much as I was. Eleni jumped and barked if he got low enough to splash water on her face. The scent of the rain replenished my soul.

Ahead of us the canopy opened, and a massive tree stretched higher than all the others. An intricate castle was built surrounding the tree. No trees were cut down to build this massive structure. The builders wanted to worship the earth god. Even the inside of the castle was created with the forest in mind. Some of the rooms had only ceilings to protect from the rain, but the walls were left open to bring in fresh air and the forest breeze. Winding staircases were built around trees that led to the more private rooms high in the trees.

This had been my home. The palace of the Forest Fae.

We made it all the way to the castle's main entrance and were greeted by a group of sentinels stationed by the opened gates under a large archway. The gates were only symbolic in structure. Rather than the sentinels covering their full body in this armor, burnished bronze plates connected with leather straps protected their most vital organs. Their bare powerful legs had sandals strapped to their feet and their helms decorated with bright plumes that resembled the tropical birds that flew free above. They held bronze crescent shaped shields like their armor. Long spears were tipped with polished darkstone and accent feathers. They were unbothered by the rain. They'd be used to the daily downpours. They were all undeniably, lethally beautiful.

Seeing the burnished armor again reminded me of the day I first saw Garren when I arrived in Kanevvluk. That was the last time I was around the sentinels. They'd accompanied my father and I to the Snowhaven Fae. My first impression of Garren was a haughty, arrogant prince who smelled divine but seemed bored with his life. I remember thinking to myself that at least I wouldn't have to spend my life with someone ugly. And he did smell good. I smiled at the memory.

I didn't recognize any of the sentinels, not that I expected to. My father kept the sentinels on a constant rotation to keep them from growing complacent and it had been forty years.

My heart pounded. Ugh. I hated how nervous I was. It was truly ridiculous.

Here goes nothing.

I took a steady breath. Stepping forward in front of our group, I said in my native tongue, "I'm here to see the queen."

I knew they wouldn't prevent me from entering the palace. Even with the brutish males behind me, covered in visible weapons. Access to the palace was a privilege granted to all living and visiting the Laeto Selva. It wasn't until one reached the inner layers of the palace where permission was required from the king. There was something in me that wanted them to know who I was, it might be the only way I got their attention.

Neither sentinel spoke or made any indication they'd heard me. Maybe my hood obscured too much of my face for them to see me clearly. My binding mark warmed as I felt a flash of irritation from Garren. He understood why this moment was important. I'd been told my whole life to keep quiet and follow orders. Well, not anymore. I was no longer a place holder or something one could possess. I refused to be ignored or to apologize for being me. I was the princess and heir to the Forest Fae of Laeto Selva. Now I just need to keep this confidence until I cross paths with my father.

I lifted my chin a touch higher and started to speak again.

The one on the left interrupted me. "And who are you to make such a demand?"

Eleni growled, sitting on the toes of my boots.

I dropped the hood of my cloak. The rain was cool against my face. I lifted my head higher to draw attention to my tribal marks better. "Princess Katuri Harland, heir to the Forest Fae crown."

Pride radiated from my bondmate at my back.

The sentinel raised a brow, but recognition crossed his face. My tribal marks were almost the exact same as my mother's—two horizontal marks around the bridge of my nose, a vertical line on my forehead and down the middle on my bottom lip. The only difference were the swirls on the outside edges of my mother's eyes.

In a sudden, sharp movement, all of them pounded a fist to their chests and dropped to a knee. Eleni huffed in approval, her head held high mirroring my own.

"Katuri, is that really you?"

I'd recognize that voice anywhere. A short male ran from the palace entrance. Although he only stood about four and a half feet tall, I knew he wasn't to be underestimated.

"Rylis?" I asked in disbelief.

He laughed as he stopped before me. The wood nymph gave a low, sweeping bow. The curled horns that sprouted from his head almost brushed the ground, he bowed so low. When he stood again, his deep plum eyes radiated with delight. He was slender like the massive palm trees that surrounded us. His skin was a woody brown and looked rough. His hair—the exact shade of his eyes—was twisted into intricate braids and hung past his shoulders. Long, pointed ears stuck out from each side of his head. Unlike Fae ears, they were about four inches long and drooped a little at the points.

"Welcome home, Princess," Rylis said with a jovial smile. He looked as if he was about to sweep me into a hug. "Your father is away but should be returning tomorrow evening."

I didn't care where he was. I didn't want to see him. Not yet.

Rylis reached forward and gripped my hand. Garren growled from behind me. The taste of salt spread across my tongue. No doubt his lips were pulled back, and his sea dragon was slipping through. Eleni mirrored my bondmate but stayed put by my side. She knew Rylis from when I was younger, but that didn't keep her from being protective if Garren was on edge. My sweet, territorial bondmate.

Rylis had been my father's royal adviser for many, many years. How he came upon the position always interested me, though I never was able to get the story from him. Not that my father was against other magical creatures and hierarchy of power, it was that Rylis was the only of his kind in such an important role.

Wood nymphs didn't have magic like the High Fae, but something uniquely their own. Shapeshifting and divination were just a few. He also had an affinity for growing all sorts of plants and medicinal herbs. Skilled with potions, he was able to calm a restless room with a simple thought. Many of the wood nymphs in our kingdom were healers.

"Where is my mother?" I asked, instead of commenting on my father's whereabouts.

"She's on the credenza with your brother."

Prince Logan Dimitri Harland.

Second born.

My baby brother.

I hadn't seen him since he was three years old. I hadn't forgotten about him, but I'd been so focused on keeping a level head with my father that I hadn't taken the time to consider how seeing my brother would be.

Rylis gave another low bow. "This way, my Princess."

I didn't need an escort but didn't say anything as he led the way. We walked through a large, curved archway that led into the main courtyard. I felt myself bottling everything up with each step. A round fountain sat in the center. White clay walls stretched vertically as the palace broached the sky. The terracotta tiles were a contrast to the deep green of the rainforest canopy. Windows and doorways were all brilliant archways. Here we were shielded from the rain. Tropical plants lined the pathways made with exquisitely hand-painted tiles.

As a young girl, I'd watched artists paint tile after tile. Each was meticulously detailed. Some were repeated patterns that formed elaborate medallions. Others were as unique as each leaf of the forest.

Several servants appeared from the main entry and took the horses from us as we came to a stop outside the front doors. They wore the same bronze as the sentinels.

"Be sure to have our guests' belongings settled into rooms near the princess' quarters," Rylis said in a clipped tone before he added a smile and wink to a young male.

"Of course, Sir Rylis," he said to the royal adviser.

I handed Sundance's reins off to the young male servant. When I walked through the towering double doors of the palace, the walls felt as if they were closing in. Being in the palace again sent my emotions into a tailspin. I heard Evren behind me gasp. It was the grandest entry I'd seen compared to all the places I'd traveled to. Vaulted ceilings. Crystals hovered in the air, spelled with a soft light that changed throughout the day. Aura flew from Evren's shoulder upward, pecking at the crystals. Every inch was a work of art, from the tallest ceiling to the carved baseboards. Smaller fountains were scattered throughout the courtyard and the palace itself. The bubbling sound combined with the rain outside surrounded us in a low hum.

Hallways branched off the main courtyard that led to various staircases. They spiraled like a fiddlehead of a fern. Only the garden, entry hall and Temple of Anruin were on ground level. Everything else was stretched toward the treetops in spirals like spokes of a wheel. Some were left open, others were enclosed, lit by torches spaced evenly along the walls. We split off to a corridor to the right with a wide staircase. Branches and vines twisted to form a tunnel. The railing was carved with butterflies and hummingbirds. It took a few seconds to adjust to the darkness, even with the glowing torches.

After quiet minutes of winding upward, the tunnel opened up and we came to massive, frosted glass doors. Rylis pushed them both open in a grand flourish to reveal my mother's favorite mezzanine. She'd always spent so much time here. The palace was massive, so if I couldn't find her, this was the first place I'd looked.

My mother, Queen Nefali Harland, sat at the table, back straight. She exuded elegance and beauty.

"Katuri!"

The shock of my presence was clearly written on her face and then she began to glow with joy. Literally glow. I'd always loved her passive power of light. It was as if it was only yesterday we'd seen each other. Her motherly warmth washed over me.

I dipped at the knees into a curtsey. "Mother."

She smiled and then her face twisted. I laughed.

"What *are* you wearing?" my mother said with a look of undisguised disgust.

She was always fussing over my clothes as a child and how I always managed to be covered in dirt. Her power was so clean and effervescent; mine is messy. Her judgmental eyes traveled up and down my body.

I looked down at my clothes. Beneath my weathered and dirty travel cloak, I wore brown breeches and a calf-length, forest green tunic that had a skirt with a high slit in the front. A leather corset and a belt with my weapon. It was more common in Kanevvluk. Warm, functional layers compared to the styles in Laeto Selva.

My mother was draped in thin layers of nearly transparent light weight cotton. The only reason you couldn't see through them was each panel was draped over one other, concealing the most intimate places. White, green, and deep purple. A tight breast band instead of a corset. I couldn't wait to get out of my corset. I was sweating in all these layers.

My mother's eyes stopped suddenly at the gilded binding mark. I fought the desire to hide it behind my back. Any warmth I felt toward my mother and our reunion froze like the icebergs in Kanevvluk. Had she known what my father had planned when she let me board the ship across the sea to the Snowhaven Fae? She had to have known I was to be bound to Garren, but how quickly and against my will? That was a whole different story I wasn't really ready to hear at this point.

My mother was hard to read. She was a perfectionist when it came to masking her emotions and the true meaning behind the things she said out loud. I wanted to believe she hadn't known. I wanted to believe that she had my best intentions in mind when she kissed me goodbye. Doubt held me in merciless grip.

My binding mark was no longer a symbol of my loss of freedom. No. Not anymore. Now it was something special between Garren and me. My bondmate and I. And I didn't want to share it with her even if she was my mother.

Suddenly, a male came running from the same corridor we'd just exited from. He skidded to a halt before me. My mother shot him an irritated look. He was breathing hard but straightened when we all turned to him.

Seeing my brother was like a punch to the gut. He looked exactly like our father with dark skin and dark eyes. Long, black hair twisted into braids. His tribal marks were different though. It was traditional for the males to have different marks based on what the seers saw in their futures, while females took on similarities to their mothers. Logan's weren't as dangerous looking as the warpaint type my father possessed.

"Logan?" I exclaimed at the same exact time he shouted, "Kitty Kat?"

The nickname he'd given me as a toddler sent a pang of happiness to my gut. His face split into an oddly familiar smile. He hesitated a moment before he swept me into a swift hug. Warring emotions. Love for the little one I'd left behind toward a grown male who resembled the father I truly hated.

"Wow. I can't believe you're here. When did you arrive? Why didn't you send a message that you were coming?"

"It wasn't a planned trip," I lied.

Eleni sat between my feet, looking back and forth between my little brother, mother, and me. Her fur bristled. Alright, she was becoming worse than Garren. She'd known Logan and my mother before we left, when she was only a pup, but the combination of my hesitancy and their startled faces, she wasn't happy. Logan was slightly taller than me. My mother, who'd placed her diplomatic smile back on her face, was eyeing Delrik and Garren with suspicion.

"And who are your traveling companions?" my mother asked.

Garren pressed his hand to my lower back and warm comfort flooded me. Logan had to look up to my bondmate and he took a step back. I could only imagine the glare Garren was giving my brother. He didn't like anyone near me, even if they were blood related.

"Queen Nefali," he bowed his head but didn't lower himself to her level. A clear acknowledgement of her status but making it clear of his own as well. "I'm Garren Eckhardt, son of High Ruler Eckhardt of the Snowhaven Fae in Illoterra, your daughter's bondmate and consort."

My mother stood and nodded a shallow bow back at Garren. Logan reached forward to take Garren's hand. Eleni sensed my hesitation before I even noticed it and a low grumble erupted.

Apparently, I didn't like anyone touching my bondmate either.

"And these are my friends: Nazneen Zathrian, future High Ruler of Arcelia, her brother Delrik Valhar, and his bondmate Evren Valhar. Her brother is the High Ruler of Rivamir and the River Fae."

"You've traveled so far! Come sit down," my mother gestured to the table. She returned to her seat and a maid silently appeared next to her.

"Please bring a full lunch service for our guests."

The maid scurried away and returned with plates of sandwiches and fruits. Their fragrant aroma filled my nose as they were placed in front of us. Another servant followed behind the first with trays of glasses and brightly colored beverages.

"Thank you, Queen Nefali. Everything looks delicious," Nazneen said.

She was always the most comfortable in making conversation. She would be an excellent High Ruler when her time came.

We sat around the extravagant table. A young female casually stepped out onto the credenza, but froze at the sight of us, her expression falling. Her eyes immediately dropped to her feet. She was too finely dressed to be a servant or maid, but she exuded submission.

"Marselina, come," my brother said. "Katuri, meet my future consort. This is Marselina Moriko."

The young female walked over and stood behind and to the left of my brother, the same position my mother took when my father was in the room. My brother was younger than me and his future consort had to be around nineteen or twenty. I wondered if her powers had even developed yet. I recognized her family name; she came from a powerful bloodline.

She gave me a quick smile but didn't raise her eyes or greet anyone else at the table. She leaned over and placed a small vial on the table next Logan's glass. As she pulled back, Logan took her fingers and squeezed them. It was the briefest of interactions, but one of gratitude. He emptied the contents of the vial into his cup and swallowed it down in quick gulps.

"Headache potion," Logan said when he saw me looking at the glass in question.

The Moriko family were a long line of healers and alchemists. Passive powers, yet quite valuable. When a young female deemed suitable came along—one to continue the precious royal bloodline—the opportunity wasn't passed on. I wondered if she was being forced into the blood binding the same way I had been. I felt sorry for her. The fact that females didn't have a choice who they were being bound to infuriated me. I'd been lucky, being bound to Garren. I knew others weren't as fortunate.

Nyla had explained that the act of blood binding had once been meant only for bondmates, but once those in power realized it combined magic powers, an act once of love and trust became a forced ritual. Blood binding ceremonies weren't known for being romantic events. While bondmates were a gift from the Powers Above, two souls as one, the blood binding ritual could be done even between strangers.

In the past, they'd simply been ways to combine powers between two Fae and make strong connections between kingdoms. I'd been sent to the Snowhaven Fae as prophesied by the royal seer to complete the blood binding ritual, fulfill a political treaty between the two kingdoms, and forever combine our two powerful family bloodlines.

"The blood binding ritual will take place in three weeks time. Will you still be with us then?" my mother asked.

"I'm not sure," I said honestly.

I'd been told Garren and I were fated to be consorts, but the instant he first touched me, I knew we were truly bondmates. A primal shift took place in me that drew a line between us. Soul recognition.

With that single touch, my entire world condensed and expanded at the same time. The awareness I'd been feeling on and off the last six months grew tenfold. I felt as if I was unraveling. I knew he felt it too, because his eyes went wide. A spark of energy passed between us and his breath caught.

Garren winked and my face heated. He knew what I was thinking. A wave of devotion came through our connection.

Would my brother have as much fondness for Marselina? I prayed to the Powers Above that my brother only inherited my father's physical traits and not his personality. Based on this brief interaction with his future consort, I would guess no. Though, I would give him the benefit of the doubt until I got to know him better. I'd learned not to judge people by the situations they were forced into.

I had only been home for a few hours, but I realized how much I missed it. I missed the air and the smell of the trees. I drew in a deep breath. I didn't want to leave Laeto Selva now that I'd returned, but I knew we needed to find as many relics as possible before Hadeon. First things first, I need to see my father about the earth relic.

TWELVE
GARREN

It was only early afternoon, but we were ushered to bedchambers to bathe and relax for the remainder of the day. Delrik, Evren, and Nazneen were in two rooms across the hall from Katuri and me. It appeared this wing of the palace was rarely used. Katuri and I stepped into a massive room that a servant, another wood nymph, led us to. She was even shorter than Rylis, but had the same deep brown skin, plum hair, and eyes. She informed us that this is where we'd be welcome for the duration of our stay in Laeto Selva. Then she departed on quick, scampering feet. The whole wall along the western side of the room was missing, leaving us open to a stretching balcony within the canopy of the forest.

"How far off the ground are we?" I asked as I stood on the threshold of the balcony and leaned out to peer over toward the ground. From this height, I could see the sweeping city far below us. We climbed so many stairs. So. Many. Stairs. Thankfully, there'd been some sort of mechanism that moved the stairs upward as we climbed. This place was a labyrinth of twists and turns. How had Katuri navigated this palace as a child without getting lost?

"Only a couple of hundred feet," Katuri shrugged.

I turned back to her wide-eyed, but she wasn't paying attention. She was absorbing her surroundings. Kat's mother had been a stark contrast to her daughter. Queen Nefali was tall and lean like a warrior, while Kat had toned muscles that showed her strength. And Kat's hair hung free and wild instead of being woven into braids, hung down to her hips. The only thing the mother and daughter shared was their tribal marks. Where Kat had soft features, her mother was full of sharp lines with high, regal cheekbones, dark brows that framed a piercing, calm gaze. Her eyes held an aloofness as she scrutinized all of us—especially me.

Her brother looked exactly how I remembered Kat's father. Logan's consort was a mousy thing. She hadn't even said a word, only given a submissive bow when Logan introduced her. She hadn't sat while we all ate; she just stood behind Logan with her head bowed. I always hated how the earth fae treated their females when it came to arranged consorts. Many of the older kingdoms followed the same tradition.

Katuri's mother informed us there would be no formal dinner that evening, and we would be served dinner in our chambers. I was fine with that. I'd had enough of the family reunion. I wanted to be alone with my bondmate. My protectiveness was on high alert in this new place. It was an odd feeling. Though I was unfamiliar with Laeto Selva, I could feel the presence of home from Katuri's bond.

Nazneen, Evren, and Delrik had agreed to join us for dinner once they were settled. That left me a few hours alone with my bondmate. I could feel how overwhelmed Katuri was with being back in her old home. Old wounds were being opened.

I didn't know a lot about her childhood. We hadn't really had a chance to discuss that far back over the last several months, but I imagined from the brief interaction I had with her father that her childhood was not particularly happy. Rigidity and order seemed more appropriate for a description.

I watched my bondmate examine the room. Eleni sniffed the perimeter and then plopped down in a sunny spot on the floor. She stretched out all four legs, arching her back with a happy groan. The rain shower had been brief but left the dense, green canopy dripping. Drake emerged from nowhere and rolled across the balcony. I snorted a laugh at his goofiness.

"This is my old room," Katuri said as she walked deeper into the space. Our packs had been placed neatly by the door on the floor.

She trailed her fingers over stacks of books—old fairy tales on top of random piles of High Fae histories. Her preferred choice of light reading back home in Kanevvluk had been romance novels.

"My reading preferences have changed a lot since I was young." She looked over her shoulder and smiled. "These are a far cry from my current reads."

I picked up a hardback with a dark blue cover about a water nymph from the top of the pile. "Is this where your love of romance novels stemmed from? Fairytales?"

"Maybe?" She gave me a playful, wicked grin. "Though I had to sneak those books. Father didn't approve of me wasting time on such frivolity."

I returned the book and reached for an old journal. A quill made from the enormous macaw feather was pressed between the pages. Someone had been cleaning in here because there wasn't a speck of dust anywhere.

An elaborate circular bed with thin, white fabric sheets suspended from the ceiling sat in the center of the room. They moved in the breeze coming in from the forest. Katuri ran her hand up the smooth wood of a wardrobe, and plumes of purple orchids bloomed and arched over. There was a carved desk on the other side of the room. A massive, gilded mirror hung above it. There was no fireplace. I guess there was no need, considering this kingdom never saw snow.

I reached out through our bond to her and felt nostalgia and sadness. I moved to my bondmate's side and gripped her elbow gently. The moment my fingers touched her skin, her body relaxed. She peered up at me. The sadness melted away and was replaced by home. I was her home, just as she was mine.

"It's just so weird being back here," she said. "So many feelings returning and new ones that I hadn't even known I was feeling all this time." I felt the myriad of emotions bouncing around her mind.

She turned fully to me and wrapped her arms around me. Her fingers delved beneath the tail of my shirt, gently tracing and exploring my spine. I knew she was tracing the ink of my sea dragon tattoo by memory. Her touch was the only thing I could focus on. It was warm against my skin. My blood roared, and all I wanted was her. Forever. Always.

My teeth teased the sensitive skin right below her ear. I pulled back, and Katuri's lips formed a sweet, seductive smile.

My bondmate's facial features shifted, and she became a different female. Demanding. Sexy. Bold. The young girl who once lived in this towering palace was no longer. She was now, and forever, my lover. I wanted to ravish her on every surface. I swept her up in my arms and carried her to the bed, where I kissed every inch of her body until all her thoughts drifted away with the rain.

The same maid who'd shown us to our room brought dinner right as the sun was setting. Delrik, Evren, and Nazneen had joined us. My hair was still wet from my shower.

Nazneen sat behind Katuri on the couch, braiding the damp strands of her auburn hair down her back. I looked over to Katuri sitting on the couch opposite me. I gave her a rakish grin. Showering hadn't been the only thing we'd done.

Through the bond, I sent a visual of her naked in the shower, head dropped back in glorious pleasure, her leg draped over my shoulder as I feasted on her...

A sharp tug on Kat's braid broke my lustful connection with my bondmate.

"Stop with the dirty thoughts, you two," Nazneen chided.

How did she even know?

"I have no idea what you're talking about," I said innocently.

What I'd done to her in the shower was anything but innocent.

"Well, if you're anything like these two," Nazneen pointed to her brother and a blushing Evren, "I know you got frisky. I'm going to have to sound shield my room as long as we share a wall."

Challenge accepted. Tonight, when I was finally alone with Katuri again, I would put Nazneen's aberration magic to the test. I planned to make Kat scream my name over and over and over.

THIRTEEN
KATURI

Filtered sunlight caused me to stir the following morning; Garren's heavy arm was draped over my waist. I'd fallen asleep tucked into Garren's arms with thunder and lightning as our only company. Eleni had gotten tired of our love making and left us to our ecstasy. She was probably roaming the palace seeking out food or getting into some sort of trouble.

Thunder rumbled off in the distance. I'd forgotten how much I loved watching storms. It was so beautiful. The blizzards in Kanevvluk were just blinding whiteness. The lightning made everything bright with color. The smell of the morning dew brought back a flood of childhood memories.

The soft sound of my bathing chamber door clicked open and Corynne, my long-time maid and closest friend, appeared. Eleni trotted alongside her. My heart leapt with happiness. I would've jumped up, but I was trapped by Garren. Corynne was back in the traditional garb of her kind, flowing layers in soft shades. She looked renewed and refreshed, even after being apart for only six or so months. I wondered how her family was doing. I'd have to get a full report and maybe even go visit. There was a fresh glow about her. Being home suited her. I hadn't realized how much I'd missed her.

She was a boto encantado, a river dolphin shifter native to Laeto Selva and the warm waters of southern Quinterre. Boto encantado had special magical powers that allowed them to enchant and spread the feeling of love and lust. They could use it for their own gain, but they could also share it among those they cared for. Corynne, in particular, was especially strong when it came to manipulating emotions. Apparently, she could read my moods.

Corynne had been with me since I arrived in Kanevvluk. I'd asked her once why she came all the way to Snowhaven Territory with me. She simply shrugged and said, "I wanted to offer the princess protection."

Boto encantado were known for protecting those who were kind to them; though they could be vicious when provoked. Not much was known about their magic. I'd heard different versions of the same story of how those that double-crossed an encantado wound up being led to the water and were found drowned at the bottom of the river. They typically stayed close to the river that ran through alongside our city, but several worked in the palace. By some miracle from the Powers Above, Corynne had been selected by my mother to travel to Kanevvluk with me. She'd been a stranger, but we'd grown close with ease. Corynne was the one that held me while I cried myself to sleep every night on the voyage from Laeto Selva to Kanevvluk. She'd been my bright spot during the endless, dark days of winter. She loved music and dancing. I'd often find her singing in our native language while she went about her tasks. Her soft and hypnotic voice made it easy to get lost in the ups and downs of her melodic songs. That's probably how the encantado tricked their enemies to their watery deaths—entrancing them with ethereal voices.

There was a smirk on her face as she took in the scene before her. Me, naked, draped with Garren, also naked. When we'd parted ways on our arrival in the City of Proux months ago, I was still wanting to strangle Garren with my bare hands. The only letter I'd sent her was when we'd decided to leave Proux in search of the relics and that we'd eventually be making our way back to Laeto Selva. I hadn't had time to give her a full update. She'd been the only one I'd trusted with our travel plans.

Heat came to my cheeks, and I tried to cover my face with the sheet. Unfortunately, it too was trapped beneath Garren's arm, and my efforts caused him to stir. Corynne hadn't ever been shy about nudity, sex, or passion, so I wasn't sure why I was so embarrassed. Maybe because all I'd done the last forty years was complain about how awful the male on top of me was.

Garren let out an adorable groan. He slept as soundly as Eleni. The wolf stretched like a cat, not the wolf she was, hopped up on the end of the bed and curled up in a ball at Garren's feet. Corynne bent and scratched Eleni behind the ears as she walked over to the open-walled balcony. Minimal sunlight trickled in through the clouds but Corynne still glowed. Her beautiful skin was a soft pink in color; and her hair almost matched her skin but was streaked with coral and orange highlights. She winked at me. Nothing slipped past her.

"It's too early, Little Flower," Garren whispered huskily, distracting me from my familiar and my closest friend.

Corynne covered her chuckle with the back of her hand.

"Love..." I started.

"Hmm," Garren hummed as he lifted himself enough to shift the rest of his body over mine.

I tried to protest by pushing against his bare chest. The too thin sheet began to slip lower on his waist.

"Since I'm awake, we may as well make use of our time." He bit my shoulder as he wedged his hips between my thighs. I protested by trying to clamp them closed. It didn't work.

I shrieked, "Garren! We aren't alone!"

He paused and then spoke to my maid without moving. "Good morning, Corynne. It's lovely to see you again."

"Your highness."

"I'm sure you're wondering..." he began.

"Oh, I'm not wondering anything." She was bouncing around the room, tidying the clothes that Garren had unceremoniously thrown as he stripped them off me last night after dinner. "I knew you two were an eventuality. I'll bring you both a small breakfast, but the king is expecting you in two hours."

"Perfect. That's enough time to ravage my bondmate before being forced to interact with anyone."

"Come on, Eleni," Corynne chirped to the wolf.

I saw Corynne give a curtsy before departing as quietly as she'd appeared. "Enjoy the ravaging."

She waved her hand in a delicate arc through the air and an invisible wave of euphoria sprinkled across me like a cooling drizzle of summer rain. The sudden urge to smother Garren with something other than a pillow overcame me.

Corynne arrived to fetch us exactly one and a half hours—and fully ravaged—later to inform us that the king had arrived home in the early hours of the morning and was chomping at the bit to see the two of us. She sat with us while we breakfasted, and caught up. Everyone else was keeping to themselves this morning. Corynne had also provided them breakfast, and we'd planned to meet up with them after visiting my father.

She escorted us toward my father's office. I had to see my father eventually. This would be the first time since the blood binding. Putting it off would only make it worse.

"How long have you been back at the palace?" I asked Corynne.

"As soon as I received your letter saying you were leaving Proux, I came back to make sure everything was prepared. I would've been here yesterday afternoon, but I was having dinner with my sister."

I smiled. "I'd love to meet her while we are here. I want her to meet Garren, too. And how are the kids? I can't wait to finally meet them."

Prior to leaving Laeto Selva, I hadn't met Corynne's family. It wasn't proper for the princess to wander the rainforest. During the voyage to Kanevvluk, she told me stories of her family and home, and shared letters with me when they arrived. I never received letters from my own family.

Garren, who wasn't paying attention, just nodded and kept a firm gaze. I walked arm in arm with Corynne and Garren followed close behind us. I could feel his tension. Eleni had stayed behind to keep Nazneen company since Corynne worked her magic on Delrik and Evren. I didn't think my father would appreciate my familiar; he never liked how the animals seemed to be drawn to me by my earth magic. I think the fact that I would one day be stronger than he would ever be, made him nervous and jealous.

Corynne stopped outside my father's office. Located on one of the middle floors of the palace, the whole floor was well guarded by only the most trusted sentinels.

She placed her palm against my cheek. "Good luck, princess."

I took a deep, steadying breath. First things first. I'd deal with my father and then get the relic. I knocked firmly.

"Enter." I flinched at my father's voice.

I hardened my features and rolled my shoulders back. I could do this.

I opened the door and walked through the threshold, Garren close behind me. The Forest Fae King sat behind a massive desk. The room was so dark; unlike the rest of the palace. There were no windows. Only dim torches lit the space. Shelves, spanning two of the four walls, reached up the two-story high ceiling. I'd never been allowed to touch the books here. They are the written histories of the Forest Fae. I wondered why they weren't in the regular library where everyone had access to them. The third wall opposite of where I stood was covered in painted portraits of past kings.

The heavy tang of magic hung in the air. I remembered the pain of his compulsive magic and had no desire to be near it again. I was thankful he didn't try to embrace me. I didn't want to get close enough where he could touch me.

The last time he'd touched me was during the blood binding ceremony with Garren. His vicelike grip would forever be burned into my memory. It was the only way his magic worked to my knowledge. If he wasn't touching me, I was safe.

The compulsion still hung heavily in my memories. I wasn't sure how I would have reacted. Being this close to his domineering presence was painful.

"Katuri!" His mouth formed a saccharine smile. He spoke in our native language. "What a joyous surprise to have you home. And with your consort."

King Kairos Julian Harland, my father, stood, arms raised in greeting, a glass of amber liquid clutched in his fingers. It was a little early for a drink.

"My bondmate," I corrected him in our native tongue.

I saw Garren's nostrils flare with his sea dragon temper, but he remained motionless. He would allow me to face my father head on without stepping in. He trusted me.

"I can see that." His eyes dropped to our joined hands where our binding mark was glowing faintly.

I disliked using my native tongue, not because I was ashamed, but because Garren couldn't understand. My father was purposely putting Garren down without doing so. I tampered down my mounting indignation at his jovial welcome.

"Ave sal." *Hello.* "King Kairos, thank you for welcoming us so generously."

My head whipped to my bondmate so fast it sent a spasm down my neck.

My father laughed with delight and clapped his tumbler down on his desk. Who was this? This king before me was a different male than who I remembered.

Garren didn't smile or laugh. He held himself stoic and still. "What kind of bondmate wouldn't even speak the native tongue of his Ashlyra?" Garren said, again in our home language.

My father switched back to the common tongue.

"I'm glad to see even as a second born you aren't an imbecile. Not going to lie, I was a little worried at first when the seer told me you were a second born and then seeing you in person...well, I wasn't convinced. Giving the heir of the Forest Fae to a second born. Ha! But I see my trust in the fates has paid off."

He strode over to us, beckoning us further into his office, and gestured for us to take a seat on a nearby couch. His boots scuffed off the stone floors that were veined with a shimmering material. "Your timing is excellent. I'd just returned from Kosmima," my father said. "So why have you returned home?"

We sat on the couch. My back was rigid, and I couldn't stop my fingers twisting themselves in nervousness. Garren quietly took my fingers in his and pressed them to his mouth before resting them on his leg. He sat close to me, his thigh pressed to mine.

This wasn't my home. Garren was my home now. I'd realized that the moment our bond snapped into place. Although Laeto Selva was where I'd started, I only belonged with Garren. Wherever he went, I'd go too. But now was not the time to bring that up. We were here on a mission: to find the relic gifted from the gods and prevent Hadeon from adding it to his collection. He'd already failed at retrieving the fire relic. We'd fail again.

"I know you know of the relics of the gods," I started. "The ones that open the veils located in the Temples of Anruin."

"Yes. The four relics of the gods. Why are you asking about them? The veils have been closed since the Uprising more than 700 years ago."

"And the relic given to the Forest Fae? Do you know where it is?"

"Of course, Daughter," the king nodded. "The Harland bloodline has ruled the Forest Fae since the gods first gave the High Fae magic. The relic was trusted to our family and in our family it has stayed."

Garren spoke up. "I know you must have heard about the chaos Hadeon Allerick is causing in eastern Quinterre. He's searching for the relics. He wants to use them somehow to further his cause, whatever it may be, and we need to prevent him from getting his hands on them."

We knew Hadeon's plans but had decided to not share that knowledge. I had a hard time trusting my father after everything he'd done to me in the past.

"I can assure you, the Cattleya's Key is safe here in Laeto Selva."

"Can I see it?" I felt a sudden surge of desire to hold the object , to feel its weight and power.

My father watched me carefully for a moment. "I don't see why not. As heir to the Forest Fae Kingdom, you have the right to see and understand what you're protecting."

I may be the firstborn and heir to the crown, but we both knew Logan was the preferred leader. Any male would be better than a female in his eyes, but he didn't need to worry about that. With his long lifespan, he had plenty of time to shape Logan into the king he wanted him to be and find something else for me to do to be out of the way.

He stood and made his way to the door, beckoning us. I followed behind my father, Garren by my side. We walked silently down to the first floor of the palace. Unlike other kingdoms, the palace was built surrounding the Temple of Anruin. The priestesses wandered about freely amongst the rest of the palace staff.

All the other temples I'd been to were white or cream stone. This one, on the other hand, was made of dark topaz with smooth columns and curved archways. The fire from the torches made the walls look like they were moving. And instead of being walled off, the temple was open-aired. Anyone from Laeto Selva was welcome in the temple. Dainty vines and flowers crawled along the space, a blessing from the earth goddess. The ground was soft, lush grass. It was more beautiful than I remembered.

All along the curved archways and columns were meticulously carved words of the essence scroll. As a youngling, I'd sat for hours, trailing my fingers of the words that told of how the High Fae came to be and the history of our realm. I'd always seen it as resplendent. Now, knowing how Goddess Aluxyeras was betrayed and banished, how her existence had been erased, I had a harder time seeing the beauty. I wondered if those who were set with the task of embedding the words into the stone had known the full truth. How Eryx, the god of fire, murdered Aluxyeras's lover in cold blood and then banished her to the Mortal Realm when she retaliated against him.

Probably not.

Sentinels were posted at each archway. They bowed as we approached, a pounding of their fists against their chests echoed in unison. My father didn't even acknowledge them. I, however, greeted them. I tried to make it a point to learn the names of the men who might one day be willing to lay down their life for me as queen.

Father led us to a turning stairway, the exact stairway from the other temple into the chamber of the veils. Down we went.

Unlike the temple in Proux, whose stairway had been full of dust, cobwebs, and forgotten weeping candles, these stairs were illuminated brightly. Each step was free of dust and pooled wax. We spiraled down to the heart of the temple.

Garren leaned in close and groaned. "If we keep walking up and down these spirals, I'm going to puke."

"You'll get used to it, my love," I said sweetly.

We finally reached the bottom of the stairs. The chamber of the veils—one of the five places in our entire realm that connected the Mortal Realm of Naśbar to Aesira, the realm of the gods.

The chamber was immaculate. Every surface was polished, the same topaz as above. So clean. Fresh candles. A priestess who had been dusting off one of the pedestals quickly stood, bobbed in a low courtesy, and then made herself scarce. Ancient magic saturated the air, more so than in my father's office. It seemed to thrum in the air all around us. My elemental earth surged forward to my fingertips in response towards the relic.

"It's so clean. Are you showing it to someone?" Garren asked.

"Respect for the gods for when they decide to return. We will be ready," my father said.

Is that the real reason he was holding so tightly to the relic? Did he know something I didn't know about the veils? Goddess Haizea hadn't mentioned anything about returning to the Mortal Realm.

"They said they would never return," I said.

"True. But they also hadn't planned to intervene in the Uprising. I like to be prepared just in case. I'd hate for them to return to see their place of worship in complete disarray."

I was hesitant to leave Garren's side, but I wanted a closer look. I hadn't known this place existed. I knew of a heavily guarded area in the temple, but I'd never gotten the nerve to check it out. I withdrew my hand from his, he squeezed my fingers before finally letting go. Garren hung back at the perimeter of the room, leaning casually with his arms crossed against his chest. A gesture that I knew was a show of holding his composure. I could feel his tension in our bond. He looked casual to anyone who didn't know him. I, however, knew he was a second away from killing anyone or anything that came near me.

The floor was the same smooth topaz as the walls above us. Candles lined the entire circular room. My father made his way to the center. I took one step forward. I looked down at my feet and made the decision to slip my shoes off, so I was skin to stone. I began to follow the engraved circle along the outer points of the pentagon, the symbol of our gods. As I moved clockwise, I sent a prayer to each god as I approached the empty dais: the god of fire, the goddess of air, the goddess of spirit, the goddess of water, and then a polished arch. I reached out and brushed my fingers along the edge. The same runes from the Essence Scrolls were carved into the dais and arch.

"The veil to Aesira," I said in a reverent tone.

Beside the dais sat a raised pedestal topped with dark emerald velvet. The relic sat, undisturbed and calling out to me. The power I had felt when I entered was emanating from that sacred place.

"Cattleya's Key."

It wasn't the shape of an ordinary key. In fact, it was two separate pieces cradled next to one another. My fingers tingled as I moved closer, itching to slip the pieces together. They were made of brass, twisting leaves and vines warped around each one. Glistering emeralds encrusted the head. Firelight from the torches made them dance with glowing oranges. I didn't advance, though. My father knew I was an elemental, but I didn't think he knew the extent of the pull the relic had on me. He hadn't asked once about the elemental power in our short reunion. I was glad about it. He didn't deserve to know anything about my magic.

"Are you expecting to see another war?" Garren asked my father. Through the bond I could tell he was thinking the same thing.

My father turned to him. "Of course not. But with the whispering of Hadeon and his fiends, one can never be too careful. I have no doubt you are safe in Laeto Selva."

Garren pushed off the wall and came to my side. "That's presumptuous."

"I would do *anything* to protect my kingdom," my father said. He stood straighter and faced Garren head on. "I'm sure your father would do the same."

"Hadeon was in Agni," Garren said.

My father went still. "How do you know that?"

"We were there. He burned the city to the ground. There's nothing left."

My father turned thoughtful. He took a sip from his glass that he'd carried from his office. "That's...unfortunate. King Ziven was a commendable ally."

He seemed genuinely upset by the news.

"I didn't say the king was dead," Garren said.

"I only assumed since the city is gone. What cowardly leader would abandon his kingdom and flee?"

That was fair. I didn't see my father fleeing the palace if Hadeon attacked. He may not be a good father, but he was an excellent king, or at least that's what everyone said who lived here in Laeto Selva.

How much did he know about what Hadeon was up to? Did he know how far into the continent he'd infiltrated?

My father cleared his throat to get my attention.

"When are you going to introduce me to your friends?" Father asked.

"You weren't here yesterday when we arrived," I replied curtly.

"Don't get an attitude," he snapped.

Garren growled.

"What I meant was Mother met everyone yesterday. I'm sure we can arrange a time when you aren't busy."

"One is a fire elemental." It wasn't a question.

"How do you know?"

"Rylis."

Of course. Rylis would give him a rundown on who the new High Fae were in the palace. After he'd accompanied us to my mother and Logan, he stepped back. He was always ears for my father. He heard everything we'd discussed. No doubt he relayed it to my father as soon as he'd arrived back home.

"And the dark one?"

Garren straightened, ready to defend his best friend. "Delrik Valhar."

"He has a unique type of magic," I answered.

I hadn't seen Delrik use his shadows once since we've been here. I wondered how Rylis had known about them. Or if there were more spies without the palace I wasn't aware of.

"Dark magic isn't welcome in our kingdom, Katuri."

"There is nothing evil about his magic," Garren finally chimed in.

Father turned his attention to my bondmate once again and they held each other's stare for a long beat.

"I meant no offense," my father said.

Garren only hummed in response.

FOURTEEN
NYLA

All I could hear was the pounding of blood in my ears echoed by heavy, ragged breaths from the exertion of our climb. Desperately, I tried to pull air into my lungs, but I felt like I couldn't expand my ribs completely. My body was stiff and sore from sleeping for days. And from being nearly mauled by a fiend. Desmund had slowed his pace as the slope increased, but I still struggled to keep up. To his credit, he didn't utter a single complaint each time I stopped to catch my breath.

Ironic; I was an air elemental who couldn't breathe. He briefly explained there was no other way to Laeto Selva the first time I'd paused, but had said nothing more. We had to go over the mountains. There was no other choice. The Baxmar Range stretched the entire length of Quinterre. If I'd had my powers I would've simply flown, but that wasn't an option. Thankfully, the sun had warmed the slopes. I was sweating under the wool cloak Desmund lent to me. I couldn't think of anything worse than fighting for every breath and shivering in the cold.

Not only was I powerless, but I was also weak and had no purpose for my bleak future. I didn't know who I was or where my home was outside the temple. This was a first. I belonged to the temple within moments of my birth. I'd devoted my life to service. And now, nothing. The last 600 years was simply a waste. I'd led a very isolated life, though it was a good life, nothing I could protest about in particular, no hardships. So why had I been so unhappy working in the temple?

And, to top off everything, while it may seem minor, I only had pants to wear. It was the straw that broke the camel's back.

"We'll stop here for tonight," Desmund said.

Thank the Powers Above!

"What? Why?" I asked, panting.

Despite how hard I tried, there was no hiding my glee at the thought of sitting down for a few hours.

He pinched his lips together. Was he suppressing a smile?

Jerk. Not all of us could look like that and be perfect after climbing a mountain all day.

He was bright faced and breathing normally. There was a breeze, when it touched his face, he seemed to lean into it. How could he look so at home while I struggle to breathe?

Fuck him.

"You seem winded," he said with a cheeky grin.

I shot him a glare.

I *was* winded. I was clearly out of shape for the steep slopes. I planted my hands on my knees and let my head drop in resigned defeat. Fine. I gave up keeping the facade of being alright. Everything hurt. And he'd seen me, was seeing me, at my most vulnerable.

When I finally looked up, I noticed we'd arrived at a small clearing near a stream. A small break in the trees showed the Baxmar Range endlessly stretching across the horizon. All I could see were mountains and trees in every direction. It was so...isolating. It was also comforting and captivating. The beauty in the view.

Desmund reassembled our tent and started a fire in no time. Just because it was a warm day did not mean that the temperature wouldn't plummet as soon as the sun disappeared. I'd originally planned to help rather than simply be a burden on our trek to Laeto Selva, but I knew I'd just be in the way. I knew how to set up a tent as much as I knew how to gut a fish. I was useless.

Instead, I made myself comfortable on the soft mossy ground with my legs tucked beneath me and sank into a meditative state. I faced my body the west and the setting sun, absorbing its energy and glow.

My mind felt sluggish and thick. As the minutes dragged on, my head began to pound, and the usual smooth details of my thoughts grew clumsy. My air magic was out of reach, flickering like a breathless whisper. At least I could *see* it out of reach. It was practically visible to my knowing eyes. I hoped that meant it would return soon. Desmund had guessed it would return once all the poison had been drawn from my wounds.

I let out a frustrated breath through my nose. I couldn't maintain my focus. Everything around me was a distraction. The subtle shift of the wind. Each step Desmund took was a crackle of earth beneath his feet. The movement of the water in the stream.

I heard, and felt, Desmund walk to stand beside me. His presence wrapped around me like a pair of warm arms. I pressed my lips together and tried even harder to relax my mind.

"Struggling?"

I should ignore him, but his presence was undeniably the biggest interruption of all.

I huffed. "No."

I opened my eyes and looked up to him towering above me. For a split second, the figure was shrouded by something. His eyes were dark and bracketed by secrecy. A haze hung over his face and body. He loomed over me and fear threatened to choke me.

And then it was gone, like a gust of wind whipping it away. It was just Desmund next to me. I released a slow, controlled breath.

"Even the most experienced struggle with recovering from Bloodthorn poisoning."

I pressed a palm to my chest to steady myself. "How do you know it was Bloodthorn?"

"Just a wild guess based on how your body reacted to it."

I lifted a brow.

He shrugged. "I know a few healers."

It was the first thing he'd offered about himself besides his name. Clearly, he did more than just 'know' the healers. He'd obviously learned a lot from them.

Desmund sat down in front of me and mirrored my cross-legged position. He was close enough that his knee touched mine. I waited a beat, waited for him to pull away with a mumbled apology. He'd been reserved in touching me this whole time besides the healing.

Surprisingly, he didn't back away and put space between us and neither did I. A yawn suddenly overcame me. Between the hike and the meditation, I was exhausted. I pressed my fingers to my temples and closed my eyes again. I could feel his concentration on my face.

Why was he watching me?

"You alright?"

"You know, for someone so grumpy and aloof, you seem very concerned with my well-being."

He didn't respond.

I dropped my hands to my lap. When I opened my eyes, he was watching me closely. I held his gaze.

"I'm a seer. Or I had been," I said.

Desmund pressed his lips together in a pinched line. His eyes grew darker, somber. I was taken aback by his sudden shift of countenance. He turned his gaze to the darkening sky. The two moons were barely visible near the horizon in the waning light.

That wasn't the usual reaction I got when people found out I could see the future. Maybe I shouldn't have told him about being a seer. I didn't think about the consequences of a stranger knowing part of me, it just slipped out. I wouldn't tell him about my elemental magic. Though if he had indeed watched me fight, he already knew I had some power.

It had taken me years to control my seeing powers. I'd practice on my own for hours on end, until I couldn't stay awake. From the rise of the sun to the setting of it. The days I couldn't devote to meditation, I was at the mercy of the fates. The visions knocked me to my knees so often it stopped being painful when my knees hit the ground. Even in sleep, they plagued me in the form of nightmares.

But overtime and with practice, I learned to control my reaction to how quickly the visions came on and how to separate them from the rest of my mind and thoughts. I was able to categorize them and store them away like tomes in a library.

I pushed on in hopes his relaxed, joking mood would return.

"I can't seem to access my magic. Could Bloodthorn remove my visions as well as my physical powers?"

"I suppose it could sever the connection you have with the fates. It definitely had you on the brink of death. Whatever it was, stifled your magic. It's still there but useless with the poison in your system." I saw his shoulders relax an inch or so. "The stream looks clean if you want to wash. It should be warm. We are close enough to Agni and the volcanoes," he offered, completely changing the subject.

A bath would be nice. I still felt filthy even though Desmund had cleaned me up the best he could while I'd been unconscious. I tried not to think about how much of my naked body he'd seen. I wasn't opposed to my nakedness; it was more the vulnerability of being unaware of it.

He stood and walked back to the tent. I closed my eyes for one more minute, seeking out my magic one more time. I thought Desmund had been finished with our conversation until something dropped at my side.

I jumped. I hadn't heard him walk back over to me. How'd he move so quietly?

He'd dropped a bundle next to me. My pack. "I found this while I was exploring the area before we departed."

What? How? When?

"And you're just now giving it to me?"

He shrugged. "At least you'll be clean before you put on fresh clothes."

"Did you just stuff it in your own pack?"

He shrugged again.

Ugh, he was infuriating!

"Where did you find it?"

"It was tucked behind some rocks about twenty minutes away from our campsite."

Evren must have left it behind for me. Or they didn't want the added weight. I wasn't sure what their line of thinking had been, but I was thankful none-the-less. I'd have fresh clothes.

"There's a note."

I scrambled to reach for my pack, with immense protest from my aching body, and pulled the folded paper out in a flurry.

"Wait." I paused what I was doing to scrutinize him. "How did you know about the note? Did you go through my things?"

"Yes."

Yes? That's it? That's his only explanation?

I swear if he shrugged again, I'd push him off the next cliff and take my chances with the mountains. I turned my back on him to refocus my attention on the paper in my hands. Desmund turned on his heels and walked away, giving me a private moment to take in my friend's words. I was livid that he'd gone through my things, but I was more excited to find out what was left for me, so I pushed my frustration aside.

I opened the note and saw Evren's graceful handwriting.

Nyla,

It may seem like we gave up hope. Like we left you behind. Friend, I am so sorry. We searched for you, but with the fiends near we could not stay long. I know in my heart you are not gone. I would feel it, which is why I am leaving this note. We are heading to Katuri's homeland to continue our search for the missing pieces.

We trust Knox and Haizea will keep you safe. We will see each other again.

Your loving sister, Evren

I reread the note several times before I stood and followed Desmund down to the stream.

"You can bathe first," Desmund said, interrupting me. Again. What was with his pushiness tonight? I don't think he'd utter this many words since we'd met.

He'd busied himself gathering wood, started to unpack his pack, and prepare a meal. He'd set a few snares not far away along our way. He'd get twenty or so feet ahead of me on our hike. By the time I'd caught up with him, he'd have a snare set and he was waiting quietly for me.

Once the fire was roaring to life, he sat with his back to me at the tree line, giving me privacy to bathe while offering protection as the sky grew darker.

Thank the goddess I had a bar of soap, as well as a towel, in my pack. I grabbed both and made my way to the shore.

I stripped off my borrowed clothes, ignoring Desmund sitting less than twenty feet away. My skin prickled at the chilly air. I stepped into the warm water with them bundled in my arms. I might as well clean them too. Desmund had been right. The water was almost as hot as a bath thanks to the geothermal nature of the volcanoes in the Fire Fae Kingdom. The stream was deep enough that it came up to just under my breasts. It felt wonderful against my sore feet and stiff muscles. I scrubbed the soap into my palms, creating a lather. The familiar smell of vetiver and citrus relaxed me. I used the first round of suds to wash Desmund's shirt and pants. I scrubbed at the dirt and dried blood. I made sure they were thoroughly rinsed before hanging them on a low branch to dry overnight.

I inhaled and sank beneath the water. The gentle current tugged my head backwards with the weight of my soaked hair. As I surfaced, the unease from the last several days rinsed away. I looked over my shoulder; Desmund was sitting less than a hundred feet from me. His back was still respectfully to me but his shoulders were tense. A sudden lustfulness took root. I turned toward him. I was tempted to call out to him, just to see if he'd tense up even more.

My fingertips massaged my scalp, and I practically moaned at how good it felt. I didn't often have the luxury of soaking in a tub. While I had a private cottage near the temple in Proux, I was often too busy for such luxuries. I lathered the soap over my arms and shoulders, careful with the stitches that were almost healed. I washed down my chest and over my stomach. I felt filthy everywhere. I scrubbed my feet and dug my thumbs into their arches. That time I did release a moan. It felt too amazing not to.

After I cleansed every inch of myself at least three times, I climbed from the stream and wrapped my dry towel around myself. Shivers moved down my spine as the water evaporated off my skin. I made my way over to the fire to warm up. Desmund had already seen me mostly naked, so I wasn't worried about being only in a towel. To his credit, he kept his eyes firmly on my bare feet. Is that why I felt heat creeping up my limbs? Or was it actually the fire?

"Why were you traveling to Agni?" Desmund asked casually.

I let out a laugh. "Who said I was heading to Agni?"

"Why else would you travel north?"

I eyed him with suspicion, but went with my gut. "We were actually on our way to Laeto Selva."

He watched me for a beat, then stood and made his way to the stream without responding.

While Desmund washed, I dressed and sat by the fire. The comforting softness of my own clothes made me feel better. As the sun set, a colder wind bit into my flesh. I shuddered and pulled Desmund's cloak tighter around my shoulders. I hadn't bothered retrieving mine from my bag. His was far warmer.

Out of the corner of my eye, I saw corded muscles and a carved stomach. The firelight danced on his chiseled body as Desmund pulled a tunic over his head. His body rippled with masculinity. He'd bathed much faster than I had. I didn't dare turn my head to get a better look no matter how much I wished. Though, he wasn't hiding himself from me. He could have easily gone inside the tent to dress. I could smell my soap on him. I'd left it on the bank of the stream in case he needed it.

He was tall. So tall. And powerfully built. Warm chestnut skin stretched over substantial cut muscles on his torso, with toned arms and massive thighs. While there wasn't a shred of fat on his body, I also wouldn't call him thin. There was nothing small about this male. Thick and wide. I'd seen many naked males' bodies in my 600 years but Powers Above, *he* was flawless. I couldn't stop thinking about his massive hands. They had been so tender and caring, delicate and precise. I wondered if they could ravish me as well as they cared for me?

FIFTEEN
DESMUND

I was famished, and not only for food. When I turned toward the stream and saw her begin to lift my shirt up over her head, I immediately averted my eyes. My imagination was running wild. Even the task of setting a fire and preparing a meal hadn't kept my thoughts pure. I hadn't peeked while Nyla was bathing. I forced myself not to notice where her towel fell at her upper thighs or her cleavage pressed higher as she held her arm across her chest. I had no business looking at her body. I'd seen so much of it already.

Her creamy skin was flushed pink from the warm water. It was impossible not to see her beauty and imagine her. I didn't need to. I'd seen her while I searched for and stitched up all her wounds when I first discovered her. The more scraps of fabric I'd pulled off her mangled body, the more wounds I'd found. But I'd been able to look past all the gore and blood. She was beautiful with long, elegant limbs. Creamy skin with silvery runes. Absolute perfection. And now she was standing in front of me naked with only a thin piece of fabric between her and my curious stare.

I could picture it all in my mind. But what I loved the most were her eyes. I dragged my gaze from her adorable feet up to her eyes. They were not only unique in their coloring, but they were full of knowledge. Way more knowledge than her youthful appearance suggested.

It had taken a lot of self control to walk away from her. So much so that I hadn't hesitated to grab her bar of soap to cleanse myself with. And now I smelled just like her.

By the way she watched me get dressed, she desired something too. My pulse spiked at the thought. I'd intended on getting dressed in the tent but when I caught her spying on me out of the corner of her eye, I gave her a small taste of the torment she'd given to me.

We ate in companionable silence. Nyla wasn't afraid of the silence like so many were. She also didn't complain about the bland meals I'd prepared. She always accepted them with gratitude. I hoped I would snare a rabbit overnight so we could have a hearty breakfast.

Nyla took my empty bowl from my hands, rinsed the dishes and pot in the stream, and sat them on the rock to dry near the clothes she'd washed. While she was doing that, I smothered out the fire and made sure all our belongings were inside the tent for the night.

Nyla was sitting with her legs crossed in front of her—the same position she was in earlier today—reading the note left in her pack by her friends. I knew exactly what it said. I'd read it of course. I was too nosy. I didn't understand the cryptic message. I assumed it was disguised since it didn't make a lot of sense. What was Katuri and what were they missing?

"What did Evren mean by the missing pieces?'" I asked.

Nyla clutched the note to her chest and scowled. Her chin lifted slightly, popping her perfect nose into the air. "It's none of your business."

I lifted my hands in supplication and moved to lay out on the bedroll. I crossed my ankles and tucked my hands under the back of my head.

Nyla cleared her throat from across the tent. Her eyes were darting around. "Um?"

I patted the roll beside me. "I don't bite."

She blanched.

"Where do you think I've been sleeping this whole time you were unconscious?"

Her brows shot to her hairline. "Are you serious? You slept next to me? In the same bed?"

"Well, it technically isn't a bed."

"Are you serious?" she repeated.

"Don't be a prude. I didn't do anything. It let me keep track of your fever and breathing while I slept."

"And the last two nights? You didn't sleep with me. You didn't even sleep inside the tent."

I shrugged, simply because I knew it would make her temper flare. "It wasn't that cold the last few nights. I'd be insane to sleep out there tonight."

She jumped to her feet like an agile cat. "I'll be fine outside."

There was no way I was letting that happen, but I maintained my calm exterior. I pushed myself into a seated position. She was going to bolt. "You are not sleeping outside."

Nyla went to turn away from me, but I caught her by the arm. She halted on the spot. I brushed my thumb against a pulse point on the soft skin inside her wrist. I could feel the flutter quicken. Slowly, I pulled her down so that she was kneeling next to the bed roll. Next to me. I didn't take my eyes off hers and she slowly acquiesced to my request.

"I'm not going to do anything to hurt you," I said. My voice was low, coaxing her to believe me.

Her weary eyes searched my face. I was a little surprised at her hesitancy. I'd done nothing to suggest I'd harm her. She'd literally stripped in front of me to bathe and I hadn't even watched. She was so hot and cold. One moment she was flirty, the next she was pulling away. I couldn't pin down her actions.

"Do you at least have another blanket I could use?" she asked meekly.

The corner of my mouth tipped into a half smile. I had another quilt folded at my feet. I leaned over and handed it to her.

"Thank you," she whispered.

She switched back and forth between a spitfire and a timid, mewing kitten so fast it made my head spin. Her lack of magic must be messing with her mind and confidence.

Nyla took the quilt, laid on top of the other blankets, and rolled so that her back was to me.

I settled onto my pillow, my hands tucked under my head again. I didn't bother hiding the smile that spread across my face. I won.

"See? Much better than sleeping outside."

"Shut up."

I let out an amused laugh. She scooted even closer to the edge of the bed roll. Stubborn, beautiful creature.

"Good night, Nyla," I said.

It wasn't long until she'd settled, and her breathing slowed to a steady pace. I lifted the quilt from her and tucked all the covers snug around us. The only sounds were the even in and out of her breathing and trills of hooting owls in the night.

The next morning, I awoke surrounded by the delicious heat of Nyla's body. In the middle of the night, she'd given up staying on one side of the bedroll and had wrapped her entire body around me. Her front was pressed against my side, leg draped across my waist, and her head nestled in the space between my shoulder and arm. Her hair was thick waves of golden rays spread in a wild fan around us.

Fuck me. I bit into my bottom lip and willed my body, and cock, to relax. It didn't help that her thigh was lying on top of it. I turned my head to the side and pressed my face into her blond waves and inhaled deeply. She smelled of a crisp, fresh breeze on a spring day. The hint of her soap lingered, too. The soft waves tickled my nose. As the swell of her breasts rose and fell with each breath, I studied her beautiful face. The color had returned to her cheeks. The dark circles under her eyes were gone. In fact, they were perfect. I tried to regain any sense of regularity without moving. I didn't want her to wake. Not yet.

She stirred and let out a precious yawn, stretching out her limbs and fingers like a house cat waking from a nap. I smiled down at her. Fuck. She looked pure and innocent with her sleepy doe eyes. Her once dry and cracked lips were soft and pillowy. The bottom was slightly more lush than the top one. I wanted to touch them. I wanted to kiss them. I wanted to trace them with my tongue. She was more seductive than a siren. There was something about seeing her fresh in the morning that sent a thrill through me. Was it possible to fall in love this quickly? I'd never been in love.

Then she realized where she was, who she was with. She sprang up so fast I worried for her health.

I let out a huge belly laugh.

Her pale skin was painted a deep, dark red. I wasn't sure if it was a result of fury or humiliation. "Powers Above, Desmund!" she screeched.

SIXTEEN
KATURI

The City of Laeto Selva

I lay on the oversized couch facing the open balcony. Rain came down and the familiar sounds of the canopy enveloped me. The pitter patter and droplets hitting the thick, green leaves were a soft melody. Birds chirped and monkeys called back and forth to each other.

Then my earth elemental surged. My blood hummed. My magic recognized Garren's presence without me even seeing him walk into the room. I didn't turn towards him. I heard his footsteps grow closer. Then his delicious scent wrapped around me. It brought with it contented bliss.

The lightweight blanket lifted and Garren's body folded against me from behind. He propped his chin on my bare shoulder. He had been catching Delrik, Evren, and Naz up on the conversation we'd had with my father.

"Little Flower."

I was mentally drained from dealing with my father. Seeing him face to face brought back all the pain and sadness from all those years ago. I'd held so much animosity against him over the last decades. Today was different. Though, not in a good way. He was too kind. Too welcoming. Something felt wrong and I couldn't pinpoint what.

Garren gently brushed a kiss against my skin. He knew exactly what I needed. He always did. Don't get me wrong. I loved his dominance and the edge we treaded, but right now I needed softness, and he gave it willingly without me having to ask. I needed to get out of my head and my heavy thoughts.

His lips traveled down my arm. "Come show me your favorite places," he said between kisses.

"I'd rather stay in bed," I grumped.

I was too lost in my thoughts to traipse through the rainforest. Actually, traipsing through the rainforest would distract me perfectly , but I wanted to wallow for just a while longer.

"Oh come on. You know I could stay in bed and fuck you all day."

I quickly interrupted him, "I'm not in bed."

"Actually I could fuck you anytime and anywhere, but I want to see where you grew up."

"Anywhere? Anytime? Cocky much?"

He rolled his hips against my ass. It was one of my only weaknesses.

"How about we go for a hike?" he prodded.

"It's pouring."

"So?" I felt him shrug. "It's a rainforest. It will stop soon. And if we get wet, I'll just strip you out of your wet clothes and..."

I groaned in reluctance. "Fine."

"Yes!" I almost couldn't take his level of energy.

I looked over my shoulder at him and was met with a goofy grin. My crankiness melted away.

"I'll take you to one of my favorite spots hidden in the forest. Drake will love it."

Garren jumped from the couch like a kid told they were getting ice cream for breakfast. Eleni appeared and barked and yipped while running circles around him.

"Now look at what you did. You got her all riled up," I said as I pushed myself to a seated position and patted my hand on the couch beside me. Eleni promptly ignored me for the attention from my bondmate.

Garren was now on the floor, rolling around, and speaking baby talk. "Do you want to go explore, Len-Len? Yes you do! Yes you do!"

Where was Drake? I needed his assistance in wrangling these two. The sea dragon was obsessed with the amount of rain and water sources surrounding the palace. I'd hardly seen him, though I knew he was nearby. He must have felt me thinking of him because he appeared on the balcony, jumping from a tree to the slippery stone and sliding on his belly. Each puddle he hit sent water flying into the air. It splashed off the magical weather barrier leading into the bedroom.

I dressed in the clothes of my people, the Forest Fae. I hadn't noticed how I'd grown used to the layered clothes of the Snowhaven Fae. I felt so exposed in the dress Corynne had laid out for me. It was made of the same fabric as my mother's, except mine was light sage in color. Long, sheer panels draped over my shoulders and were held on with a wide belt.

Garren, on the other hand, couldn't tear his eyes off my body.

"Honestly, if you're going to keep ogling me, I can change."

"Powers Above, don't you dare. I love seeing you like this."

"Barely clothed?"

He waggled his eyebrows and reached around me to grab my ass. I squealed and smacked at his hand.

By the time we'd gotten dressed and moving, the rain had ceased. Everything was wet with droplets of rain. I led Garren through the rainforest, away from the city center. I hadn't been into the city yet. We'd only been in Laeto Selva for two days. Getting into the city was one of my top priorities in being home. I'd be queen one day and I wanted to know my people. Though I'd spent the majority of my life in the bitter cold Kanevvluk, the forest and city called to my soul. I wanted Garren to see everything about the city. We hadn't talked about it, but this is where we'd spend the rest of our lives once I took over the throne.

I took Garren's hand and led him toward my favorite waterfall. I discovered it as a child and learned to swim there. Tropical trees and plants were thick along the familiar trail. Fruits and flowers bloomed on each plant that touched my fingers. The forest was as happy about my return as I was. Animals scurried from hiding places to peer at us. Colorful birds called to each other above our heads. But my favorite, many species of orchids, covered the trunks of trees. Their blossoms open wide and every color of the rainbow.

Garren had been right. I heard the roar of the waterfall before the water came into view. When we finally parted the fronds of a low palm, we were met by the dark blue and brown of the towering waterfall. The rich minerals with healing properties had changed the color of the rocks over time. Compared to the bitter cold turquoise waters of Kanevvluk, this water I knew was warm and welcoming. Though, I couldn't help but miss the sparkling majesty of the icebergs and the fjord.

"I want to kiss you under the waterfall," Garren said. His face lit with excitement.

"Dark hells no!"

His face morphed to disappointment. "What? Why?" He was adorable when he pouted.

"Trust me. It isn't as romantic as it sounds. That water hurts."

He crossed his arms over his broad chest and stuck his nose up into the air. "I don't believe you."

"Fine. Suit yourself."

I gestured toward the rushing water. I knew better than to swim directly under it. It wasn't the tallest waterfall in our kingdom but that didn't mean the water's power should be underestimated. Garren brushed a soft kiss over my cheek. Sensual, light, and lovely. Then he swatted my ass and then dove fully clothed into the water. I laughed. He tossed first his sopping wet shirt, then his pants at my feet. They landed with a wet slap against the bank. I watched him swim with graceful strokes toward the waterfall.

I sat down on the shore in a bed of ferns and admired the feathered leaves. The humidity felt so good on my skin. The fiddle heads were speckled with seeds. I reached out and touched the fronds, a glow from the ground radiated upward and toward my fingers. The fern extended out to me.

A small black and white furry animal popped its head out of the brush. A lemur's piercing blue eyes met mine. It tipped its head in a curious way. I plucked a fig from the nearby tree and held it out to the inquisitive primate. It took it from my fingers and took a bite. Juices dripped from its little fingers. I was interrupted by Eleni as she splashed in the shallow water, biting at the little fish. Drake popped out of the water and then splashed water toward Eleni with his tail.

I was distracted by the sound of Garren screaming.

"What in the circle of dark hells!"

He was standing near the waterfall, holding the top of his head in his hands. I laughed so hard my stomach was cramping. The water pounded down on him. During his attempt to extricate himself from the beating water, he slipped and dropped below the surface. He popped up a second later, sputtering and flailing. For a sea dragon, he wasn't very graceful in the water.

"I told you so!" I laughed from the safety of my bank.

He rose from the water, moisture dripping from his hair. Barefoot and tempting, glistening with droplets of water. Fuck, he was breathtaking. Garren flopped down next to me. He shook his head out like a dog and splattered water all over me. I squealed and wiped the moisture from my face.

"You look so at home here," he said.

I smiled. "I may seem at home in the rainforest, but you are my home now, Garren. You. Whether that is in Laeto Selva or Kanevvluk. I'll follow you anywhere."

I paused, scanning my bondmate's beautiful face. "I don't trust my father," I said.

"I don't either." Garren paused. "You know what I do know?"

"What?" I asked with a smirk.

"That you are the most beautiful thing in this entire forest." Then he winked.

"That was lame."

"Lame, but true."

"You know all you have to do is ask for sex. You don't have to woo me with your cheesy lines anymore," I said.

He climbed on top of me and pressed me down into the earth. My skin sang at the contact of his body above me and the earth below. "I will woo you forever and eternity."

A primal growl came from him. He snapped his teeth and his sea dragon shone through his eyes. Then with a wicked smile, he rolled us over and over, down the bank until we splashed into the water.

I shrieked but didn't try to escape his arms. We were swallowed up by the cool water. Eleni and Darke jumped in after us.

When we broke the surface, Garren held his arms wrapped around the tops of my thighs, lifting my head above the water. My hands were on his shoulders, and I was looking down at him.

"Let me have my way with you, Little Flower. Let me adore you the way I'm meant to."

SEVENTEEN
KATURI

Garren loosened his hold around my thighs, and I slid down his chest until we were nose to nose. Every part of my body exploded with awareness at the slow drag of skin on skin.

"Always," I whispered against his lips.

His strong hand came to my face. He gently cradled my chin. He dragged his thumb across my bottom lip. My lips parted and he pushed his thumb into my mouth.

I quickly wrapped my lips around the digit and sucked. Hard. His eyes flared, shifting to slits and darkening with desire. I smirked around his thumb and sucked harder, hollowing out my cheeks, teasing him. His thumb pressed against the back of my tongue, thrusting it deep. My hands flattened against his chest, but I took it without question. I swallowed and tears pricked at my eyes with the deep invasion of my throat. I loved how Garren pushed me right to the edge but never over it.

A whirlpool formed around us, swirling with the intensity that we felt. The water lapped against our bodies with sweeping suction, and I sucked on his thumb again.

He abruptly pulled his thumb from my mouth with a pop.

"You are so beautiful, even if it isn't my cock shoved down your throat."

All I could do was whimper and squeeze my thighs together to relieve the pressure building.

"You are going to come on my cock now like the good Little Flower you are," he commanded.

"Yes, please," I begged shamelessly.

Garren spun me and pressed my front against a nearby rock. His rough hands pinned my hips to the hard surface. It bit into my skin. Garren sunk his teeth into my shoulder and growled. I dropped my head back, giving him even more access. I loved that I could turn him feral. One hand snaked up my front and wrapped around my throat. The other pulled at the waistline of my undergarments, pulling them down over my hips, just low enough that my ass was free. He cupped his hand between my legs. I tried to widen them, but my undergarments prevented it. I groaned in frustration and Garren rolled his hardened cock against my ass. His finger traced along my folds. Even in the water, I could feel the smooth slickness of my arousal. With him in control, I could release every ounce of control and willpower I mastered outside of our relationship. I could be vulnerable with Garren. He had me. He'd give me anything and everything I'd ever need, even if I didn't know what that something was. It was liberating.

He dipped a finger inside me. I tried to thrust against his hand, but he had me pinned too tight against the rock.

"You're feeling greedy today, aren't you?" he hissed in my ear.

"Only for you. Always for you. Please, Garren."

The waterfall's mist sprayed us. It was cool against my burning skin.

Suddenly a fierce battle cry cut through the thickness of our lust.

EIGHTEEN
KATURI

Just then a barbaric battle cry pierced the air. Delrik came bursting through the trees, launching himself off a rock and cannonballing into the water. A tidal wave came over us, dousing our heads and the mood.

"I'm sorry, brother. Did I interrupt something?" Delrik said.

Garren threw his head back and growled. Scales skittered along his face and his sharp-pointed teeth threatened to tear Delrik to pieces if he came too close.

"Later, my love," I said, spinning in his arms, kissing his shoulder.

I straightened my clothes, ensuring I was completely covered. Then I swam to shore. Nazneen and Evren appeared arm in arm, dressed in the traditional clothes of the Forest Fae. Evren wore cream and Nazneen a soft coffee color. They were beautiful as always.

"Don't be mad. We brought food," Nazneen said as she held up a basket. "Aura was flying and saw you up here. She told us how to get here."

The little bird pecked at Garren's ear lovingly.

"So it's your fault that I didn't get lucky," he said to the bird.

Eleni climbed from the water and shook out her fur, sending droplets over us. Drake, on the other hand, who'd been churning up little tide pools along the bank hunting for tiny fish, ignored everyone in his pursuit of a snack.

I hadn't seen the others since my father had confirmed he had the earth relic in his possession. I'd spent the afternoon hulled up in my room with my mind whirling. Now that we knew where it was, we could move on, but where next?

"My father has the earth relic. Cattleya's Key."

Nazneen took a bite of guava. I knew Corynne had packed them especially for me, since they were my favorite. "Do you think he'll actually let us have it?"

"Probably not. That would be too easy."

I thought for a moment. I knew my father wouldn't let such a powerful item far from his hands.

"Are we going to steal it?"

"I don't know if that would work either. There are sentinels standing guard over it day and night. I'm sure there are wards around it too."

"We will figure it out. I wouldn't mind a few extra days here either while we lay out our plan," Evren said. "It's too beautiful here to leave so quickly."

Delrik climbed over her, pressing her back into a bed of ferns. Her lush black wings spread beneath her. Shadows caressed her body. "Not as beautiful as my Ashlyra."

"Gross, you two," Nazneen complained. "I swear, between the four of you, someone is always mounting someone."

"How do you make it look so easy?" I asked Evren.

I was flustered, I couldn't help it. I'd surrendered my powers to Garren and vice versa, but we'd yet to completely trade powers. He's caressed my magic with his elemental water, but I've yet to be able to access it. And the thought of giving up my earth magic terrified me. Being so vulnerable like that.

"Swapping powers with Delrik. I mean, you've been in a partial shift since we figured out how to do it," I said, motioning to her wings.

"I just love how beautiful they are. They remind me that even the heaviness of our elemental powers hold unique elegance."

"We do have a certain responsibility with our elemental magic, don't we," I said thoughtfully. "And knowing we can move them from person to person...It just baffles me."

"My mother always said that the first time you use one another's powers is a special moment. More so than the blood binding itself. It's showing true trust and devotion to your partner," Nazneen said.

Delrik reached over and squeezed her hand with a smile. "You sound exactly like Mom."

Nazneen continued. "For bondmates, it's the final step in being completely joined in body, magic, and spirit. You'll be at your most vulnerable, trusting your partner with your life. What was once yours becomes something shared."

"Calia, with all her wisdom. It had really helped having her there by our sides," Evren said. "She encouraged me to focus on the origin of my power and visualize it moving into Delrik. It's hard to explain. At this point it just feels so natural. Our powers effortlessly flow back and forth between us."

"You have to completely let down your guard, let down your shields? Do you block Garren from every part of your mind?"

"No. Yes? I don't know. Maybe. I haven't really ever thought much about it. I feel his magic," I responded.

"Then that's the perfect start," Nazneen said. She'd moved from her casual position to sitting alert and ready to jump in to assist.

"Here, try this. Garren, come sit in front of Kat," Evren said.

I was surprised he didn't object or make a snarky comment. I knew he'd wanted to share our powers, but never pushed me on the topic.

"Touch hands. Just reach out with your minds. Kat, just like training in Kanevvluk. Relax. Now, with your powers, let it find your bondmate, your Ashlyra," Evren instructed.

The ultimate act of trust. I did trust Garren. In every way possible. I'd resisted him for so long but he was my life. I stretched my earth elemental through our bond. The binding mark flared and warmed against my skin. Garren's fingers tightened in mine and I felt the heat of his own binding mark against my palm. It was like he was opening the gates to his soul for me.

I drew in a deep breath. Why was I nervous? Was it because though I'd said the words "I trust you" and "yes, I give you my everything" there was a big difference between saying the words and showing them to be true? I hadn't realized how much I had been holding back from Garren. Not purposefully of course. I truly believed I'd given him every last part of me. This way proof to myself, and to him, I hadn't relinquished that last part of my me.

I focused on our binding marks, joined together, just as the priestess had wrapped our hands in the gilded cord the day of our blood binding ceremony. My heart twisted and I felt Garren's grip on my fingers tighten. That day had been so full of fear and sadness and betrayal. But I also remember Garren's presence at my side and how steady he was for me, even then.

I imagined the gilded cord tying our souls together, how it stretched from my elbow all the way to his. I followed it from my soul and into the expanse of his. I stood at that precipice and looked out over the endless awe of our mating bond. As if it were guiding me, I lightly ran my fingers along the bond, following it toward Garren.

My earth elemental magic trailed behind me in a glittering swirl of autumn leaves on the wind.

Like the parting of the sea, his water elemental made room for me, for my magic. I stood on the bank. My earth to his water. Our powers intertwined together. Though my magic was gone from my body, I was surprised at how I didn't feel empty at all. I felt safe, protected, and cherished. I knew Garren wouldn't let anything happen to me.

The part I wasn't expecting was Garren's mind to embrace me. With the flood gates open, he also stepped into me. Our minds melded. I could feel his overwhelming joy and passion. Tears streamed down my face.

"Shh, Little Flower," he spoke into my mind. *"I've got you."*

My eyes sprang open only to be met with the teal ones of my bondmate. My Ashlyra.

"Do it again," I whispered.

He offered me a goofy smile.

"I love you, Princess Katuri Harland."

The press of Garren's lips to mine broke my concentration. With a sudden wave, my magic sprang back to me like an elastic band. I gasped at the suddenness of it.

"Good! Just like that. Did you feel the difference?" Evren asked.

All I could do was nod. I was too startled and breathless to form any words.

"It will come easier the next time. It just takes practice."

NINETEEN
DESMUND

Nyla and I had fallen into a routine—wake, breakfast, climb, tend to Nyla's wounds, rest. The higher we climbed, the colder the nights became.

By the third night, Nyla had given up pretending to be offended by me suggesting that she sleep next to me. It was too cold. Thank the gods for the spelled tent to keep our body heat trapped inside. The higher altitude winds made the tent whip and snap with the storms that relentlessly pounded each night, but the heat never escaped. Its nightly howling was as eerie as a wolf's lonely howl.

Tonight was no different. We'd hunkered down before the sun even began to set and ate our dinner inside the tent.

Nyla tucked the note from her friend Evren under her pillow. It was well-creased from her rereading it. She probably could recite it backwards from memory at this point.

"I think it's safe to remove your stitches," I said once we'd both finished our meal.

"Really?" she said with a touch of excitement in her voice. "I hope this means my powers will be returning sooner rather than later."

I wish I had that answer for her. Bloodthorn was a difficult poison to navigate, especially when I didn't know the dose or potency the fiends had used, or if they had mixed it with something else. In smaller doses, it would wear off after a few hours. On the other side of the coin, a tablespoon of pure Bloodthorn oil would be lethal. I was thankful to the Powers Above that hadn't been the case for Nyla.

This time, when she laid back on the bedroll for me, she didn't stare at the ceiling in silence. Instead, she watched me intently as I focused on removing the sutures. Only three raised scars remained across her chest. All the black veining from the poison was gone. And while the runes didn't line up perfectly as before, I was happy that it wasn't horrid looking. Her bicep, to my utter delight, barely had a scar.

Once I'd taken out the last thread, Nyla grasped my fingers. "Thank you."

The contact made a spark of emotion sweep through me. What emotion, I couldn't pin down. "You don't have to thank me."

She squeezed my hand. "I owe my life to you."

The sincerity in her eyes drew me in like a moth to a flame. I shook my head, and I brushed a piece of hair from her forehead. "I'm honored to have had you as a patient."

Nyla pulled the blankets back, lifting them for me to join her. I lay down beside her and she snuggled deep into my chest. I didn't hesitate to wrap my arms around her. Her warmth washed over me and I sighed with contentment. This is where I belonged. We'd been together for roughly five days in total. Five days and she'd altered the course of my existence. She'd become all I thought about. Even in my dreams, she was there.

TWENTY

KATURI

Exploring the rainforest had been an excellent way to lift my spirits. I hadn't expected Nazneen and Evren to show up, but having them help guide me in opening myself to Garren had immensely improved my mood.

I'd let Garren into my life several months prior after so many years of animosity between us. I didn't think there was a way to surpass our connection until I'd freely given him my earth elemental magic. It was liberating.

I was now hand in hand with Garren as we meandered down the cobbled street toward the city center. Eleni trotted happily beside me. Drake, since being shown the waterfall, had chosen to venture there today instead of the city. Evren and Nazneen had gone ahead of us. I could see them off in the distance standing at a market cart. A nymph was offering a piece of fruit to Nazneen.

I took my time walking and peaking into the stores and all the carts scattered around the street. We weren't near any of the residences yet. The market and heart of the city formed a semicircle around the southern side of the palace. Then, as you walked east, the homes and neighborhoods started. Tiny apartments and townhouses turned to farmlands full of dense trees and crops the further you got from the city.

A chimed grabbed my attention. I turned my head and saw Marselina ducking out of a nearby herb shop.

"Marselina!" I called and waved to my future sister.

She looked around at the sound of her name until she spotted me. She offered me a sweet smile and then a low curtsy.

"Don't do that. You'll be princess soon. There is no need for such etiquette."

"As you wish Princess Katuri," she said softly.

"Kat," I corrected.

"Kat."

"Care to join us? We were just exploring. I'm sure you're more knowledgeable about the city than me. Everything has changed so much since I was a girl."

"I was actually on the way to the apothecary to drop off some herbs."

"Oh that's perfect. I'm in need of some more tea."

I released Garren's hand and took Marselina by the elbow. "Mother mentioned you are a member of the Moriko Family. You come from a long line of healers, correct?"

"Yes, princess...I mean Kat. My family is known in Laeto Selva as healers and high level alchemists."

"I've never studied the healing arts."

A smile broke out on her face. "It's quite fascinating. Though I was born with healing powers, the subject in school always fascinated me. I knew I'd eventually have the magic of healing once I came of age, but I still couldn't get enough about how facets of the earth all around us could be combined in different ways to cure illnesses."

I could sense the joy the subject brought to her.

"Is that how you met Logan?" I asked.

A blush crept up her cheeks. "No. I attended the city schools. Prince Logan had private tutors."

Of course he did. I knew this. I was just gauging her reaction to my brother. He'd seemed cold toward her on the day we'd arrived. I stayed silent, waiting for her to continue.

"I met Logan about a year ago, maybe? He came into the apothecary I help restock occasionally." She looked up beneath her lashes at me. "It's a boring story."

"No! Please continue. I don't know anything about my brother. We haven't seen each other since he was so little. I'd love to hear about the male he's grown up to be."

"He'd come into the shop looking for tea for headaches. I'd had my back turned and I hadn't realized it was the Prince who'd come in. I was on my tip toes on a ladder reaching for a jar of ginseng. When I looked over my shoulder to respond to his greeting, I literally fell off my feet."

"Powers Above!"

"And your brother caught me. It was like a cheesy line from a romance novel. I wouldn't have believed it if it hadn't happened to me."

"Oh, are you a reader too!?"

"I am. Logan says I spend too much time with my nose buried in books, both academic and...not so much."

"He's just jealous you're so well read," I said.

She let out a sparkling laugh.

"Here we are!" Marselina exclaimed.

She pointed across the street to a small shop with large windows that were pushed open. We were almost caught up to Nazneen and Evren, so I called out to them.

"Marselina and I will be at the apothecary."

Nazneen waved in response. "We'll be there momentarily."

Marselina quickly took the lead and guided us across the road and dipped into the shop. The scent of herbs hit my senses, but not in an overwhelming way. Garren and Eleni had been distracted by a cart of grilled meat. Eleni was bouncing up and down next to Garren as he tried to take a bite, she practically took the meat out of his mouth. I left them to it, so it was just Marselina and me. She squeezed my hand before popping behind a curtain into the back. I stood, spinning in a small circle, and taking it all in. I'd never been in an apothecary before. Glass jars and clay pots lined every available space along the walls. Each one was meticulously labeled. Some words I recognized. Others may as well have been in a different language.

Evren and Nazneen appeared in the doorway, each with a skewer of grilled meat.

"This city is amazing. It's huge compared to Arcelia," Nazneen said.

"It's definitely the biggest city I've ever been to," Evren said.

The curtain Marselina had disappeared behind rustled and then was pushed aside. She appeared with someone in tow.

"Marselina! How are you?" Nazneen said. "It's nice to see you again."

Marselina dipped into a small curtsy. "Nazneen. Evren."

"Evren?" The voice came from the figure behind Marselina.

"Yes. That's me."

The dainty, feminine figure stepped around Marselina. Linen robes draped from her shoulders all the way to the floor. Even the tips of her toes were covered. Long, billowing sleeves went down her arms all the way to her wrists. There was a loose-fitting hood that covered her head and a mask covered her nose and mouth. Only her eyes and forehead were showing, though they were shadowed from the hood.

I hadn't noticed the cane at first. It reminded me of the cane Salina, Nyla's mentor, had used in Proux. It was a smooth-polished wood. The handle was a dark stone with a tiny hand held on it. The female took another step forward and I recognized a limp.

"Evren Byrnes. I've heard so much about you," she said.

"Me?" Evren said, looking from Marselina to Katuri, then back to the female.

"I'm Rhea." She passed the handle of her cane to her opposite hand and reached out for Evren. Her skin had a blueish hue to it that reminded me of coastal waters near the sea.

Evren, ever polite, took her hand without hesitation.

"How do you know my name?" she asked.

"Oh." She shifted awkwardly on her feet.

A tension hung in the air.

"I'm sorry, I thought you would recognize my name. I knew your brother."

Evren immediately lit up. "Adaris?!" How did you know Adaris?"

She batted her hand around in nonchalance. "Nevermind. It was a brief meeting. Not important."

She seemed almost dejected, like Evren should have known who she was.

"No matter. Princess Katuri, Marselina said you were in need of a tea or tincture?"

"Um, yes." I felt there was still something hanging unsaid but I let it pass. "Tea. Yes. Fertility tea. Or I guess a tincture would work too, whichever you have."

"Wait?! Fertility tea? What are you *not* telling us?" Nazneen piped in.

"It's nothing. I just wanted to have it on hand."

I hadn't even mentioned to Garren I was going to get the fertility tea. It kind of just sprung to my mind when Marselina mentioned the apothecary. Maybe based on Nazneen's reaction, I should get the tincture to prevent pregnancy instead. I knew she had a good stock of it herself with as frequently she'd taken lovers. Nazneen was also much older than me. I was young for a High Fae and hadn't quite reached my prime for fertility.

Why was I even thinking of this now?

"I'd be happy to whip up a batch for you," Rhea said.

"No, it's fine. I don't actually need it." I couldn't help the flush that was creeping across my body.

"So Rhea, how did you say you know Adaris?" Nazneen asked.

She was clearly focused on this connection more than my issues. Again, I thanked the Powers.

Rhea's eyes darted from side to side, and then backed away a few steps.

"I've got work to do. Marselina, thank you for the herbs. I'll chat with you soon."

"You ladies almost done?" Garren said, popping his head into the shop.

Fuck. Could this get any worse?

"If you say anything..." I said through gritted teeth and under my breath to Nazneen.

"We're fine. Be out shortly," Naz said.

Thank the Powers she was willing to *not* stir the pot for once.

"Come on. Delrik is getting hungry and we all know how he'll spiral if we don't feed him," Garren joked.

Evren and Nazneen rolled their eyes, but followed without putting up a fight.

As we turned to leave, Rhea with the stealth of a spy, slipped a vial of fertility tincture into my hand. My fingers instinctively wrapped around the amber glass. I looked at her. Her face was friendly and open now that we were the only two remaining in the shop.

"Just in case you change your mind. Your secret is safe with me," Rhea whispered.

"Thank you."

I blinked against the day's sunshine until my eyes adjusted. Garren was back at the nearby meat cart with Delrik, Evren, and Nazneen. Eleni was begging at Garren's feet. He plucked a piece of sizzling pork from the stick in his hand, but before he could pass it to her, Aura swept from the sky and swiped it from his fingers.

Marselina appeared at my side from the apothecary. "Rhea is very talented. She somehow can make the worst tasting tincture bearable."

"Did you find what you need to get for Logan?" I asked, avoiding the topic of the fertility tincture I'd slipped into my pocket.

"I did."

"Do the headaches bother him often?"

Her mouth turned down at the corners. "They've been getting worse the last several months when we first met. I'm not sure what's causing them. He's been under a lot of stress. Your father, I mean the king, has put a lot on his shoulders."

I didn't know what to say to that. I didn't know anything about my father and brother's dynamic.

Suddenly Nazneen released a squeal of happiness. She darted across the street to a local bakery. She pressed her face against the window.

"Oh gosh! Is she okay?" Marselina asked in concern.

"She's fine. She's obsessed with baking so she gets a little excited when she finds a bakery," I said.

"Luiz is one of the head chefs at the palace. This is his family's bakery. He makes the best brigadeiro."

"What's that?"

"Oh it is the most decadent fudgy ball of whipped chocolate covered in chocolate sprinkles."

"Well, that is exactly up Nazneen's alley as far as dessert is concerned."

Eleni, peeved at Aura from stealing her tasty morsel of pork, abandoned Garren for Nazneen. She raised her front paws to the windowsill and mimicked Nazneen's posture with her nose pressed to the glass.

"Do you want some sweet treats too? Maybe a nice carrot cake?" Nazneen cooed to my spoiled familiar.

"We should probably head back to the castle before Nazneen buys the whole city a dessert."

Nazneen didn't bother turning, but yelled out to me, "I heard that!"

TWENTY-ONE
GARREN

It's been almost three weeks since we arrived in Laeto Selva and I'd insisted on continuing daily training with Katuri. She'd never been in combat before, and I knew we'd be dealing with Hadeon again sooner rather than later. I wanted to make sure she was prepared. Sometimes, we trained with everyone. Today, I snuck my bondmate away from our friends. I wasn't sure if it was the lack of privacy we'd had since we arrived or if the surge in Katuri's elemental magic that had me wanting to have her undivided attention.

Katuri and I had been in the small courtyard training for about an hour. Her golden skin glistened with sweat. Three weeks of being in the sun—and not the snowy abyss of Kanevvluk—had darkened her complexion so that she looked more like her mother. Kat didn't really need my instruction today, but she needed to burn off some energy. She was on edge. Between her father's overbearing, overkind attention to Nyla's continued absence, it was more often than not Katuri needed a distraction. She flipped back and forth between a sullen mood and a preoccupied mind. We were getting closer to departing Laeto Selva with each day. Yesterday, Katuri had selected a small group of sentinels to scour the Baxmar Range along the border in search of signs of Nyla.

Kat was mindlessly blocking my blows with an escrima training stick. Her eyes were glazed over and she seemed far away from the courtyard.

"We also could use the practice with joining our powers," I said. I swung my stick in a halfhearted attack from the left. Good thing, because she completely missed it. I stopped its momentum just before it struck her. "Katuri."

"What? Sorry," she stammered.

I dropped my escrima stick to my side and took a step closer to her. Rather than reaching for her hand, I pushed against our mental bond, pressing my elemental water toward her. She smiled, now focused on me.

"We should practice swapping out powers and using them together."

After that afternoon when Kat had sat with Evren and discussed in detail how her and Delrik shared the fire and shadows back and forth, we'd openly been trying to pass our powers and open our mental connection even more.

Everyone was scheduled to meet us after lunch. Nazneen had made friends with some of the weapons masters and trainers. She'd taken advantage of being in Quinterre to make connections as future leader of Arcelia. She was quite good at it, too.

"I have no problem reaching out for your elemental when it's just us, but it's when there are other things going on, I get distracted and can't focus."

"That means we need to find a way to disrupt your focus so you can practice with a distraction."

She planted her hands on her hips. "And how are we supposed to do that?"

A mischievous smile spread on my lips. "My inner sea dragon has a few ideas," I purred.

"Wow. That was rough," she teased.

She secretly loved my perverted thoughts and cheesy lines. I wiggled my brows at her. The air between us sparked with energy. Kat recognized the sudden change immediately.

"Sharing powers is the ultimate form of trust," I said to my bondmate. "You're at your most vulnerable."

Almost more so than the blood binding itself. It shows true trust and devotion to your partner. You're at the most vulnerable without your magic, and you're trusting your partner with your life. What was once yours becomes something shared between you both. For bondmates, it's the final step in being completely joined in body, magic, and spirit. And while we'd swapped powers in the past, neither of us were pros at wielding the other's magic.

"I have a few ideas."

Katuri rolled her eyes.

"Garren. That's not what I meant."

TWENTY-TWO
GARREN

I stalked toward my bondmate. "I know exactly what you meant. You need to practice your power control while having distractions."

She stepped back away from me, but I was in front of her with three quick, long strides, my hand around her throat.

Her mouth popped open in surprise, but her pulse spiked beneath my palm. My Little Flower loved when my hand was wrapped around her throat. I was thankful for the ridiculous, gauzy dresses of the Forest Fae at that moment. They allowed easy access to my favorite place in the realm—between my bondmate's thighs.

I slipped my hand between the sheer panels and cupped her heat. Her nipples peaked through the flimsy fabric.

She let out a not-so-quiet moan. I released her throat and quickly pressed my palm over her mouth.

"Shh, my love. We aren't in a very private part of the palace. Someone could easily come upon us."

"We're going to get caught," she said, muffled, looking around. But her heart was still pounding hard.

"And? Do you want me to stop?"

I would stop if she asked me to. She never wanted me to stop. I knew how to bring her right to the edge and dangle off the cliff. My bondmate loved the thrill.

She smiled beneath my hand, then bit into the flesh of my palm. The sharp pain of her teeth only spurred me on. Then she planted a soft kiss where her teeth had just been. She was too sweet for her own good.

I quirked a brow in question and she nodded in understanding.

"I like this kind of training." She trailed her fingertips past the hem of my shirt and teased the skin of my back just above my waist band. She scraped her nails against the flesh.

I growled and pushed my cock against her stomach. At the same time, I thrust two fingers deep inside her.

"Summon your earth power," I commanded.

She was panting and moving her hips against my hand. I withdrew my fingers from her because she wasn't focusing.

"What? No!" she gasped into my hand.

"I'll only keep going if you summon your power," I said.

Her head dropped back against the wall away from my hand and she whined. "Fine."

She pressed her hands to the wall and delicate flowers arched from her fingers. I pressed my fingers back into her slick heat. I kept my heated stare locked on her.

"Good girl."

I stroked gently against that spot deep inside her and she moaned. The flowers spread, weaving higher and higher all around her. The higher I brought her, the more intricate they became. Small pebbles from the courtyard rose into the air, hoovering off the ground. But I wasn't going to let it be that easy. I slowed my pace and removed my fingers again. The small stones dropped back down to the ground.

I brought my fingers to my mouth, and while staring at my bond-mate, I put one finger in my mouth and licked it clean.

"Powers Above, do you know how good you taste? Sweeter than all the fruits of the rainforest."

She opened her delicate mouth, silently asking for a taste. Fuck, she was perfect. I slipped my middle finger through her parted lips and they closed around it.

This time it was my turn to groan. "You were created just for me."

I thrust my hips forward, my cock hitting the apex of her thighs. Powers Above, I wanted to bury myself in her heat. But I had other plans. I dropped to my knees. I lifted one of her legs and draped it over my shoulder.

"I'm going to give you pleasure now, Little Flower. But you need to do something for me. You need to use not only your elemental, but mine too. Do you understand?"

She looked down at me and nodded. While keeping my eyes locked on hers, I parted the fabric panels and ran my tongue across her slit.

"Yesssss," she whispered, dragging out the word and digging her fingers into my hair.

I pulled back and just looked at her. She was drenched. All for me.

"Garren," she pleaded.

I pinched the back of her leg right where her ass met her thigh. She flinched. “Shh! No talking. Only conjuring. Focus.” My voice was all gravel as I took in my bondmate. “Stay quiet and do what I told you.”

She was trembling in my hands. I let my warm breath ghost over her opening.

Finally, I couldn't take it anymore. I had to taste her. I flicked my tongue against the bud at the apex of her thighs, and she jerked in pleasure. I brought her so close to the edge just moments ago and she was still teetering. I'd have to slow down if I wanted to actually get any practice in.

“Be a good girl while I take what I want.”

She nodded and closed her eyes but I could tell she still wasn't centered or engaging our powers.

“Focus, Katuri. Don't try to control the power. Let it be one with you. Let it flow through you.”

“Yes, sir,” she choked out.

She growled, but took a deep breath and closed her eyes. I felt her reach through our bond, her magic caressing mine. The binding mark on my arm warmed and my elemental water reached out to her. Our two powers entwined together. She lifted her hands from me and held them, palms facing up.

I stroked her languidly with my tongue and watched as swirling water and earth appeared in her palms. I sucked hard on her clit and she gasped. The magic flared higher. I alternated sucking, flicking, and biting. Every time she began to recognize the pattern, I'd change it. She ground against my face, unable to stop herself from seeking out more friction. I gave her what she sought. Soon we were surrounded by an elaborate display of water and ice and mist with flowers and earth. They were woven together the same way our souls were. The ground beneath my knees was quivering with my bondmates strength and power.

“Eyes on me, Little Flower.”

Her eyes snapped open at my command. The look on her face made everything more intense and our elemental powers pulsed.

“Who do you belong to?”

Her pussy fluttered as I spoke the words against her.

“You. Only you. Always you,” she panted. “I love you.”

“I love you, too.”

My cock was painfully hard in my pants, but this was for her.

“Show me.”

She moaned.

"Show me how you control our magic."

I kept up my pace and her thighs began to tighten. She lifted her hands higher and earth and ice erupted from her fingers.

"Garren."

Fuck. When she said my name like that...

"That's it, Little Flower. More."

An unseen pulse of energy shot through the courtyard, almost like lightning. "Get your hands off my sister."

TWENTY-THREE
GARREN

Katuri, my gorgeous bondmate and consort, had woven our elemental magic together the same way our souls were. I felt her reach through our bond, her magic caressing mine. The binding mark on my arm warmed and I opened myself up to her. My elemental water reached out to her. The two powers entwined together. She lifted her hands from me and held them palms facing up. Soon we were surrounded by an elaborate display of water and ice and mist with flowers and earth. She lifted her hands higher and earth and ice erupted from her fingers.

An unseen pulse of energy shot through the courtyard, almost like lightning. "Get your hands off my sister. How dare you expose the future queen of Laeto Selva in such a disgusting way."

A furious voice broke into our circle of bliss. A hard hand landed on my shoulder and a current shot through me. My sea dragon took over. I spun on my heels, using my body to block the intruder's view of my bondmate. Thank the Powers Above I hadn't stripped her down. My eyes were slits, scales rippled into place down my arms and across my face. Talons sprouted from my fingers and my teeth lengthened into deadly points. The enraged hiss that emanated from me along with my appearance made the male stumble back.

Logan.

What the fuck was he doing here?

Katuri's control of our powers slipped and ice shards, greenery, and stone fell to the ground in a circle around us.

My inner sea dragon did not like being interrupted. And this tiny thing of a male who thought he was a bad ass simply because he was a prince had another thing coming if he thought he could come between my bondmate and me. I didn't care if he was Kat's brother. The primal urge to rip out his throat even stumbling upon us, much less interrupting, was barely being held back. That was only because

I figured Kat would be upset by seeing her brother strung up by his entrails.

"*My* bondmate."

"Just because she's your bondmate, doesn't mean you can treat her that way. And in public much less."

"Go away, Logan," Katuri said.

"Yes, princeling." I stepped closer to him, drawing his focus to me rather than his disheveled sister. "I'm the one your father sold your sister off to. She is mine now. You will never get her back. And I will do whatever I please to make your sister scream my name."

"What's going on here?" Delrik. Good. He could help me rearrange this child's face.

I felt the coolness of his shadows reaching out between us to create a visible barrier, not only separating Logan and me, but covering my bondmate, and giving her privacy. I knew he wouldn't stop me if I tried to move forward but it was enough of a barrier to have me breathing and calming down...just a touch. The pulse of energy I'd felt became a visible blue streak within the shadows.

"This doesn't concern you, dark one," Logan ground out between clenched teeth. His eyes never left my face.

The Forest Fae didn't trust Delrik, but I trusted him with my life. We'd saved each other's asses enough times in the past. King Kairos had made that very clear from day one. I hadn't missed the extra sentinels posted throughout the palace.

Delrik casually crossed his tattoo and shadow-covered arms over his massive chest. "Actually, it does concern me when you threaten my family. And right now, Katuri is being threatened."

Logan's attention shifted to his sister, hidden behind shadows and my body.

"Run along now, Princeling," I said.

Though I was calming down, I left my sea dragon visible to make sure the prince knew who he was going against.

Logan stood stock still, silent seconds dragging into minutes. Standing off against the beast that was me. Finally he found his words. A bolt of energy arced from Logan's fingertips to the ground, splitting the stone. It veined out from where it struck like a spider's web.

"My father will hear about this." He sounded like a petulant child.

He glared for only a minute longer before turning on his heel and stomping—yes, stomping—down the corridor, leaving the three of us behind.

"Are you in need of any more assistance?" Delrik asked.

He kept his back to Katuri and me, but his shadows remained in a protective circle.

"Ugh, you two are sickening," Delrik drolled, his back still to us.

"And you have room to talk?" Katuri snarked back. "I'm good now. Thank you, Delrik."

She looked perfectly put together as if nothing scandalous had occurred. Stepping forward through the shadows, she brushed her fingertips over the scales along the side of my face, down my neck, and across my collarbone. My elemental water rippled at her touch before dissolving the scales.

"You're lucky Delrik appeared, otherwise I might've not been able to hold back from clawing out his eyes," I said sweetly.

She pursed her lips and scowled. "He's still my baby brother."

"And that's why I would've only clawed out his eyes."

"Do we need to worry about him interfering?" Delrik asked.

"I'll handle it," Katuri said, planting a quick kiss on my lips. "Where's Evren?"

Delrik's expression dropped and his brows pinched. "Her and Nazneen have been flirting with the temple sentinels to see if they can figure out how frequently they trade posts."

"So, acting completely normal for Nazneen?" I asked.

Katuri smacked my chest.

"What?! She's been trying to get laid since we arrived," I defended. "I thought we'd decided it was impossible to steal the relic."

"True. But I'd rather have a plan in place just in case," Katuri answered.

She was right. If shit went down, we'd need a quick way to grab the relic and leave. I knew Kairos wouldn't willingly part with the relic. We'd have no choice but to risk our necks to steal it.

Part Three

TWENTY-FOUR
DESMUND

I was woken in the early hours of the morning. Nyla was thrashing her head back and forth. Her face was pinched as if she were in pain. I brushed my fingertips across her cheek, and she settled back against my chest, but the dream plaguing her didn't cease. Her chin tipped up, giving me an unobscured view of her face. Her eyes under her lids moved rapidly back and forth. Her lips formed silent words. The runes that decorated her soft skin glowed gently. I could see them down her neck and across her arms.

What in the dark hells was going on? No. It couldn't be. This was too real. Too familiar. I wanted to run but I couldn't leave her side. Not like this. She was having a vision. I knew it all too well.

Then, without warning, Nyla's eyes popped open. They were solid white and every rune on her body ignited with vivid, shining light. And a scream as loud as thunder burst from her lips.

TWENTY-FIVE

NYLA

I woke up with a scream clawing up my throat. My body jolted upright, giving my mind whiplash. My head spun and the scream was replaced with nausea. My runes glowed brightly in the dark tent. My body felt as if I was being torn in two—reality and spirituality. A distorted scene from a broken vision flashed before me.

Dark crimson eyes. Fire. Havoc. Katuri's face came into my mind. Then Nazneen. Arik. Those haunting eyes again, like the dark scarlet wine swirling in a glass. The same eyes that had been taunting me *forever.* Pain, torment, and stretching expanse of warped hell.

A steady, warm hand landed on the center of my back.

Desmund. I was with Desmund. I was safe. The instant his hand stroked my back, the mayhem within me evaporated.

Thank the Powers Above.

It took concentrated effort to slow my heaving breaths.

"My visions..." I shook my head, applying pressure to my temples with my fingers. "I think they are returning."

I sighed and laid back down on the bed roll next to Desmund. He looked like a startled animal in the moonlight. His jaw clenched, trying hard to mask something on his face.

Finally, Desmund settled beside me. We rolled to face each other. Silence draped over us like a warm blanket on a cold night. He was so calm. Startled, yes. But also oddly quiet. Why wasn't he freaked out? People who'd never seen a seer in the midst of a vision were always taken aback. And with my runes, I was an oddity when it came to having visions. I didn't know any other seer who literally glowed the way I did. But he was too calm. His jaw was clenched. I brushed against his clenched jaw and he visibly relaxed. Had he been around seers before? Did he know one? Or maybe he'd had experience with seers while learning from the healers in his homeland. It wasn't uncommon for healers and seers to cross paths and work together since many healers worked within the temples.

Then Desmund's voice, rough from sleep, spoke into the quiet. "Are your visions always so...violent?"

I shook my head. "They haven't overwhelmed me since they first started to manifest."

"When was that?"

I thought back. "I had my first vision when I was around three years old."

"Whoa! So young for such a powerful gift."

It was. That combined with my air elemental powers, and I was an anomaly. My mother had foreseen my elemental magic. She was a seer too. Not as powerful as me, though. That's why my parents had traveled to the temple, and she gave birth to me there. She knew I would need guidance. My predicted magic was well beyond her capabilities. It was a shock to us all that I was a seer as well, just like her.

"They didn't become a regular occurrence until I was in my teens. That's when I discovered the meditations from my priestess training was the only way to maintain control."

"That's why you keep meditating."

A small smile lifted the corners of my mouth. I'd been hoping that my visions wouldn't catch me off guard if I kept up with my meditation work. My meditation practice was more important than ever.

"Part of the reason, yes. Now I can control when my visions come for the most part. And I can search within the wisps of the realm. Or at least I could."

"Wisps?"

"Wisps are like the strings of our realm. They're all around us, connecting everything together like a giant web. I can use the wisps, ask them to do my bidding."

"I've never heard of them before."

"They bring me information provided by the gods, guide my path. I don't know if it's because of my specific type of magic that they are easier for me to interact with. They speak to me." I paused. "They *used* to speak to me."

"It will come back."

I wasn't sure if I believed him. My visions may be returning, but my air elemental was still absent. Not knowing was frustrating. Before, if I had questions, I could simply focus on my powers. I felt stranded and abandoned, without them. And Knox. The hole in my soul where he resided was more noticeable with each passing day.

I still hadn't told Desmund about my other magic. I wasn't sure why. With each passing day I trusted him more. I guess if I didn't voice the loss, I figured it would have less of an effect on me. Yeah, that made no sense at all. If I trusted Desmund, then I trusted him.

I took a deep breath. "There's something else."

"Something else?"

"I am an air elemental too."

His eyes went wide and then a broad smile.

"That explains so much," he said, scrubbing his hand over his jaw.

I stared at him curiously. That was not what I was expecting.

"I um...I saw you. Fighting in the valley with the fiends."

I pushed up on my elbow, so I was higher than him. "I knew it!" I blurted and pointed at his face. "I knew you had to have seen me. How else would you have found me?"

"Thank the gods I did! I don't think you would've made it far being so wounded."

"True."

"You were incredible! I knew there was something special, but watching you."

He just shook his head back and forth in awe. Then his features shifted.

"And watching you get blindsided by that fiend." Fury flashed across his beautiful face. "I couldn't get to you in time. I had to just watch it take you down and drag you away."

I pressed my palm to his cheek. "I'm alright now. You saved me."

He turned and pressed his lips to my palm. Heat rushed from the place his lips touched my skin all the way to the tips of my toes.

Had he just kissed me? I wanted to lean into him and replace my hand with my lips. I wanted his mouth on mine. I stroked my thumb across his cheekbone.

I was now attracted to this stranger. Okay, it isn't the end of the world. I didn't know much about him, and he wasn't *really* a stranger anymore. I could handle this attraction and still get to my friends. He already agreed to take me to Laeto Selva. I wasn't embarrassed by my attraction, more frustrated with my magical weakness. I lowered back down onto the sleeping mat and snuggled my back into his chest. He stiffened for a moment before relaxing and wrapping himself around me. I propped my head on his bicep and inhaled his scent.

I'd adjusted to a quiet life. I'd gotten my kicks every now and then with males who either looked past my odd appearance or were too drunk to care. I'd gotten used to the looks I received from others, between my runes and my two-toned eyes. I could feel the stares behind my back.

Desmund, however, was the first to ask outright. I loved how he never beat around the bush.

"So do all the people where you came from have runes?"

"Excuse me?"

I tried to push away from him to look in his face but he tightened his arms. What started out as cuddling for warmth became cuddling for the comfort of his touch. I let out an irritated huff. He pushed my hair away from my neck and glided his nose up the back of my neck. I closed my eyes and released a soft sigh.

"I've never met a seer with runes. Is it common where you're from?"

I shook my head. "Do you know a lot of seers?"

"Not a lot, but yes. I know a few." Desmund said.

I rolled over to face him again and he let me this time. His arm cradled the back of my head. I watched him closely.

Something flickered across his face. The same trick of the light like yesterday. I squeezed my eyes shut. That poison had really messed with me.

"Are you alright?"

I cracked open one eye to glare at him "You ask a lot of questions." I swallowed. "Yes." I opened both eyes but didn't look up at him. Instead, I focused on the hollow dip at the base of his throat. "I'll be fine."

He traced his finger along my collarbone where the fiend had sliced into me. I couldn't tell if he was attempting to be intimate or if he was checking his handiwork with a needle and thread. Although we were quickly becoming more comfortable with each other, he hadn't once come on to me.

"Desmund?"

"Hmm?"

"Whatcha doing?"

He froze. He muttered something under his breath, released me, and rolled away from me.

"Sorry," he said as he stood. He raked his fingers through his hair.

I had to hold back the small laugh. He looked almost embarrassed touching me.

"Desmund?" I asked.

He ignored me as he looked around the tent for his shirt. It was in a puddle next to the door. He quickly pulled it over his head.

"Desmund?"

He whipped around and our eyes locked. The air pulsed. He studied me for a moment with his mysterious eyes. His hair was a tousled mess. I could tell his mind was running a million miles a minute.

Tense silence stretched between us.

I smiled at him coyly. "I don't mind. You didn't have to stop touching me."

He swallowed audibly. His features molded into what seemed like pained restraint. His jaw locked and he took a small step back.

That time I did release a small laugh. "It's just an offer since you seemed interested. I won't tackle you if you come back to bed."

The wind howled around the tent. A storm had started during the night. Only a short while ago, I would've assumed the storm was caused by my elemental air, but I hadn't been the one to cause this storm. I could tell it was morning. Even with the dense clouds and snow, the soft light coming in through the tent's fabric. It appeared we wouldn't be walking today. We were stuck inside this now too small tent with sensual, heady tension between us.

"It isn't that I haven't thought about it," Desmund started. His fists opened and closed at his sides.

He looked uncertain. I never asked how old he was. It was hard to tell among High Fae since we had long life spans. I didn't even know what kind of magic he possessed. What I did know was I was going to give into this gravitational pull between us just because of the look of innocence on his face.

He rubbed his hand across the back of his neck.

Powers Above! He was nervous! He was nervous about touching me. It was cute.

I sat up so I was on my knees on the bedroll. The blankets dropped away. I was wearing one of Desmund's shirts—the same one he'd given me the first night after he found me. My knees were slightly parted, and my legs were bare where the shirt hem had ridden up during sleep. I hadn't needed pants or shorts with how long the shirt was on my short frame and the warmth in the tent.

I bit my bottom lip. "Desmund? Do you want to touch me?" I teased.

His eyes, which had been roving over my bare legs, snapped to my face.

The energy in the tent was like a jolt of lightning.

"Nyla. I've never..." I could see the words getting stuck in his throat. He shook his head back and forth.

My eyes popped wide before I schooled my features back to normal. Powers bless him. He'd never touched a female. Now that he said it, I could see it. The way he acted around me. How he seemed to float around me with inquisitive stares. His lingering looks that I knew he was giving me. He didn't hesitate to touch for healing purposes. He was confident when it came to stitching me up and examining my injuries.

I tipped my head to the side playfully. "I can teach you."

"*You* can teach me?"

"Desmund. I've been in this world for six hundred years. I have a little bit of sexual experience."

His cheeks flared at the word sex. "Six hundred?"

I nodded.

"I don't want to take advantage."

"You aren't taking advantage of me if I offer it."

His tongue roved over his bottom lip, his gaze dropping to the ground. Then his eyes found mine again, and in an instant, he was moving toward me. I remained perfectly still, afraid any movement would scare him off. He lowered himself down to the bedroll and I dropped back to sit on my heels. He kneeled in front of me so that our knees were brushing slightly. He ran his palms down his thighs. I placed my hands on top of his.

"We don't have to do anything, Desmund."

"No!" He practically yelled. Then in a calmer voice, "I want to. It's all I've been thinking about since you first looked at me with those beautiful eyes."

His gaze searched my face. I leaned forward and brushed my lips to the underside of his chin. His head moved to the side, and I dropped my mouth lower. I wondered if he tasted as good as he smelled. His scent made me light-headed. My tongue darted out to taste his skin. I couldn't help it. He smelled so good. He tasted even better.

I felt a rumble in his throat, and I smiled against his neck.

I slid my fingers up his arms and over his shoulders. I entwined my fingers through the hair at the nape of his neck. I pulled back just enough to look at his face. The corner of his mouth twitched.

"Is that all?" he asked.

Now he was teasing me.

He leaned forward and he brushed the tip of his nose against mine. His eyes bounced from mine to my lips a few times.

"Your turn," I urged.

His hands were pressed firmly into his thighs, not touching me, holding himself back.

Then he pressed his unbelievably soft lips to mine. It lasted only a moment. Then he did it again. A third time. He kissed the corner of my mouth. Powers Above, my heart was going to pound right out of my chest.

Each time I kissed him or stroked my tongue against his, he mirrored me.

"You're a fast learner."

"I have a great teacher."

"Have you seriously never been with anyone ever?"

He kissed me briefly again and then laid down next to me. "I've never had the opportunity."

I pondered what he meant by that. I traced a finger down his chest. "Well everyone is missing out. You have a natural talent."

"Teach me more?"

"I suppose I could, considering we are snowed in."

TWENTY-SIX
NYLA

Most of my encounters were fast-paced, grabbing hands, less kissing and more...rough. Usually bent over a piece of furniture to avoid being completely nude. No emotions beyond simple, erotic, primal pleasure.

Desmund touched his palm to the side of my throat. His hand was so large it almost spanned the circumference. The pad of his thumb, rough with callouses, stroked along my pulse point. When he gently pressed down, the most delicious pleasure swept through me like a gust of wind. I couldn't suppress the purr that left my mouth.

A wicked smile curled his lips. "Like that?"

"Mh hm."

He pressed his mouth to mine again but this time I parted my lips. I traced my tongue against his bottom lip, encouraging him to follow. When he began to deepen our kiss, I laid back on the bedroll. Desmund planted his hands on either side of me on the ground and hoovered above.

Each sweep of his tongue against mine was tortuous bliss. I moaned into the kiss.

He still hadn't actually touched me. I pressed my palms to his chest and gently pushed him to get his attention. He immediately drew back.

"Did I do something wrong?"

"Gods no. But you are allowed to use your hands. Allowed to touch me. Let me show you."

Teasingly, I slowly ran my hands from his chest down his sides and beneath the hem of his shirt. I tucked the tips of my fingers into the waistband of his pants and urged him to rest his weight against me. He followed my wordless instructions perfectly. Once he'd settled, I took one of his hands and pressed it to my breast.

While his gaze was focused on his hand squeezing my breast, I kissed the sweet spot directly behind his ear, one of my favorite places.

"I like to be touched like this. You don't have to be gentle. You won't break me, I promise."

He squeezed my breast again and my nipple pebbled under the thin shirt. I gasped as he continued to massage me. Then he dropped his head and sucked my nipple through my shirt.

"Powers Above," I moaned.

He chuckled against my chest.

"More. Keep going. Trail your mouth up my neck."

He obeyed...beautifully. His mouth continued sucking kisses across my chest to my other breast, then up to my collarbone. His kiss along the wound there was more healing than any salve. There was a sensation of his tongue at the base of my throat.

"Yes," I encouraged, running my fingers through his hair, guiding him higher.

When he reached my chin, he broke away. He leaned further and resting his forearms on either side of my head, caging me in. I leaned forward and sucked his bottom lip.

He repeated my movement.

"You're a fast learner."

"I have a great teacher."

"Have you seriously never been with anyone ever?"

He kissed me briefly again and then laid down next to me. "I've never had the opportunity."

I pondered what he meant by that. I traced a finger down his chest and teased the waistband of his pants.

"Well everyone is missing out. You have a natural talent."

"Teach me more?"

"I suppose I could, considering we are snowed in. After all, you will never know how to give pleasure if you have never received it."

My finger pulled at his waistband.

"Now, where shall we start?" I continued to tease him by dragging my finger up and down his chest.

I pushed his shoulder so that he would lie back and then I climbed to straddle him. His hands hesitantly landed on the tops of my thighs.

"Don't feel like you have to..."

"I *want* to give you pleasure, Desmund."

His throat bobbed as he swallowed.. "Unless you don't want me to."

"Powers Above, Nyla. I do."

"Well, I'm going to suck your cock. If for any reason you don't like it and want me to stop, just say so."

"You're going to put my cock in your mouth?"

"That's the plan."

His eyes rolled to the back of his head. I lifted off him and began tugging his pants down off his hips. His cock was already hard and throbbing. It laid heavily against his stomach. A thick vein ran up the underside of it and the smooth tip was glistening with the arousal he was feeling. This was all from kissing me. It was heady knowing I could do this to him without even really trying.

I nestled myself between his thighs and lowered my head until I was just inches above him.

I kissed his neck slowly as my hand reached into his pants pushing them below his bulge and releasing his cock. He moaned at my touch. I trailed kisses down his chest and abdomen as I took his cock in both hands stroking it. He released a sharp hiss of pleasure when I gave it a squeeze.

"So you like it a little rough?" I asked, laughing a little at the shy look in his eyes.

I lowered myself between his legs and continued my kisses up the side of his thickness and finally right on the tip. I took one final look up at him before I dove in. The look of anticipation was more than enough to fan the flames of my desire.

I slipped him into my mouth slowly. I swirled my tongue around the smooth head and across the slit at the top before pushing a little bit more of him into my mouth. I repeated it, testing to see his reaction, letting him feel every sensation for the first time. With each pass, I push him deeper into my mouth. I was halfway down his length when I stole a look up at him. He was staring down at me like he was seeing a god.

When our eyes met, the thick vein pulsed against my lips. With our gazes still locked, I relaxed my jaw and throat and pressed him all the way to the back of my throat. Tears stung at the corners of my eyes at the intrusion but I relished it.

"Oh god, Nyla I don't know how long I can last like this," Desmund strained. His fist gripped the blankets tight like it would hold off the inevitable.

I hummed in approval and swallowed. The motion of my throat made him let out a sharp gasp. I smiled around his cock. He dropped his head back and released an animalist groan.

I paused and waited, giving him a chance to compose himself. I wasn't going to let him finish just yet. As soon as his breathing settled and he was able to look at me again, I pulled back completely to the tip and slid back down. I kept a steady pace speeding up as his breathing increased. The pulsing of his vein on my lips quickened. His hands dove into my hair holding my head and his instincts took over. He thrust upward into my mouth. I allowed him the control as he grew closer and closer to climax. His pace grew erratic before he convulsed beneath me. He thrust forward one last time, deeper than all the other times before. I tasted his release in the back of my throat, thick and hot. He stayed there for a minute completely still, his cock releasing every last ounce of his pleasure. I swallowed it all down.

Eventually, he pulled himself free and rolled over to his side, propped his head on his hand. He looked down at me. I'm sure I was a flushed and wanton mess. I didn't care in the slightest.

TWENTY-SEVEN
DESMUND

I stood out on an outcropping of the rugged mountains, overlooking the dense trees as the sun peaked over the horizon. Behind me where the mountains climbed toward the sky, everything was painted white. Before me, the earth was deep colors of browns and grays and greens in the early morning light. I shivered at a breeze that swept down the mountain. It was as if it was pushing me forward, urging me to Laeto Selva and the destiny that awaited me there. A destiny I wasn't sure if I wanted.

Nyla was still asleep in the tent. I hadn't been able to relax my mind enough for sleep. The closer we got to leaving the Baxmar Mountains, the more my anxiety grew. Also the closer we got to the Forest Fae Kingdom, the faster pace Nyla walked. Yesterday she was actually walking ahead of me rather than trailing behind me. I had to keep redirecting her course to prevent her from leading us in circles. Maybe I should let her lead us in circles to slow us down. No. I couldn't do that. She was so eager to see her friends again.

Another shiver rippled up my spine from the chilly breeze just at the same moment Nyla appeared from the tent.

"Good morning," she said in a scratchy morning voice I'd grown to look forward to.

She wasn't dressed yet. She had a thick blanket wrapped around her bare shoulders and her hair was a knotted mess. There was an imprint from my lips and teeth on the spot just above her collar bone—the one where the fiends had almost stolen her from me—where I'd sucked and kissed last night. I loved that her pale skin showed every love mark I gave her.

Last night was the first night it hadn't been below freezing outside. I'd actually gotten too hot sleeping with Nyla wrapped around me and thrown the covers off the bedroll. Seeing her wrapped in our discarded blanket this morning made me have trouble controlling my pulsating urges. The breeze lifted her hair off her shoulders and a strand shipped across her face. She closed her eyes and leaned into the air. Her scent made its way to me, full of promises of tender love and desire.

"Is that the Forest Fae Kingdom?" she asked.

I pointed to the horizon. "That sliver of trees right on the horizon is the rainforest where the palace is."

"That's so far! We'll never make it," she said, her shoulders drooping.

I couldn't help but laugh. "We'll be there soon. And we'll be in the Forest Fae Kingdom much sooner than we will be in Laeto Selva." I walked over and wrapped her in my arms. "You're stuck with me for a bit longer I'm afraid."

Nyla dropped her head back in a dramatic fashion. "Oh what a fate I'm subjected to."

The fluffy snow of the mountains had given way to a misting rain that dampened our cloaks as we approached the palace. Nyla and I had been slowly making our way to Laeto Selva for almost two weeks. I won't lie, when we started our descent from the peaks and I first laid eyes on the rainforest and saw the shimmering barrier of the Forest Fae Kingdom, I was almost disappointed. I knew the closer we got to the Forest Fae palace, the less time I had with Nyla. Only about a week left unless I slowed us down. Powers I wanted to slow down. I wanted more nights with Nyla.

Everything would change once we arrived. I wasn't ready for my time with her to end. In three weeks, Nyla had become my everything. I wished I wasn't tied to the life I had. I wished there was a way to change. I would do anything for Nyla. Anything she asked of me. I'd sell my soul if she told me to do so. But some parts of me couldn't change and those parts would be what turned her from me in the end.

I took a deep breath of the morning air.

The closer we got to the rainforest, the faster Nyla walked. About ten feet ahead of me, she spun herself in a circle with her arms spread wide. I smiled at her. We went from sleeping with our backs to each other to falling asleep kissing every night. She was quite an excellent teacher.

It wasn't hard to find the Forest Fae palace. I'd been here several times on errands for my father. I'd always been given specific instructions to head straight for the palace and to not dally in the city. Business first, then fun. Not that I actually found fun.

It was late afternoon and as we walked through the city's cobbled streets, I had to keep guiding Nyla away from all the distractions—shops, food vendors, fountains with little ones playing. A gentle hand on her lower back was enough to have her bypass those things.

As the massive tree that housed the palace came into view, I nervously patted my chest where I'd stowed my father's letter to the king. I'd pulled it from my pack this morning so I wouldn't have to dig through everything.

It was even easier to walk into the palace itself, although there were guards scattered around. They didn't seem concerned about two strangers, who clearly didn't belong in Laeto Selva, roaming freely. Such a contrast to my own heavily guarded home.

The main atrium doors were thrown open. We strode right through the front doors and into the foyer with vaulted ceilings and insanely intricate decor. I had a gentle grip on Nyla's hand. She had her head tipped all the way back and a smile of elation at the beauty of the atrium. I admit, the first time I was here, I too was overwhelmed by such grandeur.

Suddenly, the clashing sound of steel on steel and fierce voices echoed from the courtyard. Nyla's face, for some reason, split into the biggest, gleeful smile. She ripped from my grip and took off in a full-speed run.

"Nyla! Wait!" I called after her.

Was she insane? She had to be. Who in their right mind would run *towards* fighting? One moment she was there, the next she disappeared in the blaring sunlight. Damn, she was fast for a tiny thing.

"Oof! Put me down you buffoon!"

Nyla sounded like the air was being crushed from her body.

Oh, fuck no!

I turned the corner not ten seconds later. I had to squint into the daylight pouring into an open-air courtyard.

A male taller than a mountain had his arms wrapped around Nyla's torso, her arms pinned to her side, and her feet clean off the ground.

"Release her!" My voice rumbled like thunder through the open courtyard, but the male didn't heed my command. Instead, sharp, teal eyes met mine in a flash of fury. A stare as lethal as lilura steel. My whole body was trembling, on the verge of exploding to protect my Nyla. It took all my concentration to hold on to my composure and magic.

"No!" Nyla let out a strangled laugh. "No, Desmund. I'm fine. Garren, put me down right now."

The male shifted his steely gaze to Nyla and immediately his features softened.

I froze. Once I heard her say she was safe, my mind stopped racing with the worst case scenario. I recognized him from the Baxmar Mountains, but I didn't dare drop my guard. Good thing, too. In my haste to get to Nyla, I'd missed a second male to my right in my peripheral vision. He was dark, dangerous, and fuming. I wish I'd thought of having a weapon. I didn't because I was simply a messenger. I'd never once been threatened while in the palace.

Then the male disappeared before my very eyes.

I blinked in confusion.

I whipped my head back to Nyla. The dark male was now flanking her, his chest was pressed to her shoulder. She barely came up to their shoulders. These were the same males from the valley who had gone looking for Nyla. At least I knew they wouldn't harm her. I relaxed a fraction with that knowledge.

Both males were shirtless, broad and muscular. The blond's bare chest and torso were covered in a snarling dragon tattoo.

But the other one...brutal scars and tattoos covered his entire body. In the valley, he had been wrapped in a thick cloak and a hood that hung low over his scarred face. Seeing him in broad daylight, he was a completely different male. Sinister, yet familiar, he had a deadly, haunted way about him. I hadn't been imagining anything—his eyes were solid black now as they bore down on me from across the courtyard.

Ice and smoke. Light and Dark. Death and...more death.

Darkness pooled around his feet. It trembled and rolled. An entity of its own waiting to be released on an unaware prey. He had an otherness about him that was familiar, yet foreign at the same time.

My eyes zeroed in on a leather pouch around his neck. I didn't need to see what was inside to know what it held. The Relika Stone. I could feel its power. It was so familiar.

Nyla's voice broke me from my memories. "You two are such brutes."

"I'm glad you aren't dead," the blond one said.

She slammed her tiny fist against the icy one's chest. He stumbled back in fake hurt.

"Is that how you greet me after being apart for weeks? I thought you would've missed me."

"Only a little."

The dark one hugged Nyla's shoulders. "I'm glad you're safe."

Just then, something crashed into my legs, and I landed flat on my back on the ground with a hard thwack. The air punched from my lungs and the back of my head bounced off the stony ground.

A reddish, brown wolf bound across the courtyard. As it ran, it grew in size.

What the fuck was happening?

Its front paws landed on Nyla's chest. It yipped and barked happily as Nyla hugged it.

"Eleni!" she squealed.

"So, the mutt gets more love than me. I see how it is." The blond rolled his eyes.

I stood, brushed myself off, and started towards Nyla. The wolf dropped to all fours and turned its snarling head in my direction. It was huge! It had *not* been as large as a pony when I saw it last. And what was with all the aggression? I'd brought their precious Nyla back to them. I, at least, deserved a warmer welcome.

"Not you too, Eleni," Nyla chided affectionately for the vicious canine.

The wolf plopped its rear end on top of Nyla's booted feet and lifted its head up to stare at her. A line of white fur trailed from its chin straight down its chest. A bright pink tongue hung from the side of its grinning mouth. When it looked at Nyla like that, it didn't seem scary at all.

As if it could read my mind, its eyes sliced to me again and one side of its upper lip curled.

Nyla pulled her toes from under its rump and stepped around the wolf to come stand by me. She slipped her hand into mine and all was right in the realm again. Shock and confusion must have been written all over my face.

She whispered, "Play nice," into my ear, pinching the back of my arm.

"Who's the hottie?" a female voice came from behind me.

I looked over my shoulder to see three females. I hadn't seen them this close while in the valley. Not only were they each beautiful in their own way, but I could sense their power radiating from them.

This is why I'd come to Laeto Selva. They were why I was here. Elemental High Fae. At least that's what the missive said from my father. Yes, I'd read the letter. And after reading Nyla's letter, I was curious as to what they were doing here too.

The one with short auburn hair wrapped Nyla in an embrace. I didn't release her hand.

"I knew the gods would return you in one piece. But this one," she not-so-subtly nodded my way and lifted her brows suggestively. She dragged her eyes from my feet all the way up. "Is a delicious bonus. Please tell me you've let him have his way with you."

Ha!

Alright. She was a keeper.

"Rude, Naz!" the blond remarked.

Nyla's cheeks flamed. That was enough of an answer. She couldn't deny it even if she'd wanted to. My scent was all over her despite the fact we hadn't actually had sex yet.

Nyla cleared her throat. "Guys, this is Desmund. Desmund, meet my...friends."

The last word came out almost as a question.

The redhead kissed Nyla's cheek. "More like an unwanted family. I'm Nazneen. It's so nice to meet you."

She took my hand in greeting. Her grip was firm and authoritative.

"Nazneen Zathrian, heir to the Mountain Fae and Arcelia." The voice came from the scarred, dark one.

So, they were from Illoterra, the other continent in the Mortal Realm.

The silver-headed female with looming onyx wings standing next to Nazneen turned to him. She was the one who'd used fire.

"Ashlyra," she admonished.

He scowled in my direction but then quickly turned to the winged female—his bondmate, his Ashlyra. The battle scar running across his once perfect face would no doubt draw fear from the most stoic of warriors. With his focus on her, I studied it closer. It started at his brow and swiped down his cheek. It even continued over his shoulder, where it was met with countless others. He'd evidently been victim to brutal torture.

Quicker than a blink, he was at her side. "I'm Evren..."

"Sister to the High Ruler of the River Fae," he interjected. His powerful arms, covered wrist to shoulder in ink, crossed over his naked, puffed out chest. A clear challenge. A gilded binding mark shining brightly was the undeniable proof that they were bound to one another.

Evren placed a gentle hand on his forearm. The black tattoo across his shoulders shifted up the side of his neck and then moved down the arm with the binding mark. When the moving darkness made it to Evren's hand, it appeared to travel into her, her fingertips turned black. Her wings flared slightly. That wasn't an ordinary tattoo. It looked to be some kind of dark magic. I'd seen dark magic. I was not a fan of it. My hackles rose again thinking of the potential threat it posed to Nyla.

Evren extended her hand in greeting, the same ruby from the mountains nestled on her finger.

"And this is my Ashlyra, Delrik Valhar."

I recognized the famous bounty hunter's name, even all the way across the realm. The Master of Death and Darkness. A vicious bird of prey resembling an owl or falcon or something in between swooped into the courtyard and landed on Delrik's shoulder. He shifted slightly under the avian's weight. It clicked its beak.

"That's Aura. Don't get too close. She bites." Nazneen whispered. Aura's sharp eyes that flashed in fire pinned their glare on me. "Thank you for bringing our Nyla back to us."

Nazneen reached out and laced her fingers through Nyla's free hand. It was as if she had to be touching Nyla, needed to feel that she was indeed safe and sound.

The blond male stepped forward and pulled the remaining unidentified female to him. She had the same tribal marks on her face as the king and prince. A white line tattooed down her forehead and down the center of her bottom lip, along with the two parallel lines across the bridge of her nose marked her as Forest Fae royalty. The thin ring of twisted silver in her septum glinted in the light, along with the multiple piercings along her pointed ears.

"Garren Eckhardt, second son of High Ruler Holden Eckhardt of the Snowhaven Fae. Eleni," he ruffled the fur atop the wolf's head who was still eyeing me like a snack. A miniature sea dragon appeared from thin air on the wolf's back. It stretched out on its belly and nuzzled its face into the auburn fur. Garren pointed at the sea dragon. "My familiar, Drake. And my bondmate, Princess and future Queen Katuri Harland of Laeto Selva."

Yup. She was King Kairos's daughter.

The princess smiled warmly at me. "Welcome to my kingdom, Desmund."

Maybe this wouldn't be so bad after all.

TWENTY-EIGHT

NYLA

Desmund had grown quiet, closed off. Of course, he wouldn't have been able to get a word in with how much Nazneen was talking. Even Delrik was more chatty than usual. Desmund tried to hang back as we were led down a corridor, but I took his hand and interlinked our arms, so he was forced to walk side by side with me. I wasn't necessarily nervous, but Desmund was a steadying presence. Being around everyone again reminded me that I was still lacking my elemental magic.

Evren walked beside me, her velvet-soft wing brushing against my arm.

"What brings you to Laeto Selva?" Delrik asked.

"Diplomatic mission," Desmund replied curtly.

"Care to elaborate?" Delrik asked.

"I have matters to discuss with King Kairos."

"Lucky you found our Nyla on your way," Delrik looked skeptical.

"Lucky enough."

"Is my father expecting you?" Katuri asked.

"I believe so. My father sent a missive prior to my departure."

"Where are you from?" Katuri asked.

I felt Desmund stiffen under my hand, but our conversation was interrupted by a handsome, young male who turned the corner and stopped. His eyes narrowed and darted between Garren and Katuri before he plastered a fake smile on his face. He clasped his hands behind his back and lifted his chin high. He was dressed regally. He had tribal marks of his own, but where Kat's were delicate, his were thick and looked more along the lines of war paint.

The newcomer's gaze stopped on Desmund and me. If I thought it had been tense when we first arrived, I'd been wrong. If it was even possible, Desmund straightened more before he bowed at the waist.

"Prince Logan Dimitri Harland. It's a pleasure to see you again," Desmund said formally.

Katuri's younger brother. I remembered her mentioning him. I'd pictured him as a younger, friendly face. He was awfully haughty for someone so young.

"Desmund. When did you arrive?" Prince Logan replied.

"Just now actually. I was on my way to see your father."

"You know each other?" Katuri asked, looking between the two.

"Yes. Desmund and I are well acquainted. Who is your lovely friend?"

It took a lot to hide the disgusted look on my face as he took me in.

"Logan, this is our friend I was telling you about. Nyla, this is my little brother Logan," Katuri said.

Logan strolled forward, brushing past Garren and Delrik. Neither looked happy. Logan took my hand in his and brushed his lips over my knuckles. Desmund took my hand from Logan and stepped between us. Apparently, Desmund wasn't happy about Logan's presence either.

Males were so territorial.

"It's wonderful to meet you Nyla, seer and air elemental."

My eyes were on Katuri. It would make sense she'd told her family about me.

"My mother..." Katuri began.

"The Queen," Logan interrupted his sister.

She shot him a glare. "*Mother* insisted I tell her all about you. And Corynne. I can't wait for you to meet her. We've updated my family on our mission to find the relics."

"Relics?" Desmund asked.

I hadn't told him why we'd been heading to Laeto Selva. Again, not because I didn't trust him. I'd been too swept up in my own problems and his kisses. He hadn't asked about the 'missing items' since the night he found the letter from Evren.

"Perhaps this is something we should discuss in private," Delrik said, eyeing Desmund again. He clearly didn't trust the new arrival. Whether that was Desmund or Logan, I wasn't certain which.

"I need to find King Kairos anyways and let him know I've arrived," Desmund said. He squeezed my fingers and then released my arm. "I'll find you when I'm through." He spoke this last part to me in a lower voice, before leaning in and pressing his mouth to my forehead.

I nodded. I didn't want to be separated from him, but I knew he had work that needed to be done.

"Yes. I'll accompany you," Logan said as he nodded his head in a bow.

Desmund held Logan's gaze for several beats. Then they were gone.

We watched in silence until they turned the corner.

"Well, that was tense."

Leave it to Nazneen to speak her mind. She had her eyes trained on Desmund's back, despite her quip to release the heaviness in the air.

"Come on. I know you must be famished. We hoped you'd make it here eventually but were fully ready to send out a search party."

Katuri piped up. "I may have already sent out said search party."

We all stopped and looked at her. "What? I was worried!"

"When did you all arrive?" I asked.

It took Desmund and me three weeks to walk all this way. I knew they were going to Agni first. Or at least that had been the plan.

"We got here a few weeks ago. We have so much to update you on."

I rubbed my forehead. Everything was coming at me too fast. My head was beginning to throb. I needed food, meditation, and sleep.

"Maybe we can update you in the morning," Evren said gently, sensing my distress.

"You just missed dinner, but I'm sure we can find something in the kitchens," Katuri said. "I'm sure you're exhausted. Let's eat and catch up on non-important things."

I nodded. I appreciated my friends being so understanding. They didn't even know about my powers being gone and yet they still wanted to take care of me.

"I think that hunk of a male is something important, but that's just my opinion," Naz quipped.

Kat led us up tall spiraling stairs that had me wishing for the steep mountain peaks. We bid goodnight to Garren and Delrik, and all four of us girls piled into Nazneen's suite.

The second the door clicked closed, Nazneen burst, "Holy Powers Above Nyla!" She dramatically threw her back against the door and fanned her face. "Where did you find that male?"

"Don't mind her. She'd been deprived of sex for way too long. The sexual tension is clearly unresolved."

Nazneen slid her back down to the floor in a puddle of lust. Powers Above, I've missed her antics. I laughed.

"Tell us everything. Please tell me he fucked you senseless."

Heat sprung to my cheeks. Nazneen was one of the only people I'd talked to about having a crush on someone. Mainly because she wouldn't stop prying until you spilled every last secret.

"There's nothing to tell," I lied.

She pinned me with a glare.

"A few kisses here and there."

"Liar. The way he watches you says it was more than a few kisses."

The sun was setting, streaks of light barely penetrated the dense forest. Desmund had wanted to camp one more night, but I was anxious to be reunited with my friends and to sleep in a real bed again. He wouldn't be beside me. I'd grown so used to him, using his chest as a pillow.

"Nyla, you're thinking about it aren't. You're thinking about his cock. I can see it written all over your face."

"I'm not. Well, not directly."

"Suuuuurrre." I was impressed with how Nazneen dragged out the word.

"Nazneen. Stop picking on her. She just got here. Let her breathe," Evren said, from her perch on the edge of the bed.

"But I need to know. It's been so long," Nazneen whined.

Katuri walked past Naz and plopped down next to Evren on Nazneen's plush bed. Eleni licked at my fingers and then pranced off to the balcony I somehow missed when we walked in. We were literally in the trees! All I could see was green interrupted sporadically by brightly colored flowers.

"It hasn't been that long since you and..." Evren began.

"Don't you dare speak his name." Nazneen's playful demeanor vanished in an instant.

Evren's features turned soft. "I just meant to say, you've gone longer without having sex."

Nazneen rubbed her hands down her face. "Ugh. *Why* did I have to fall for the guy with the manners of a starving osomal?!" She exhaled quickly and shook her hands out in front of her as if she was shaking away the thought. "I need to go out tonight."

"Go out tonight?" Katuri asked.

"Yep. I need to get laid. I need a new conquest. Do you think Corynne would do my hair?" she asked.

She sprang up from the floor and strode to her wardrobe. Throwing open the doors, she began tossing all sorts of clothing items to the floor. Was she looking for something specific? Where had she even fit all those clothes in her pack? A sexy little red dress hit the floor. Why would she have packed that? I laughed at the image of Nazneen packing for every occasion. I had never owned anything that revealing. Desmund would melt in my hands if I wore something that scandalous for him.

"You're thinking about him again, aren't you," she said over her shoulder to me.

Of course I was. But I wasn't about to admit it. Plus, we'd moved on to her.

A soft knock sounded on the door and a female's head appeared. She bustled into the room but stopped in her tracks.

"Oh! Nyla!"

The creature before me wasn't Fae. Or Nymph or Sprite. I recognized her from my readings. Boto Encantado.

She rushed over to me, gave a small curtsey, and wrapped me in a warm hug. I felt her magic engulf me in warmth and welcome and I instantly relaxed. I knew Boto Encantado had the ability to alter emotions, but I wasn't concerned about her magic affecting me. I welcomed it.

"Nyla, this is Corynne. She is one of my dearest friends," Katuri said.

"Oh hush." She pushed back and held me at arms-length, looking over me like a doting mother. "Princess Katuri has told me all about you. I'm so glad you made it safely to Laeto Selva." She stopped for a moment and tipped her head to the side. "You have a companion with you."

It wasn't a question. How did she know? Could she smell him? Could she sense the lust we shared?

I nodded. "He's with the king right now."

"I'll set up a room for him across the hall from yours. And make sure he has some food as well."

She squeezed me one more time, her magic blanketing me again. Then she pressed her fingertips to my forehead. Her touch had eased my mind enough that the headache was gone. I knew Encantados had magic but it was one thing reading about it and another experiencing it.

I took a deep breath. "Thank you."

"Of course, dear. Just give a shout if it returns." Her hand touched my cheek one last time.

So much physical contact from everyone had tears brimming my eyes. I sat on the couch and Eleni, now back to her normal size, immediately jumped up and laid her head in my lap. Aura, who was now too big to sit on my shoulder, perched on the back of the couch. She clicked her beak, then nuzzled against my cheek. Their greeting warmed my heart and made me miss Knox all the more.

"What happened? How did you get away from the fiends? I saw you go down, but I couldn't get to you. By the time it was safe for us to search, you were gone."

"It was Desmund. He found me in rough shape. Still am. He healed me to the best of his abilities. He had a healer kit and was able to suture my wounds and remove the poison."

"You were poisoned?!" Katuri gasped.

I nodded. "The fiends' talons had Bloodthorn on them."

Corynne arrived with a tray overflowing with food. Nazneen grabbed a piece of fruit and plopped down on the other end of the couch. She must've given up on finding an outfit for the evening.

"Thank you, Corynne," I said to the river dolphin shifter.

I looked around at my friends and tears spring into my eyes. I hadn't realized how much I'd missed them. I picked up the plate of food Corynne had brought in to busy myself so they couldn't see the tears falling down my face.

"Do you need a healer?" Evren asked.

"Not at the moment, but it would probably be a good idea to see one tomorrow."

"Okay, so start from the beginning," Nazneen said.

"The last thing I remember was you screaming my name. After that, I woke up half naked in a tent, aching all over and wishing for death."

"Shit," Nazneen cursed.

"Desmund made this drawing salve that was able to pull the poison out of the deep gouges, but it took days. It was not a pleasant process. But I'm thankful he was there. Without my high fae powers, I wasn't able to heal myself. I don't know what would have happened if he wasn't there."

"We would've flown you back to Proux," Nazneen said.

"And probably would've gotten ourselves killed in the process." Evren said. "You're right. Haizea was looking out for you."

"Now if only she'd give me my powers back, that would be great. Being completely powerless is awful."

"You don't even have a little bit of power?" Evren asked.

Out of all of us, she knew the most about being powerless. And being poisoned, come to think of it. She had been poisoned most of her life. I couldn't imagine that drugged feeling I'd only suffered a few days of for such a long period of time.

I was just finishing telling them about being healed and traveling with Desmund when a soft knock came to the door and Delrik popped his head inside.

"I'm here to steal my Ashlyra."

"I should find a bed, too," I yawned.

I could feel the pull to an actual bed. My body begged for it.

"I'll show you to your room," Evren said.

I stood and hugged Katuri and Nazneen goodnight. It appeared Nazneen had given up the notion of finding some fun for the evening. Evren took my arm. When she passed by Delrik, she brushed her lips against his cheek. He followed Evren and me down the hall away from Naz's room.

"Are you alright? Truly?" she asked.

"I will be. I'm just happy to be with you all again."

She smiled and leaned her head on my shoulder.

"Same here. Everything felt off without you here."

We continued to walk in silence past several doors.

"Here we are," she said. "Our room is at the end of the hall if you need anything. Kat and Garren are across from Nazneen where we just were." She pointed two doors further away. "Corynne is always floating around. Of course, she has a way of knowing exactly what you need before you even know." She smiled and hugged me. "Good night."

Delrik wrapped me in his arms again. "I'm glad you're here too, Nyla. Goodnight."

He gave me a brotherly kiss on the top of my head. My absence must have been hard for him if he was showing such kindness so openly. He typically kept to himself.

I stepped into the room and closed the door behind me. I leaned my back against the door and let out a long breath. My pack was sitting on the bench at the end of the bed. This place was really beautiful.

I gazed around the room. It had the same doorless balcony as Nazneen's suite. There was a large bathroom with a massive bathtub, and a shower on my left that I happily entered. I stripped off the layers of clothes and stood beneath a steady stream of water that was hot enough to turn my skin pink. Exhaustion hit me like a tidal wave. I could've fallen asleep leaning against the wall.

I turned off the water and wrapped myself in a fluffy towel. When I left the bathroom, the sight of the bed reminded me of how tired and sore I really was. Naked, I crawled under the soft, thin blankets and relaxed into the comfortable bedding. I exhaled deeply and let my heavy eyes close.

I hadn't practiced my nighttime mediation since I'd been with Desmund. At first, it was due to being too tense with him so close. Once I grew comfortable with him, he was all I needed to sleep.

I rolled to my back and propped a pillow behind my knees. I took several deep, focused breaths, inhaling deeply through my nose and exhaling through my mouth. The sensation of my rhythmic breathing was the only sound in the room. I pulled all my attention to the present, leaving behind the past several weeks and the unknown future. Starting at my toes, I visualized each muscle relaxing. I moved up my calves, to my thighs, to my back, my fingertips and shoulders. Each time a thought drifted into my mind, I acknowledged it and then let it pass. It took me longer than usual to reach the muscles in my face. I was out of practice..

After an hour, I grew restless again. My mind was finally relaxed but my body felt off. I'd grown used to Desmund's body against mine and I needed to be near him.

I tossed the covers off. My naked skin prickled in the chilly night air as I rummaged through my bag. Desmund's shirt was toward the bottom since I'd thrown all my other clothes on the floor. I slipped his oversized shirt over my head. The hem landed halfway down my thighs.

I cracked my door open and peeked up and down the hall to see if anyone was there. Desmund was directly across the hall.

"Desmund," I whisper-yelled.

No response.

Of course he wouldn't respond. He was a heavy sleeper.

I tiptoed across the hall. I pressed my ear to his door but was greeted by silence. I should've been listening to hear when he'd come back from speaking with the king. He probably wasn't even in his room yet. I wasn't sure what they had to discuss.

"Desmund?" I tried again.

Nothing.

I gently turned the handle, and it was unlocked. I crept into the room, the narrow strip of light from the opened door gave me enough light to guide my way. Once I closed the door behind me, the light disappeared. I made my way over to his bed. My heart skipped a beat when I saw him there.

Desmund was fast asleep. He was on his side, arm tucked under his head. I slipped beneath the covers and scooted myself back so that he curved around me.

On instinct, he draped his arm over my waist possessively and pulled me closer to him. He kissed my back between my shoulder blades then buried his face into my hair, mumbling something incoherent.

Now I'll be able to sleep.

TWENTY-NINE
DESMUND

I followed the prince away from Nyla, much to my dismay. But I had work that needed to be done. Logan walked in front of me rather than beside me. He massaged his fingers into his temples and then rolled his neck. He was too good to walk next to a simple errand boy. Using the opportunity to stretch my power, I summoned my astral projection from my body. With minimal effort, my astral projection became corporeal. I looked at an exact replica of myself. It winked back at me, then followed Logan on silent feet. The further it got from me, the more solid it became. Soon the sound of boots trailing after Logan tapped on the stone floor.

"He won't be happy to be interrupted, even if it is you," Logan said to my astral body without turning around.

They were about thirty feet ahead of me now.

I heard my voice reply, "We'll see, Prince."

I smirked. My astral had more snark in him than I did. I dipped down a narrow passage used primarily by the palace servants. I didn't need to be close by to hear what was being said. I could see, hear, taste, and touch everything my astral did.

I preferred to use my astral projection when dealing with unpredictable foes. And King Kairos was one of the most unpredictable people I'd ever met. He didn't often lose his temper with me, but I'd seen it flare over the smallest mishap, especially when his son was involved. My astral also protected me from his compulsion magic. As far as Kairos knew, his power was ineffective on me. The first time we met, he'd clapped my astral projection on the shoulder. I could sense his compulsion magic trying to get a grip on me, but it failed.

While I wasn't working directly with Kairos, I was the go-between him and my father. I didn't know all their plans and I preferred it that way. I was simply a messenger and, on occasion, a healer.

Prince Logan Dimitri Harland acted as if he knew me and my purpose on Laeto Selva, but he didn't know who I really was, what I really was. Very few did. Unfortunately, King Kairos was one of the few and he often reminded me so.

Four sentinels stood guard outside the king's office. As my astral projection and Prince Logan approached, one of them knocked once, then opened the door before announcing our presence.

King Kairos was sitting at his desk. He didn't bother looking up when we entered.

"Leave," Kairos ground out without looking up from his desk.

My astral didn't move. I knew the king wasn't talking to me. I turned slowly toward Logan and let just a little of my abilities shine through my eyes. The stupid smirk on his face quickly melted off as he did a double take. He shrank back under my gaze.

"Leave Logan. You're dismissed."

I didn't risk the urge to cringe at the harsh dismissal. But I also didn't bother hiding my pleasure at it either.

"But..."

The only time Kairos could use his compulsion without physical contact with the person he wanted to control was within the walls of his office. Every surface acted as a conduit. I understood the pain of compulsion. Kairos wasn't dumb enough to use compulsion on me, he'd have to deal with the fallout from my father. And even the mighty King of the Forest Fae wouldn't risk that encounter. It was also why I was in my astral projection form. The king didn't notice the difference. It was another layer of protection; even in this form, I could taste the thrumming power radiating from every surface and the king himself.

Logan turned on his heel and stomped to the door. It slammed behind him.

"Did you use your compulsion?"

He barked out a laugh. "No. He's just a coward."

I didn't respond. My astral projection just stood patiently, waiting.

"What did you bring me? The missive your father sent had zero information. Please don't tell me he wasted my precious time."

I pulled the letter from my father from my breast pocket. It seemed redundant to send a letter to tell the king I would be arriving with a second, more detailed letter, but I just did what I was told. There were other ways to communicate between long distances, but the king, as well as my father, preferred the trusted method of hand delivering instructions.

King Kairos snatched it from my hand and tore through the envelope. His eyes scanned the words before he balled it up and tossed it into the fire.

"So, you arrived with an elemental in tow. That wasn't part of your father's instructions I assume," Kairos said as he stretched back in his chair and laced his fingers behind his head.

"No. It was a mere accident that we ran into each other on our way into the city."

"Such a happy accident."

"Yes sir."

"You have a job. A simple job really. To retrieve information and bring it back to your master. I'm sure he'd love to hear about your new little friend."

I clenched my fists behind my back. "I have no master."

"You could've fooled me." He laughed cruelly as he studied me. "You are to stay here until further notice."

"Fine. If you don't have any further need of me, I'll be on my way."

"Don't forget I know who you are, boy. Remember your place," he hissed.

I turned my back on the king without permission to leave and left his office. I walked steadily and didn't slam the door behind me like his son had. Despite my fuming temper, I wouldn't show my distaste of the king or my father.

Once my astral was in the hall and free from his malicious glare, I summoned it back to myself. It dissipated into thin air with a shimmer as felt my astral return to my body in a wave of magic. To any passersby, it would be as if I disappeared without a trace.

I punched the wall. Hard. The crack of my knuckles on splintered wood was drowned out by a boom of thunder. I pressed my head against the wood. The broken bones in my hand throbbed but were already beginning to heal. Whispering a healing spell, I extended my fingers to make sure the bones straightened before they healed crooked. Combined with my High Fae healing, my bones were repaired in a matter of seconds. It wasn't the first broken bones I'd healed and it wouldn't be the last.

I made my way to my rooms, following the scent of the others. It wasn't my usual accommodations, but the servants kept me near Nyla. It only took a flash of my eyes and anger for them to scurry away to do my bidding. When I reached the room I'd been assigned, I stopped and looked up and down the corridor. The hair on the back of my neck had been standing on end since I'd entered the hall. I felt like someone was watching me. It wasn't uncommon to have Logan skulking after me or Kairos to send his right hand male Rylis to keep tabs on me. I brushed it off as nothing and pushed my door open, being sure to lock it behind me.

I peeled off my clothes, dropping them to the floor as I made my way to the washroom. I tossed my discarded shirt over the mirror that sat above a vanity. Usually, I requested the mirrors be removed before I arrived, but I'd forgotten in my haste to be closer to Nyla. These were much nicer quarters than the last time. I had a private bathroom and a luxurious bed. It even had a view.

To my surprise, a tray of food sat on the small table near the balcony. This must have been Nyla's doing. Or the princess. According to Princess Katuri, I was a welcomed guest. Little did she know, I was just here to be a pair of listening ears and wandering eyes.

Either I'd dreamt we'd arrived in Laeto Selva, and I was still sharing a bedroll with Nyla or I'd passed into Evermere in my sleep. Only Nyla's scent could bring me so much contentment. It surrounded me, filled my lungs. I could feel her against my body. Her skin was so soft. I didn't want to open my eyes.

A soft puff of breath fanned across my chest. I cracked open my eyes, blinking away sleep, to see Nyla draped atop me. Her blond hair spilled down like a waterfall. I didn't know when she'd snuck in last night, but I was more than happy she had. I was surprised I slept through it. Just proof my body was comfortable around her.

I didn't remember how long I watched her sleep. Soon she would know the truth. Soon she would never want to see me. I wouldn't blame her. My meeting with the king had gone as expected. He'd been in communication with my father, and I was here to make sure he followed through with their agreement. Easy; except now I didn't give a crap about their little scheme. My focus had shifted to Nyla and only her.

"Why are all your mirrors covered?"

There was a reason I avoided mirrors. I was not about to have a lengthy conversation about it, despite how beautiful Nyla looked this morning.

She stood and walked to the window. Thankfully, she didn't push me for an answer.

"Have you ever seen anything so beautiful?"

No. I hadn't. She was even more beautiful than before. She was clean, healed, and practically glowed.

Suddenly she shuddered, gripping her head, and dropped to her knees.

I rushed to her side.

"Nyla?"

The runes across her body pulsed with bright, sparkling blue light. I lifted her face to mine, hands on either side of her face. Her eyes were a milky white, her lips parted in an "o". Her lashes fluttered wildly. Her hair lifted on an unfelt wind. Every part of her shook. She was having another vision, but this one was much more intense than the last one I'd witnessed.

"Nyla," I tried to call to her through the vision, but she remained locked within her mind and whatever the fates were showing her.

She levitated above me while I was still kneeling on the floor. I needed help.

I darted from my room and banged on the door next to mine. "Evren. Come quick. It's Nyla."

I slammed my fist against the wood again. It groaned beneath my relentless pounding.

A door down the hall flung open and Nazneen appeared, rubbing her tired face.

I'm sure I looked insane. Barefoot and shirtless, standing in the hall screaming at the top of my lungs. "It's Nyla."

Nazneen sprinted toward my room. She was standing in front of Nyla when I came in after her.

"Don't just stand there! What's happening? Help her!" I demanded.

"There's nothing I can do. This is normal. Well, not necessarily normal. Only really strong visions have this effect on her. She isn't in pain. We just have to wait it out," Nazneen explained.

How could she be so calm?!

"What in the circle of dark hells is going on?" Garren demanded as he burst into the room, Katuri hot on his heels.

"Nyla's finally having visions again," Nazneen said. She seated herself on the floor in front of Nyla.

"Wait. Was she not having visions?" Garren asked.

"When she was injured, the fiends somehow poisoned her and it took away her powers," Katuri said.

"How did you know that?" I asked.

"Um, she told us last night," Nazneen said. "She told us everything." Nazneen lifted a brow and raked her eyes down my body.

Her perusal made me more aware of my state of undress. Why was no one freaking out? This was *not* a normal vision. I'd been around seers. Visions never lasted this long or made their person float.

"Shit! What about her elemental air?" Garren asked.

"Yup. That's gone, too. I'm assuming temporarily since her visions have clearly returned," Nazneen said.

"No wonder I haven't seen Knox," Garren said under his breath.

"Who's Knox?" I asked, confused.

"What's going on?" A sleepy Evren appeared in the doorway.

"Nyla's having a vision," Garren and Katuri said in unison.

"Oh," she yawned. "Let me know when she's recovered. I'll have Corynne bring breakfast."

Then she turned and left. Just...left.

"Recovered?" I asked worriedly. "What do you mean recovered?"

Nyla was still floating in the air, runes steadily pulsing.

"Longer visions can make her hungry...and tired. That's all," Nazneen answered.

Katuri made her way over to my bed and sat down on the edge.

Okay. Make yourself comfortable then.

Garren leaned against the wall, not coming further into the room but not willing to leave his bondmate alone with me either.

I'd never seen a seer react like that when receiving a vision. I knew the stronger the connection to the fates, the more frequent and intense the visions. Nyla must be a very powerful seer.

Nazneen sat with her legs crossed on the floor in front of Nyla.

After what seemed like an eternity, Nyla's body finally lowered to the ground and landed in a kneeling position. Her hands rested on her knees and her chin dropped to her chest. The runes flickered out and she released a rush of air. Nazneen scooted closer so their knees were touching. Jealousy flared within me. When Nyla lifted her chin, she blinked a few times. Her solid white eyes returned to their usual heterochrome state.

When she saw Nazneen before her, she smiled. My shoulders drooped in relief.

Nazneen tipped her head to the side, smirking. "Hello, friend. This is *not* your room. Sleep well?"

THIRTY
NYLA

Warm hands gripped my face. Desmund's scent surrounded me. I sucked in a grateful breath of air and sunk into Desmund's touch. His hands on my face made the visions suddenly stop their spinning collision and unravel. A fog lifted and I could see everything with distinct clarity. Each vision came and went peacefully. I'd always known that I was created to receive the visions from the fates but this was confirmation. The tranquility of each image placed in my mind by the fates reminded me of my purpose in this life.

When my visions ended, I opened my eyes. Nazneen was sitting cross legged in front of me. One of her hands was on top of mine, resting on my knee. I smiled.

"Hello, friend. This is *not* your room. Sleep well?" Nazneen asked.

She gave me a not-so-subtle wink. Clearly, she was referring to the fact that I wasn't in my bedroom, but rather in Desmund's. Wearing his shirt. Smelling like him.

His heady scent clung to my skin in the most decadent way.

"Good morning to you too," I snarked back. "I slept great. Thank you for asking."

I looked over Nazneen's shoulder and saw Desmund. He looked flustered, his hair standing on end like he'd been running his hands through it.

"How long was I out?" I asked.

"Only about two hours. Not long at all," she answered.

"They've lasted longer than that?" Desmund said in surprise.

Her hand was still on top of mine. And I did something I'd only done one other time. I shared a vision with her. To Nazneen's credit she didn't flinch or give any indication of what I'd shown her—Desmund wrapped around me and us sleeping soundly.

"More?" she whispered.

"Later." I bumped my forehead to hers.

I didn't let my smile drop. My body was drawn to him. Desmund had relaxed his shoulders, but there was tension written on his face. His only experience with my visions had been a tad unpleasant. He didn't know they weren't usually that way, so I didn't blame him.

I stood on wobbly legs, exhausted from the mental gymnastics, but, other than that, I felt great. Desmund took my arm and led me to his bed where Katuri had made herself comfortable. She'd leaned her back against the headboard, propped up by pillows.

"Good to see your visions are back," Katuri said.

"It's definitely a relief," I smiled at my friend.

"I think you should rest today," she said, standing up. "Let's sit on the balcony.

I turned and looked out the balcony for the first time. There was a wonderful view of the tree tops. Garren came into the room carrying two loungers. Sitting on the balcony and watching the rainforest life sounded like the perfect day to me. Desmund followed Kat outside and over to the group of loungers. Nazneen followed behind.

So now we were propped on loungers, chatting up a storm, while my visions filtered in and out. Some lengthy, some quick. These weren't all consuming. I was able to speak through them, telling Katuri and Nazneen what I was seeing. Desmund was pacing back and forth behind me, sneaking glances at me every so often.

Evren returned with Corynne in tow, carrying a tray full of fresh food. Corynne made direct eye contact with Desmund. She stopped dead in her tracks. I watched from the corner of my eye as she stared at him for a brief moment before offering a stiff smile and following Evren out to the balcony. Evren plopped down on an empty lounger between Kat and me.

Garren was leaning against the doorway. "What did the wisps have to say this morning? They seemed pretty chatty."

"So nosey. Always so nosey," I replied.

"You love me, and you know it," he said.

"The wisps are responsible for all these visions?" Desmund asked. He seemed unnerved by Corynne's presence.

"Not necessarily. But they are ever present," I replied.

"Kat, I'm going to go change. I'll be back," Garren said leaning over to kiss her cheek.

Eleni appeared from what seemed like nowhere and pounced onto the lounger right in the middle. We laughed and squealed as Eleni soaked up all the love like she was the princess. Drake swooped in from the trees and landed on the balcony railing. His eyes were trained on Desmund. Garren turned to leave and gave Desmund a quick nod, clearly confident the familiars would rip him to shreds if he got near his bondmate.

After Corynne sat the tray down, she went to stand next to Desmund. When he saw her approaching, he steeled his gaze, crossing his muscular arms over his chest. I could tell he wanted space from the Boto Encantado but he stood his ground.

"I'm Corynne. Is there anything I can get you dear?" she asked.

It seemed that whatever was bothering her initially was gone now.

"No thank you," he answered gruffly.

"I think they've passed," Corynne said.

"Pardon?"

"Her visions. You can relax now."

Desmund looked down at her. She barely came up to his shoulders. Smiling, she patted his forearm. He flinched a little at the contact.

I watched Desmund as he held eye contact with Corynne for several beats. She didn't touch him again like she had me, soothing my emotions. But as if she was still settling him, Desmund's shoulders relaxed and he dropped his arms.

"You have nothing to worry about. She is safe here." She paused for a beat. "And so are you."

This time, when she touched his arm, he didn't flinch. He nodded in gratitude and then lifted his chin to me. The smile on his face warmed me from the inside.

I don't think I'd ever been so happy in my life. My seer powers had returned. I was here with my friends. Desmund, someone I was never expecting, is in my life. I let out a contented sigh. I closed my eyes and tipped my face toward the morning sunshine just now peeking through the dense canopy.

Just then, I felt a vibration against my chest and something soft bumped the underside of my chin. I opened my eyes to see Knox—well, a tiny version of him—bum in my lap and tiny paws on my chest and purring. When he saw me look down at him, he tilted his feline head, dropped down to all fours and arched his back and wings in a long stretch. Then he began kneading his adorable paws against my thighs.

"Um. Where did he come from?" Desmund asked. "He literally just appeared."

I lifted the fluff ball into the air. He batted playfully at my nose. Then I pressed my forehead to his. His heavy feathery wings flared out then drooped. He'd had a hard time learning to handle them at first. I guess he'd have to learn all over again.

"My familiar."

He hadn't been this small since my powers first developed as a child.

"Knoxxy!" Nazneen squealed and snatched my familiar from my hands.

He pressed his paws to her face and nuzzled her nose. Eleni tackled Nazneen and she went tumbling backwards, laughing. "Eleni!! I had him first!" she squealed.

But Eleni won. Knox wriggled from Nazneen's grip and had a hold on Eleni's ear, pulling with all his might. He flapped his wings and just managed to hoover off the ground for a few seconds. Then the two were wrestling on the floor. For a moment, Drake looked like he was going to join in on the wrestling, but then remembered he was supposed to be watching Desmund.

"It's too early for all this," Desmund grumbled.

"Come meet Knox," I said.

I patted the space beside me. Desmund stepped out onto the balcony, around the jumbled mess of fur, and sat next to me. Knox jumped up in his lap, examining Desmund with concentration.

"Well, if Knox hasn't eaten your face off yet, I guess you aren't all bad. He's a bit particular about people," Nazneen said.

"This tiny thing would eat me?" Desmund said doubtfully.

Knox puffed up and released a tiny hiss. He bowed low, wiggling his butt in the air before he pounced forward, swatting at Desmund.

"Vicious," he said. He squinted at my familiar, stroked a finger under Knox's chin and he melted like a puddle in Desmund's hands.

My magic hummed within my chest. I welcomed the soothing familiarity. I flipped my palm upward and rested it on my knee. I tried to summon my elemental air. I felt tingling across my palm but other than that, nothing.

I sighed. "It will come back. I can feel it. And I've seen it. I just need to be patient." Saying the words out loud made me feel...less inadequate.

I saw my powers returning just this morning.

With Knox back in my arms, well, in Desmund's arms, I could feel my elemental air magic returning in shallow bursts. I looked up to Desmund. His scent surrounded me as he leaned in close. His muscles strained. He seemed to be holding himself back. His broad shoulders and strong arms took up almost my entire focus. My magic was pressing me toward him.

The five of us sat and talked about my returning power and the visions I had seen. Eleni and Knox ran in circles around the balcony pouncing on each other from behind planters and loungers. Drake finally accepted that Desmund wasn't a danger to the group and joined in by spraying them with water when they got too close. Aura watched all this from a nearby tree with her head held high like she was too proper to participate in their childish games.

Delrik and Garren made their way back out to the balcony shortly before Corynne showed back up with lunch for everyone.

After everyone had eaten far more than our stomachs could handle. Katuri spoke up, breaking into the peace that had come over the group. "I think we've done enough lazing around. Let's get dressed and go explore. I can show you the relic and then I want to take you to a special place."

Part Four

THIRTY-ONE

NYLA

I stepped from the dimmed light of the palace and into the sunny courtyard. I sucked in a deep breath of fresh air and squinted at the glinting light. Knox sat at my feet, like the proper boy he was. He stretched his ivory-feathered wings. He'd always reminded me of the clouds on the seemingly endless summer days of Proux. Desmund kept close to my side.

Nazneen and Evren were right behind me, chattering away with excitement, followed by Katuri.

"You're going to love the river! It's beautiful this time of year," Katuri said.

She was nearly bouncing with elation. Delrik slipped by her, smirking, and took Evren's hand. Garren reached for Katuri, but Eleni bounded through the door on clumsy paws, knocking him off balance.

"Really, Eleni?" He stumbled, practically crashing into Katuri in the process.

She released a yip over her shoulder as if to say sorry, and darted into the trees. I laughed. It felt good to laugh, to feel joy. I hadn't realized how unfulfilling my life had been until now. I couldn't remember a time I'd laughed while working in the temple.

"She loves visiting Corynne," Katuri explained with a shrug of her shoulders. She straightened her dress and fussed over Garren. "The littles always fill her up with treats."

"Gotcha," Nazneen laughed. She turned back toward the door I'd just exited. "You coming, hot stuff?"

Desmund, who'd been lurking in the shadows, turned bright red. He'd been preoccupied since my visions had returned. Nazneen took his silence as an invitation to pepper him with any question or thought that came to her mind. She'd made sure he was kept within our little group's circle. I smiled and stretched out my hand to him.

An offering. For a moment, he hesitated. My brows knitted together. Had my visions scared him? Or maybe it was my air elemental powers returning? My heart began to sink a little.

Before I could tell him he didn't have to come with us, he stepped forward and gripped my fingers in his. "Lead the way."

The realm felt right with his warm hand wrapped around mine.

We all made our way south through the city's market and toward the river. I spotted Marselina and Logan, hand in hand, strolling from store front to store front.

I was surprised at how close the Visola River was to the palace. It was invisible through the dense trees and underbrush, and our rooms were on the opposite side of the palace, so I hadn't seen it from above. Kat brushed away long vines, revealing the hidden gem of the river behind them.

The river was almost the width of the Temple of Anruin. And while some would describe the water as muddy or murky, all I saw was a kaleidoscope of rich earth tones eddying together. The patch work sun hitting the very changing surface, made the mundane at first glance a spectre of beauty. The water moved in swift currents that filled the air with a soothing lullaby.

A braided rope bridge with aged planks stretched from shore to shore to a small village. A cluster of thatched huts dotted the shoreline and nestled into the tangled jungle. Women and children, with the same light pink complexion as Corynne, meandered about dressed in all white.

Eleni ran at full speed toward the river and launched herself off the bank. She landed with a loud thwack on her belly, then disappeared beneath the surface. She paddled all the way across.

Katuri was the first to venture across the bridge. Evren looked as nervous as I felt about the makeshift bridge. It swayed gently under me. I gripped the rope tightly and took a tentative step. I looked down into the murky brown water. It was so unlike the waters near Proux of the Boreas Sea. There was no telling how deep the river went. How deep even was a river of this size?

Eleni easily beat us to the opposite side, and by some unknown power, was already dry. A small child, maybe around the age of six or seven, was squeezing Eleni's neck in a fierce hug. The wolf was still in her huge form but had lowered herself to the ground for the girl. Her back legs were outstretched behind her, so she was belly to ground.

Suddenly, the child squealed, loud enough to make me cover my ears. The sharp note was enough to shatter glass. "Princess Katuri!" She ran and jumped into Kat's arms.

"Princess Yara."

"I'm not a princess," she giggled.

"Are you sure?" Katuri sat the child down and then, with a swirl of her hands, wove an intricate crown of reeds and flowers from the river's bank. She placed the crown on her head. "You look like a princess to me."

Katuri had told me that since arriving three weeks ago, she's been filling her days with visiting the people of her kingdom, including the Boto Encantado.

"Mami! Mami! Princess Katuri says I'm a princess too! Does that mean I don't have to do my chores?" she belted out in a sing-song voice.

Again, I involuntarily cringed at the girl's pitch.

"You are putting thoughts into that child's head." Corynne's voice came from behind us.

Gifts from the gods. The Powers Above gave Boto Encantado many gifts, but the gift of song is the strongest.

I spun to see Katuri's maid approaching with a wide smile. She had a tiny, pink baby strapped to her chest.

"Is this the newest addition?" Katuri jumped up and down, clapping her hands. Her chubby, pink cheeks rose with her toothless grin.

"Si, Princesa. This is Larissa," Corynne cooed at the baby.

She lifted the baby from the intricate wrap and placed her in Katuri's waiting arms.

"Hello, sweet child. Are you a princess, too? Princess Larissa." Katuri conjured the same crown she'd made for Yara and placed it on the baby's head. The little one smiled at Katuri and cooed. It was the softest noise.

Another female came from the neighboring hut. She looked exactly like Corynne, except a little taller.

"Miranda! It's so good to see you. Guys, this is Miranda, Corynne's sister." Katuri went around our gathered circle. "Evren, Delrik, Nyla, and Desmund. And you already met Naz."

Nazneen swept forward and hugged Miranda tight in greeting.

"It's nice to meet you all!"

"Oh! Your wings! Can I touch them!?" Yara asked in awe. Her tiny fingers were already reaching for Evren.

"Yara!" Miranda scolded.

"No," Evren laughed. "It's fine. Yes, of course."

Yara let her fingers brush over the sleek feathers with reverence.

Then Yara reached and pulled at the hem of Miranda's shirt. "Mami, can I go swimming?"

Miranda sighed with a smile. "Si. As long as you..."

Yara was off in a flash, darting to the bridge, or so I thought. She made it a few feet from the shore before she dove into the water headfirst. Her petite body arced gracefully in a perfect dive.

"...terminar tus tareas," Miranda mumbled to herself.

"Um...does she know how to swim?" Garren asked.

Then a pink dolphin, the same size as the little girl, jumped from the water and did a front flip.

"Si. She's Boto Encantado. Of course, she can swim," Miranda answered. "She was born beneath the water. It's her nature."

Drake made a sudden appearance by dropping from the sky. He stood at the bank where Yara had slipped below the surface. He leaned close to the water, sniffing, his sleek, long tail twitching. Yara emerged and sprayed water at him, drenching him from snout to tail. The sea dragon didn't skip a beat. He dove in after her.

"Don't worry, Miranda, Drake is a dear. It's his master who is the troublemaker of the two," Corynne said, teasing poor Garren.

Drake and Yara both came jumping out of the water making a large arch then splashing back into the river together.

"Come. We prepared lunch for you," Miranda said. We started towards her hut.

I looked around at the small village. "I thought there were more Boto Encantado here in Laeto Selva." It looked almost abandoned.

"There are many of us. Most just choose to live in the underwater city, Geysa."

"There's a whole city down there?" Evren asked from beside me.

She let out a soft chuckle. "Si. It's well-hidden and protected thanks to the Forest Fae. King Kairos is worthy and many thanks from my people."

"Why would you need to remain hidden?" Evren asked.

I forget sometimes she grew up under the control of her tyrannical father. Her knowledge of our realm was minimal.

"Boto Encantado don't necessarily have a good reputation throughout Quinterre. We were once peaceful people. Unlike the merfolk and other ocean creatures. We dwelt all along the coast surrounding the continent and even in some of the larger rivers. Many centuries ago, our people were led by a group of renegades, specifically Davi del Mar. They had ideologies of our kind being better, stronger. He sought to control not only coastal waters, but also the land. They focused on expanding their territories among the water creatures. High-ranking males became aggressive. They resorted to using their magic to entrap females—fae, human, nymph, it didn't matter. They'd lure them to the water with their songs, rape, and impregnate them. When they gave birth, they would steal the children in the middle of the night and keep them as bartering tools to gain riches and territory.

"In towns where the people fought back, where reputation preceded them, they purposely spread disease and famine. They spread disease and would often hypnotize their enemies with songs to lead them into the water to drown. Many opposed their views and tactics, but we weren't strong enough to go against them. We fled from the growing factions. Some couldn't escape and remained trapped. That's when the King of the Forest Fae offered us sanctuary here in the Visola River. Our population has flourished here in Laeto Selva."

"Do you still possess the ability of song?" Garren asked at the same time Evren said, "I've never heard you sing." There was only reverence in her voice. "Only hum a song here and there."

"Yes. The gift of song and several other gifts, such as seeing through glamors and knowing the difference between truth and lies. However, we teach our young to use it only for good unless threatened."

"You used to sing me to sleep when I first arrived in Kanevvluk," Katuri said.

"I did," she smiled fondly at Katuri. "It was one of the only ways to comfort you.

"I can also alter emotions through touch or simply projecting the feelings into the room."

I thought back on when I'd arrived and Corynne had touched my forehead, the instantaneous sense of calm had swept through my addled mind and tired muscles.

"Is that what you shared with me the other day, Corynne?" I asked.

"Yes. I sensed your tension and offered you a reprieve."

I squeezed her hand in gratitude. As a seer, I knew the true meaning of mental peace. Even with mastering meditation techniques, I rarely had moments of peace. The last few weeks had made me realize the beauty of a quiet mind.

"I actually have news I wanted to share with you, Princess," Miranda said, her tone turning serious and gathering my attention. "We've heard word through the currents. Hadeon is heading toward Kosmima. He's searching for something."

I knew exactly what that something was. One of the two remaining relics.

Desmund shifted nervously next to me. Instinctively, I placed my hand on his knee. Kosmima, the capital city of the Water Fae Kingdom, was located on the southernmost tip of Quinterre. I'd traveled there many times and visited the various temples scattered throughout the kingdom.

"Mami, I'm hungry," Yara came bursting into the hut, dripping wet, and breaking the tension.

A puddle formed at her bare feet. She wiggled her toes and smiled shyly. I waved my hand and used my air elemental to dry the girl. It was second nature to reach for my elemental power, without really thinking that it was still in its early stages. I'm glad it didn't fail me at this moment. That would have been embarrassing. Knox purred at my feet.

"Wow! That's so cool! Thanks Nyla!" Yara said, and then she jumped into my arms.

The moment she landed in my arms, a wave of images slammed into me like the force of gale winds. I gasped at its clarity and strength. Desmund touched my arm. His fingers burned against my skin. I opened my mouth to scream but no noise came out. I saw the eyes I recognized, but they were rimmed in darkness. Then his face came into view. My Desmund. Scrunched eyes and a silent agonized scream. Or was that my scream? The skin on his face split and sloughed off like charred bark peeling from a tree. Soon, the male I'd grown to love was replaced by a fiend. Wicked curled horns were perched on its head. Dark, looming wings tipped with deadly talons loomed behind him. My collarbone and arm seared with lightning pain. Its hot breath fanned across my face, and I heaved. It smiled a cruel smile. It opened its mouth so wide it could swallow me whole. Fire surrounded him, obeying his command.

Yara was pried from my arms and the vision vanished.

"I'm sorry, Mami. I'm sorry!" Yara cried as she buried her face into her grandmother's chest.

I blinked at Mami holding a sobbing Yara. Tears poured from my stinging eyes.

"It's fine sweetheart," I rasped. "I'm alright," I tried to soothe the scared girl.

I reached for her, but she cringed away from my glowing rune-covered hand. My heart plummeted once again. It was like when my visions, these gifts from the fates, scared away any potential friends or playmates I had as a child. It happened so many times that I eventually gave up on those childhood friendships and kept close to the temple and priestesses.

Corynne was kneeling in front of me a hand resting on each of my knees. She pressed her magic into me, and I struggled a slow breath. Her magic felt like pulsing waves ebbed and flowed. Like a gentle breeze pushing waves up onto the shore. Corynne hummed a steady, repetitive melody. Warmth flowed from her palms up to my chest. A gasping sob released from me and the tension disappeared.

"I should have warned you. Just as I can affect emotions, so can the child. She must have inadvertently magnified your vision."

I shook my head back and forth. "It's okay. It just took me by surprise." I turned to the little girl. "I'm fine. I promise."

She still looked frightened. I didn't blame her. My first visions were jarring and I knew to expect them. I couldn't imagine having them forced upon you. It would be terrifying.

"I'm a seer. I just wasn't expecting the vision." I reached my fingers toward her and wiggled them. "I can show you how it works."

Miranda, looking skeptical, side eyed Corynne. Corynne, still kneeling in front of me, beckoned Yara to her lap and placed the girl's hand in mine.

"My eyes are going to change color, and my skin is going to glow, okay?"

Yara nodded but didn't speak. Desmund stood behind my chair looking out the window, but kept his fingers on my shoulder.

I offered a reassuring smile. I ensured my fingers were also touching Corynne so she would be able to see as well.

Then I summoned a vision. Just as I'd said, my eyes changed to white and my runes began to glow. "When you jumped in my lap, I saw Geysa."

I projected my vision into her mind. *Yara swimming down toward the glowing city.*

Yara lit up with joy. "That was just now!"

Corynne responded, "That's right, my dear."

Drake and Eleni are coming from the river, chasing each other. They stumbled over each other's feet and toppled in a tangled mess of limbs into Garren, who collapsed into the wet familiars.

"Is that the future? Is that really going to happen?" She was now bouncing up and down.

"Now, just wait a few moments," I said. "Watch the river."

We all turned to look out the open window. A few seconds passed. "Ready?"

Garren and Delrik stood near the river with their backs to us. Sure enough, Eleni and Drake arrived. And just as I'd shown Yara, Garren was taken down by sopping wet creatures. We all burst out laughing.

"Mami! I saw that! Nyla showed me that that would happen!" She ran into her mother's arms and wrapped her arms around her neck

"Why don't you go collect flowers for Princess Katuri to add to your crown?" Miranda suggested as Yara unwound herself.

"Okay! Eleni and Drake can help." She popped a swift kiss on Corynne's cheek.

She stopped in front of Desmund. His towering form looked down at her. Then, he knelt to her level.

Yara reached out and touched his cheek. Though I could only see Desmund's profile, I saw this shock when she whispered. I wasn't able to hear her voice, but I read Yara's lips. "I see through the dark."

She held his gaze for a moment. As she bounced out of the hut and ran toward Eleni out into the sunshine.

THIRTY-TWO
DESMUND

Those five little words shook me to my core.

I see through the dark.

No one else had heard the words the little Boto Encantado had whispered. Actually, Nyla probably had. They wouldn't have understood them even if they had. I didn't understand exactly what she meant. But deep inside my gut I wanted to run from Laeto Selva in the middle of the night and never return.

I'd excused myself from the little village by the river and returned to the palace ahead of everyone else. As quickly as possible. I hadn't wanted to leave Nyla's side, but I was worried about the Boto Encantado matriarch. Corynne already seemed suspicious, and then she said Boto Encantado could see through glamors. When she first met me, she seemed startled by my presence in the palace. But then she'd relaxed, even spoken to me.

I had to leave. I wanted to believe that there was a way for me to be with Nyla, but it was unlikely at this point. I should leave Laeto Selva but that wasn't a possibility. Not yet.

I meandered through the lush gardens. Paths wove in and out of the trees, keeping me far away from King Kairos and Prince Logan. I didn't often spend more time in Laeto Selva than necessary. Once I grew bored of the greenery, I returned to my room to wait for Nyla to return.

I stood at my door for a moment, then turned to the opposite side of the hall and let myself into Nyla's room. I collapsed on the end of the luxurious bed and dropped my head into my palms. We'd been in Laeto Selva less than a week and my whole world had been flipped on its axis. I didn't know where I was going from here. I couldn't go back home. I felt drawn to Laeto Selva, drawn to Nyla, and I couldn't ignore it. But I also feared my past would ruin everything.

I wasn't sure how long I was lost in my thoughts. I heard the door to my bedroom open and close with a click. Nyla returned, Knox at her heels. Nyla's powers were returning quickly if the size of the winged lynx was any indication. He was now the size of a standard house cat.

"Want to know something funny?" she said in greeting.

I dragged my eyes from the floor to look up at her. Fuck. She was stunning.

"Hmm?"

"I went straight to your room first, only to find it empty, and you here."

"Oh, I hope that's..."

"It's perfect."

"I just want to take a quick shower before the blood binding ritual," she said, breaking me from my contemplations.

"Hm mh," I mumbled. I wasn't truly listening.

"Desmund?"

"Sorry." I shook out my head. "Yes. Blood binding. That's tonight, right?"

"Are you all right?" She came over to me.

As soon as she was within arm's reach, I grabbed her hips and pulled her to me. I wrapped my arms around her and buried my face in her stomach. She didn't miss a beat. She stroked her fingers through my hair. The gentle raking of her fingernails against my scalp felt so divine.

"We don't have to attend," she said.

"No. I'm fine. It's just been a long day."

The steady rise and fall of her breaths grounded me.

"If you're sure. It'll only be about an hour. Probably less."

I nodded against her and gave her another squeeze before releasing her. She kissed my head. Nyla disappeared into the washroom. I splashed some water over my face from the wash basin. Once I heard the water of the shower turn on, I quickly walked across the hall to get fresh clothes. I didn't want to be gone when Nyla finished. When I opened my eyes and looked down into the basin, I saw my true self. The real me. In a moment of weakness and rage, I gripped the intricate edge and flipped the basin, sending it flying across the room. It crashed into the wall, Thankfully it was made of copper, so it didn't shatter into pieces. Water soaked the carpet, but I was too angry to care. I was being reckless and I knew it.

"Are you okay?" Nyla said behind me.

I jumped at the sound of her voice.

I glanced up to see Nyla standing in the doorway of the washroom. Her silver dress hugged her narrow hips. It had slits on both sides all the way up to her upper thighs, showing off smooth, rune-covered legs with each step. I knew her legs were as soft as they looked. I almost fell to my knees as I dragged my eyes upward. Strips of fabric crisscrossed over her chest. Her stomach and back were uncovered. I wanted to run my tongue over her smooth skin. *She* was the sole reason I hadn't fled this afternoon.

Nyla's beauty was enough to distract me from my spiraling thoughts.

"I'm fine. Just knocked over the basin by accident," I said, trying not to choke on the lie.

Knox padded across the room and wove himself in and out of my feet, purring loudly. His wings were tucked against his body.

"I'll be fine. Let's go," I said, stretching my hand out to her.

"I'd believe you if you hadn't used 'fine' for the tenth time."

She took my hand and a shock of power flickered between our palms. I kissed the back of her hand and led her out the door. She didn't pull away, but rather smiled brightly like she was in on a secret.

THIRTY-THREE
GARREN

Strings of glowing crystals were strung high above our heads criss-crossing back and forth. The sun had just set and the heat of the day had given way to the damp evening air. The rushing water of the Visola River hummed in the background.

"I thought blood binding rituals took place in the temple," I looked back through the entryway toward the temple at the center of the palace. It emitted a soft, golden flow in the shrinking light.

"Not in Laeto Selva. The goddess of earth gave us our magic, so we always return the blessing during the ritual," Katuri's mother answered from behind me.

Everyone was barefoot, even the servants. Katuri had always been barefoot in her greenhouse.

"And the no shoes?" I asked.

"It keeps us grounded and fully connected to the Powers Above."

When we crossed into the Forest Fae Kingdom, she immediately removed her boots. Her earth elemental had grown exponentially with the contact.

A priestess emerged from the temple. She didn't wear the longer robes of the priestess in Kanevvluk or the flowy gown. Instead, she wore the traditionally dressed as the forest fae, draping white fabric around her lithe body. Kneeling on the ground, she whispered a prayer of gratitude in the ancient language. She kissed the pendant she wore around her neck, then placed her forehead on the earth. Slowly, she stood and poured a circle of fine red powder in the middle of the courtyard.

Marselina stood off to the side out of the way of the priestess. She did look beautiful. Katuri wove flowers into her hair and she wore a gown encrusted with thousands of tiny gemstones that danced in the evening light. She stood quietly, staring at her feet, and waited to be told what to do. It was as if everyone and everything just moved around her. It reminded me of my own blood ritual in a way. Except while this mouse of a female followed without fuss, my fierce bondmate had fought with her all against her fate.

Once we'd removed the final barrier between us, she'd showed me her memories of the blood binding with me. She'd fought against her father's compulsion so much so that it was physically painful for her. And then, once she could hold out no longer, he broke into her. The pain was unbearable.

I squeezed Kat's fingers, and although she was deep in conversation with Evren, she returned the gesture. Her earth magic reached out and cradled my own powers. Such a courageous Ashlyra.

Once everything was ready, the priestess invited Logan and Marselina into the circle. Marselina jumped when she was addressed. She joined her future bondmate timidly.

We stood in a circle around Logan and Marselina. Katuri to my right, Delrik and Evren on my left. Nyla, Desmund, and Nazneen were across from us on the other side of the ritual circle. Although Naz had her own hand looped through Nyla's, Desmund had a secure, possessive grip on Nyla's other hand. The King and Queen stood proudly behind their son. There was no sign of Marselina's family.

Delrik, who'd followed my line of sight, leaned in close and whispered, "There is something off about Desmund. Did you see him yesterday, how fast he left the river? And how Corynne keeps looking at him like...like, I don't even know."

I studied the profile of the High Fae who'd rescued Nyla from a painfully slow death. He was listening to the priestess carefully, his mouth pressed into a serious expression, like he was analyzing every word.

I shrugged. "He seems alright to me. A little uptight. And that's saying something considering you're my best friend. Anyways, Naz has been keeping tabs on him. You know she is more of a super spy than you are."

Delrik elbowed my ribs and I grunted. The priestess paused and pinned me with a steely glare.

"Sorry." I pounded a fist to my chest. "Just getting choked up a little."

I shot Delrik a look. The priestess continued the ritual.

"I can't explain it. It's like a part of me...recognizes him," Delrik continued and shook his head. "That sounds dumb. It's hard to explain."

"Your hand," the priestess said to Marselina, more loudly than the previous time. She looked as if she was about to lose it at our continued interruptions.

The girl's shoulders curved forward the barest amount.

Kairos, standing directly outside the circle behind the female, shifted on his feet. I bristled at the clear threat Kairos was making. *Obey or I'll make you.* He didn't touch Marselina, but she was terrified and she followed his bidding. She must know what the compulsion feels like. Her hand darted out, nearly knocking the blade from the priestess.

"The threads of the fates have drawn you both together, across time and space," the priestess began.

When she sliced into Marselina's palm, she squeaked through tightly clamped lips. She did the same to Logan. She then pressed their hands together, threading their fingers and squeezed. Blood dripped between their hands onto the soft earth at their feet. At the offering, Marselina swayed ,the coloring draining from her face. Logan steadied her with an arm around her shoulders. She looked up into his eyes. All I saw was uncertainty.

"I've got you," Logan said under his breath. "The worst is over."

I was close enough to hear him but I couldn't see his face from this angle. Marselina nodded and the priestess continued.

"May your blood become one, tying your lives together."

The priestess wove the golden cord around their interlocked hands and forearms, up to their elbows.

I drowned out the rest of the ceremony and focused on my bondmate. Her heart was pounding. I knew Kat was struggling, so close to her father, especially now. The last time we were near a binding circle, he'd forced her hand. I focused my attention on pouring all the love and adoration I could down our connection to my bondmate. She leaned into me.

The rest of the ceremony went quickly, thank the Powers Above.

Queen Nefali had prepared a small outdoor meal afterwards. And by small, I mean lavish and over the top reception. Marselina's family had even arrived. I hadn't seen them at the ceremony though.

Evren sat across Delrik's lap, her wings draped elegantly to the side. The tips hoovered just above the ground. Delrik mindlessly stroked the silky feathers. They were murmuring into each other.

"You are my heart," Evren said into Delrik's neck.

"Ew. Why are y'all so gross and lovey dovey? I know it's a binding ceremony but get a room," Nazneen said.

Delrik flashed a dimpled smile at his sister before planting a kiss on his bondmate's lips.

"What's with those two?" Delrik whispered as he brought a glass of fresh-squeezed fruit juice to cover his mouth.

"So much suspicion tonight, my friend."

He indicated Kairos and Logan in the corner having a heated argument.

"He's probably being chastised for showing empathy to his bondmate when she nearly fainted after the bloodletting," I replied.

Delrik snickered. "Bloodletting. Wow."

I hadn't heard that one before.

"You know what I mean. Kairos is only concerned with the power in that girl's blood and nothing more."

"True."

Logan stomped away from his father and over to Marselina's side. He snatched a drink from a servant's tray and downed it in a few quick swallows.

"Did Daddy scold you?" I teased, raising my voice loud enough for him to hear me.

"Garren, don't," Delrik said, suddenly stern again.

The crystal glass shattered in Logan's hand. Remnants of wine sprayed across Marselina's gown.

I rolled my eyes and turned to find something to eat. I wasn't going to stand here and watch Logan pout. He'd tested enough of my patience, and I didn't want to ruin the night. Poor Marselina already had to deal with him.

"Throw away prince," Logan hissed.

I spun on my heel and had Logan lifted off the ground before the spineless weasel could utter another sound.

"Say that to my face, you coward," I said through gritted teeth.

"Throw away prince."

Glistening scales shifted across my forehead and my sea dragon eyes turned to slits. My teeth sharpened to deadly points. I could taste the blood from where one had sliced into my tongue, but I only let it fuel my rage.

"I'm going to wipe that smug ass smile from your pathetic face."

Logan opened his mouth to say something else, but I snapped my teeth an inch from his nose. "You know nothing of the world, little prince. All you've lived is a pampered, sheltered life. Or maybe you're projecting your feelings on me? Are *you* a throw away prince, Logan?"

I felt Katuri's hand touch my shoulder. The only reason I knew it was her was her earth power shot down our bond and encircled me. It gathered beneath my feet and wound upward, readying to back me up if needed, but also reminding me that Logan was no real threat.

"Don't," Katuri said.

Another hiss came from my lips.

"Garren," she said more firmly. "Please. Not now."

I dragged my gaze to her face and felt myself soften immediately. I went from blind rage to concentrated primal possession of my bondmate instead. My inner sea dragon grumbled with lust as he took in her figure. She dominated all of my senses. I dropped Logan, who struggled not to fall to the ground. He straightened his tunic and brushed non-existent dust from his front. Always so prim and proper.

I pressed a rough kiss to Katuri's mouth, lifted her over my shoulder, and stomped off into the dark forest with her in my arms to have my way with her.

THIRTY-FOUR

NYLA

Everyone had long since gone to bed and a heavy mist was failing around the palace. I found myself being drawn to the gods. I hadn't stepped inside the temple since I'd left my life in Proux behind. Desmund and I wandered from the courtyard into the temple.

"I am...or I guess I used to be a priestess," I said.

"Really? Did you perform blood binding rituals like that?" he asked.

"Me? No. I was more behind the scenes."

Staring at the vaulted ceiling, I could feel his eyes roaming over my face and down my neck, tracing the runes with his fingers, carefully studying me. I relished his touch.

I guided us to the stairs I knew would bring us to the chamber of the veils. Katuri was supposed to bring me here before we'd visited the river, but I'd needed rest. However, since all the temples were the exact same, designed after the Sanctum of the gods, I knew exactly where the relic would be.

Desmund didn't ask where I was taking him. He simply followed me, trailing after with his fingers holding on top the flowing layers of the back of my dress.

I sat on the earth floor in the center of the dome, looking up at the decorative ceiling. He joined me sitting crisscrossed on the floor, our knees touching.

"Did you enjoy it? Being a priestess and living in the temple?"

I shrugged. "It's all I knew. My mother gave birth to me in the temple and the only time I left, I was traveling to other temples. My life was determined for me before I was even born."

I looked at him. There was a strange shimmering over his body. I studied it, watching Desmund closely. I moved closer, sitting on my heels and leaning close. It rippled differently than the torches that lit the temple. The torchlight moved left to right, while this illusion rippled and swirled like a leaf caught in the wind. I reached forward, my fingers not even an inch away from his cheek and stroked where the ripple should've been. Nothing but air met my fingers. Desmund didn't move. A delicate wind swept into the temple and wrapped around my knees before moving up and down my arm. It was as if Haizea herself urged my hand closer to Desmund. I touched his cheek and his eyes fell shut. His skin was warm and soft.

"My life as a priestess was lonely. I lived on the temple grounds alone in a cottage rather than with the others. I found it easier to keep to myself than interact with anyone. At first, it was due to their proximity. I didn't have a good grasp on my seer powers and visions would catch me off guard. It scared them just as it had scared Yara. And I found that when I was alone, I didn't have as many visions either. Meditation practice was easier without all the distractions, too. I was young and thought that was how it was supposed to be. By the time I realized my seclusion wasn't necessary, it had already become my life. It was easier to stay quiet and not take up space."

Desmund opened his eyes and held my gaze. I had a feeling he knew about loneliness, about trying to not take up space. He'd been doing that very thing since we'd arrived in Laeto Sela. He'd held himself back, keeping to the shadows or behind me. He'd stayed quiet as if he spoke, everyone would ask the world of him. We'd led different lives but somehow parallel.

"It wasn't until Nazneen and the others showed up that I stepped out of my little bubble." I chuckled. "Well, more like Nazneen pulled me out of my comfort zone."

"She seems to be a character."

"Yes, she truly is. She's become a great friend."

Desmund nuzzled my palm that was cupping his cheek. I couldn't help but lean into him. Something about being in the temple with him felt right. It was as if the fates were whispering to me to follow Desmund, be with him. They nudged me closer and closer. I should trust him, not only with myself, but with my future. He was important somehow. I just knew it.

"I never asked. How did you all end up meeting?"

I smiled at the memory of the first time Nazneen came bouncing into my house. The desire to tell him everything about my life had the words effortlessly spilling from my lips. "They came to Proux in search of answers for Evren and Delrik. Evren had stolen the shadow magic from Alux when they were in Illoterra. Once Delrik and Evren went through the bloodbinding, the shadows seemed to become almost uncontrollable for Delrik. They were seeking ways to extricate them from Delrik. Little did we know that we'd find out about Aluxyeras, the relics, and the plan Hadeon has along the way."

"I've never heard of the relics before."

"That's why Hadeon's bondmate, Elenora, was so powerful." A pained look crossed over Desmund's face briefly, but I continued. "She had possession of the Relika Stone. She wore it in a circlet on her head. There are five magical relics given to the High Fae kingdoms as keys. They connect the Mortal Realm of Naśbar to Aesira. The relics were hidden after the Uprising and the release of the Great Chaos. Hadeon somehow stumbled upon a tear in between the realms, specifically the one between the void and Naśbar. Or at least, I think that's what is allowing the fiends into this world. He wants to collect all the relics so he can gather all the power and break into Aesira."

Desmund looked pensive, absorbing everything I'd said. Then he said, "King Kairos mentioned that the King of Agni refused to help him. King Ziven threatened to wage war if Hadeon returned to his kingdom. So Hadeon had it burned to the ground."

That's what they must have discussed when we first arrived. Logan had pulled Desmund away before I'd had a chance to ask him what their meeting was about. And after, I'd been too exhausted, it had slipped my mind.

"I'm surprised King Kairos offered up so much information."

Desmund shrugged. "So is there a relic here in Laeto Selva?"

I pointed over the pedestal near the stone archway. "That's Catt-leya's Key."

He merely gave it a cursory glance. "Well, if there is a plan for him to steal the relic, I'm sure it's safe here in the palace."

We sat in companionable silence for a while. I rested my mind in the presence of the gods and Desmund watched me.

"Thank you," I finally said.

He scrunched his brow. "For what?"

"For listening. For saving me, in more ways than one."

"You never have to apologize for taking up space. You can have all the space in my life that you want," he smiled. "Come on. Let's go to bed."

He stood, pulling me to my feet with ease. The same breeze from earlier curled around me, and I noticed wisps dancing throughout the temple. They had a soft glow to them, similar to my runes.

"Um...is this normal?" Desmund asked.

A single wisp floated between us, emanating a soft glow. Desmund poked at one of the wisps, shaped like a kitten. It hugged its translucent body around his digit.

I laughed. "They are just wisps. They won't hurt you."

"I figured as much. I've never seen them before."

He wiggled his finger at me where the wisp had a firm grip. Its tiny kitten claws dug into his skin, the mouth was gnawing on his knuckle playfully. I pried it off his finger and released it back into the air.

"They are invisible to most. Only a privileged few ever see them for what they truly are. You, Desmund, are favored by the gods tonight."

THIRTY-FIVE
NYLA

Desmund woke at the exact same time as me. We were covered in sweat and breathing heavily. Smoke filled the air outside the open balcony. If it hadn't been for the enchantments creating an invisible barrier to keep the rain out, the smoke would've suffocated us in our sleep.

A sharp and sweet smell of trees burning filled my nose and made my eyes water. The sky was so ominously dark, but the forest had a hazy orange glow. A thick layer of sticky sweat coated my entire body, making the sheets cling to me.

I flung the covers off and rushed to the balcony. Fire crept up the walls of the palace, the wood of the ancient tree crackled as the flames licked up, up, up. They moved quickly. Too quickly. The air was dry as if all the moisture had been sucked from it, strange for the rainforest. The air was thick, choking me, like I was swallowing grit. The forest around the palace trembled with unnatural energy.

"We need to leave. Now." Desmund said, gripping my arm tightly.

I hadn't felt him come up behind me, but I didn't hesitate.

"We have to warn the others." The last word was cut off with a cough.

We rushed from the room and across the hall. Evren burst from her door right as I raised my fist to knock.

Katuri's scream pierced the air. Our heads whipped toward her room, several rooms down. Nazneen beat us there, darting across the hall. She didn't bother knocking. She barged inside, Evren and me right on her heels.

Katuri was curled on the floor, screaming in agony. Her hands covered her head, like that would somehow protect her. Garren stood above her, terror on his face, his hands hoovering over her like he was afraid to touch her.

"The forest. The earth. The animals. I feel it. Burning alive. All of it is dying. All of it is burning."

Evren ran for the balcony, arms outstretched. With her hands extended, she began to call the firestorm toward her. They obeyed, flame by flame, reaching her open palms, and engulfing her completely.

I'd followed behind her and what I saw almost stopped my heart. From my room, all I'd seen was smoke and an orange glow. But on this side of the palace, the southern side facing the city and the river, the fire devoured everything in its path. A gust of hot air swept from the north. It was as if it had a life of its own. The sky was heavy with thick, cloying smoke. Birds filled the air, fleeing for their lives. They called out to each other, their voices drowned out by the roaring of the flames. Flames leaped from treetop to treetop. Ash from the burning forest fell like snow. I followed it as it floated downward and covered my bare skin.

A low wall of flames crept closer toward the city and the village where Corynne lived. The citizens of Laeto Selva stood like statues, captured by the haunting scene. Disbelief and terror were written all over their faces as they watched flames whip in every direction. They were trapped between the palace ablaze and the massive Visola River.

A tree suddenly exploded. Burning chunks of debris flew in every direction. Shrieks of panic rang out as people ran for their lives.

On instinct, I thrust my elemental wind toward the running fae, guarding them with a shield of air from the flying pieces of splintered and burning wood. Despite being high up in the treetops hundreds of feet above, the shield of air reached them fast enough, thank the Goddess Haizea.

Evren, with hurried but measured steps, climbed onto the railing. Her bare toes gripped the stone. She looked like a deadly omen standing, ignited arms and wings spread wide. Then she dove toward the ground.

"Evren!" Delrik yelled.

He ran to the railing, leaning over. His shadows tore from his body and reached out toward his Ashlyra. Evren landed gracefully on the ground. When she landed, she spun fast on her feet towards the flames and beckoned them to her away from fleeing people. Her arms glowed as the fire flowed into her. Her wings spread.

The next thing I knew, Delrik's shadows returned to him. They swallowed him whole in a swirling vortex. He disappeared and reappeared on the ground next to his Ashlyra. Did Delrik just teleport through his shadows?

"I need to get to the ground," I called over my shoulder to no one in particular. "I can't protect them from up here."

If I'd been at my full strength, I would've shifted on the spot and flown myself, but I didn't trust that I could do it. I also didn't want to drain my magic in an attempt to shift.

Suddenly, I was lifted into the air by my upper arms, the stones of the balcony disappearing beneath my feet. A massive clawed foot cradled me with unexpected care. I looked up to see the belly of a massive sea dragon. Garren. He'd shifted and grabbed me. We were plummeting toward the ground at breakneck speed, the heat threatening to engulf us. Just before we crashed to our fiery deaths, Garren's outstretched wings caught our descent and my feet landed gently to the ground. My stomach somersaulted but I swallowed back any nausea.

People were running in every direction now, probably from the sea dragon coming at them. Females scooped up children and ran towards the river. Others were using whatever they could to frantically smother the flames creeping toward their homes.

The flames roared, cracking and snapping as trees crumbled. I covered my ears at the deafening sounds. It was so much louder on the ground. Cries of panic and pain pierced the air from trapped animals, invisible beneath the thick smoke. The fire had come on so quickly, they hadn't had time to escape. There was no way this forest fire happened naturally. Something sinister was behind this. It was all too familiar. First the fiends attacked us with fire in Proux, and Agni then being obliterated; I had a feeling who was behind all this. But how had he gotten past the wards around the city?

Evren continued absorbing the fire. Her eyes were now a bright white and her wings had shifted from their sleek black feathers to towering flames. It was much too strong. She was becoming unstable. I could see the effort for her to remain in control. Delrik stood at her back, his shadows wrapped around her, holding her upright. They also stretch outward, creating a barricade between the burning edge of the trees and the homes closest to the palace. I much preferred their cold terror over Delrik's shadows mixed with this hot inferno, ravenous in its destruction. It made the magic seem so dark.

Relentless flames surged forward from my right. Unbearable heat and intense waves radiated like the fire was a physical being reaching his fingers toward me. I covered my face, blinded by the brightness. Tears dripped from my eyes to flush out the sooty debris. I thrust my hands forward and the inferno met my wall of air. Flames were forced upward into the sky, illuminating the destruction. The fire cast long shadows across the palace walls. The wall of air was enough to give Evren a reprieve. She dropped her arms and Delrik caught her around the waist before she could collapse. Fire jumped back and forth between their bond, just as the shadows moved to her to cover her alight skin and smother out the embers.

I gathered my power, digging deep within myself. While holding the shield with my right hand, my left swept upward, driving the winds in the opposite direction, forcing the fire away from the heart of the city. Both arms shook with the effort.

Garren, in his sea dragon form, swept overhead. His maw opened wide and water poured from above, dousing flames licking up the palace walls. I'd never seen him use his elemental water in such a massive way before. Again and again, with each pass above, he sprayed water along the city and the palace, soaking everything and creating a barrier that was impossible for the flames to cross.

THIRTY-SIX
GARREN

I couldn't bear it. The pain coursing through my bondmate crashed into me like a tsunami, drowning me in agony. It was by far the worst pain I'd ever felt in my life, which meant Katuri didn't have much time. I did my best to build a wall around my mind to push out all her feelings. I needed to focus on putting out this fire rather than her pain. Her pain would cease once the fire was gone, I was sure of it.

"Go!" Nazneen yelled at me. I looked up to see her kneeling beside me. "Go. I have her."

I swallowed thickly, but nodded. I trusted Nazneen to care for my bondmate with as much care as I could. She was family.

I nodded one more time and ran for the balcony. I was already mid-shift when I heard Nyla.

"I need to get to the ground," Nyla called over her shoulder. "I can't protect them from up here."

There was nothing slow about my shift. The sea dragon exploded from within me, ripping my clothes to shreds. I felt the stone walls scrape along my lower back. I pumped my wings once, twice. I looked down long enough to find Nyla and grip her arms between a front claw. Her startled squeal was quickly drowned out by the rushing air and I dove for the ground. Only seconds passed before I dropped Nyla beside Evren and Delrik.

Then I was airborne again. I pushed myself high into the night sky, past the charred canopy, past the clouds, closer to the stars. I need to be above the smoke and moistureless air.

Drake was next to me in an instant.

"No! Stay with Kat. She needs you," I said to my familiar through our mental connection.

He didn't balk at being cast away. Rather, he circled back down to the palace, spraying water along the canopy as he went. I saw him swoop into our bedchamber and back to our love.

I stretched my body and my wings and urged my water elemental to the forefront of my mind. I drew in a deep breath, tucked my wings in, and nosedived back toward the flames.

I swept from the west side of the city toward the palace, releasing a torrent of water on all the houses that were closest to the forest as I went. A singular flame curled, reaching upward, hugging my tail. Just before it touched my scales, dark shadows swallowed them up. I looked down to see Delrik's hand reaching out towards me. I snapped my jaws in thanks.

I turned and made another pass. This time, I drenched the head of the fire. My water quickly turned to steam, sizzling and crackling.

I didn't count the number of times I swept back and forth along the city's edge and around the palace's northern side. I was pushing my water magic to its limit. I knew. I could feel it. Thankfully, between Evren, Delrik, and Nyla, we seemed to be making some sort of headway.

That, combined with Nya's shifting the winds, the fire was held at a standstill. The blaze wasn't fully contained, far from it, but the city was safe. For now.

THIRTY-SEVEN
DESMUND

My heart plummeted to the ground as Nyla did. I tried to reach out and grab her, but Garren was too fast. She slipped right through my hands. At that exact moment, shadows exploded around Delrik and he disappeared. I knew nothing of his powers and I didn't have time to contemplate them right now. I had to get to Nyla. I summoned my astral projection and landed directly behind Nyla down on the ground, in the midst of the chaos. She battled the fire with such grace and power. I'd see her fight in the mountains but up close, she was magnificent. I knew she'd keep herself safe, so I focused my energy back on the palace.

My astral returned to me, and I pivoted to see Nazneen and Katuri behind me. I'd never shown my powers before. The pair seemed shocked by a copy of myself that appeared before me and then was reabsorbed.

"Now that's a cool trick...that we will discuss later," Nazneen said.

Katuri had gathered herself and was back in control.

"We need to evacuate the side of the palace closest to the fire," she said.

I nodded. We ran from room to room, waking everyone from sleep and having them aid in the efforts of warning the palace. Very few people had actually been asleep. Most were just frozen in shock. It took being told to evacuate to kick them into gear and move.

We'd made it down several floors when we came to the royal wing. The hallway was abandoned, not a sentinel in sight. Where was everyone? Nazneen and I headed in the direction of Logan's room, while Katuri ran to wake her parents.

When we got to Logan's room, he was nowhere to be found. Marselina was awake and scrambling to her feet. The same solid wall of smoke against the invisible barrier to the rainforest blocked out the view. Only a glow pulsed through the smoke.

"The palace is on fire. We have to go!" Nazneen yelled.

"How can I help?" she asked.

"Any extra pairs of hands would help, especially those of a gifted healer. Warn as many as you can," I said.

We went to find Katuri.

The King and Queen were already out of the palace. Or at least they weren't in their room, which was better than them burning in their beds.

A tree crashed down and landed, still ablaze, across the King's balcony. Sparks and embers burned through the magical barrier with a sharp hiss and landed on the floor. I quickly stomped out the embers.

I reached for Katuri and guided her out of her parents' rooms. We ran into Nazneen in the hallway, and continued down the spiraling staircase until we made it out to where everyone was fighting the fire.

Nyla, by some sheer grace from the Powers Above, was pushing the fire back with one hand while at the same time sucking the oxygen from the area, helping to smother the fire.

Evren, who appeared to be completely engulfed in flames, was walking from home to home, calling the fire to her. The flames that were slowly destroying everything jumped into her awaiting palm.

Delrik was a scary sight. His eyes were solid black and his arms from the elbows down were stained with shadows. Tendrils came from his fingers and climbed higher than the tallest flames. They pressed down, smothering the fire. The dangerous message had been contained.

THIRTY-EIGHT
DESMUND

We moved cautiously, putting out anything that smoldered to prevent anything from catching again. Soot and grime covered our faces. Devastation surrounded us. There were layers of ash on everything. The homes closest to the edge of the forest and near the palace were charred skeletons and the ground was scorched black.

Villagers picked through the carnage, surveying what was left of their homes to see if anything could be salvaged. It had been impossible to save everything. But there were no bodies in the wreckage and that was a miracle.

One wood nymph sat on a blackened stump. Behind her was rubble. She shook uncontrollably as the adrenaline wore off and the ramifications set in. So small, so helpless. Nazneen approached her, knelt in the ash, and draped a blanket around her shoulders. She sat with her and cradled the crying female in her arms.

Despite the number of people moving around, heavy silence hung in the air. Smoke still rose from the ground.

Evren stood off to the side, still ablaze.

"Ashlyra," Delrik said as he approached her without fear.

He wrapped the burning elemental in his arms. His shadows reached to her, as the fire reached for him in return. I watched as their powers evenly spread between the two through their binding mark.

"I need water," Evren said in a rasping voice.

"Drake!" Delrik called, calm as a cucumber. "Care to assist?"

The familiar, who hadn't left Katuri's side the whole time, soaked the pair in a splash of water. Steam hissed as the water landed on their skin, but soon the fire was out. The bondmates stood, embracing, and sopping wet.

"You had too much fun with that," Delrik said with an eye roll at the sea dragon.

Drake, who stood a few feet taller than Evren, bent his long, slender neck downward so he was face to face with her. He chuffed and icy mist puffed from his nostrils.

"Thank you, Drake," Evren said as she stroked his nose.

Garren was still flying above in his massive sea dragon form. He flew in smaller and smaller circles, dousing the forest to ensure nothing would accidentally catch again.

Hollowness was left in the wake of the fire. They'd have to rebuild. But Forest Fae were resilient. I'd seen it on each visit.

Katuri stood staring into the once luscious rainforest. Garren's sea dragon landed delicately with Katuri in between his massive front legs. She didn't falter as his massive body made the ground quiver. A swirl of ice and water whipped around him. Then he was standing in his Fae form beside her, stark naked and water-logged. He had eyes only for his bondmate. He swept his hand in front of his hips and shorts appeared made of soft linen. I wasn't sure how he'd done that, but I wasn't complaining.

"The forest, it aches with sorrow. I can feel the earth mourning the loss," she whispered through her heartbreak.

Garren took his bondmate's hand and pulled her down so that they were squatting. Then he pressed her fingers into the ash.

"Remember, Little Flower. Life can come from the death of the forest."

A tear ran down her cheek and hit the ground. Their gilded binding marks began to glow. Together, their water and earth elemental magic poured from their souls into the earth, replenishing it, healing it. Life bloomed in a spiraling circle around them, like ripples on the surface of a still lake.

"With you as its guardian, the rainforest and Laeto Selva will be even stronger than before."

Katuri leaned her head against Garren's shoulder.

We spent most of the day attending to the residents of Laeto Selva and cleaning up the devastation from the fire. Marselina offered to assist me with healing anyone who needed it. She was quiet, but steady-handed. She didn't shy away at the nasty burns and was more patient than me. Nyla stayed by my side, offering comfort to those she could. For one child, I watched as she shared a vision of the rainforest in full bloom again. The little boy who had been almost inconsolable soon dried his tears.

"Will the forest really come back?" he asked Nyla, his tiny hands tucked in hers.

"Of course it will. I've seen it, and now so have you. It will be bright and happy once again," she said as if she was sharing a secret.

After that, the boy clung to Nyla's soot covered skirt until his mother pried him away from her side.

Evren and Delrik walked a circle around the palace, hand in hand, and smothered all the smaller fires and glowing embers to prevent rekindling.

Katuri and Garren had their work cut out for them. Rylis had joined them as they went from home to home, taking notes of all the damage and reassuring their inhabitants that all would be done to help them recover their losses. I wasn't sure where King Kairos was, nor did I particularly care. He was too rough around the edges to offer his subjects any empathy. I'd overheard Rylis tell Katuri that her father was 'handling things' in the palace. I doubted it. Logan was still missing.

Exhausted from hours of backbreaking work, we dragged our weary bodies back into the palace that evening. The smell of smoke hung on our clothes and skin, soot smudged our faces and hands. An acrid stench still hung in the air from the burned flesh of injured animals. I wanted nothing more than to rinse the day off from my tired body.

Nyla used her elemental magic to clear the palace of the ash as we trudged our way to the upper levels where the family's mezzanine and throne room were located. It appeared the urgency of the forest fire made Nyla's powers return in full force. Katuri had not seen her parents or brother yet and wanted to search for them. Even Marselina, who'd followed us back from the city, was starting to wonder where her new bondmate was. As much as I disliked the kid, it was unlike him to not help the people of this city when they needed it.

Eerie silence punctuated by creaks of wood as the heat dissipated throughout the palace echoed off the walls.

"Who is responsible for this disaster?" King Kairos bellowed.

His voice carried down the hall. The doors were thrown open to the mezzanine that led to the throne room. Several of the sentinels stood before the king, heads bowed in subjugation.

"We haven't found the culprit yet, Sir," one brave soul replied.

Something crashed against the floor. "Try harder!"

"Yes, Sir."

The rushing of boots on stone as the guards exited the throne room. They didn't bother acknowledging us. I didn't blame them. I'd get as far away from the king as I could if I were in their shoes.

A crash resonated from behind them. The king probably was smashing anything he could get his hands on. He'd always had a temper. That must have been where Logan got his oh-so-lovely disposition. Where had he been while all of us were risking our lives to save *his* people and *his* kingdom?

Katuri and Garren walked in front of us, hand in hand, toward the throne room as the king was throwing a fit. They entered the throne room first, Garren keeping close to his bondmate. He felt as much appreciation toward the king as I did. Nazneen, Marselina, Evren, and Delrik went next. I stuck to the back of the group. If Nyla hadn't had a hold of my hand, I would have slipped away into the shadows and sent my astral projection instead. But I wouldn't be able to do that without her taking notice. I figured the first time she saw my power shouldn't be like that. Also, I didn't like the idea of the king knowing my power either.

Nazneen looked over her shoulder and scanned me head to toe as if she was assessing whether I was truly there or not. She'd kept her mouth shut about my astral all day for some reason.

The king was tossing a chair across the room. Did he even feel shame from having an audience?

King Kairos stared passed this audience and zeroed in on me with a furious glower. "This was your doing."

It wasn't a question. He was blaming the fire on me. I stood taller and felt a ripple of power start at my head and move to my toes. I wanted to be sure I was protected for whatever was to come. Nyla looked down at our joined hands. Had she felt the surge of my magic? I knew he couldn't do anything to harm me unless he was touching me. Compulsion was a fantastic power if you had the upper hand. Right now, he didn't.

"I had nothing to do…" I began.

"Silence!" Spittle flew from his mouth.

I snapped my mouth closed.

"Father. What are you speaking of?" Katuri began, looking back and forth between me and her father.

"Quiet girl!" he shouted.

King Kairos stepped forward, but I took a half step back. He was all the way across the room but even a step closer was too close for comfort.

"This is all *your* fault. You brought this destruction to my kingdom. You brought on this evil." He punctuated each word.

"I've only done exactly what has been asked," I replied, standing my ground now that I'd found my voice again.

I didn't know who was responsible for the fire, but I had nothing to do with it. It had taken me by as much surprise as everyone else. However, there was no point in trying to say so. The king only wanted someone to blame.

He finally took in a breath and exhaled heavily. He walked over to a nearby window and took in the state of his kingdom.

"Where's Mother?" Katuri asked.

"There's never been a fire in Laeto Selva's history," I heard the king say.

"Father, where is Mother?"

He ignored his daughter. His hands were clasped behind his back. I noticed he was fully dressed in his usual royal attire, which I found odd. Hadn't he been asleep in bed when the fire broke out? Wouldn't he have rushed to help squash the fire? When would he have had time to dress in his royal attire? His hands were spotless, his hair flawless. Only his cheeks were flushed from his earlier outburst.

Katuri tried a different approach.

"Evren, Garren, and Nyla managed to shift the fire away from the city, but the palace..." she tried again but was interrupted once again.

"I know the state of my kingdom," he barked.

Garren rumbled with the growl of a sea dragon.

Marselina stepped past Katuri. "Where is Queen Nefali?" she asked.

She had been standing to my right. She was so soft and quiet. I doubted the king had heard her. Yet, he answered her.

"Where she's supposed to be. Why do you always ask the most obvious questions?"

"Logan is missing too," Nazneen said to Katuri.

Katuri tried one last time. "Father, we need to..."

"I will not leave my throne to go search for your wayward brother. I've sent the sentinels to find him. He probably ran like the coward he is," the king snapped back.

Chaos sounded in the hall and two different guards came running into the throne room. One skidded to a stop and knelt before the king's throne. The other stayed by the door. He sat, waiting for the king to give him permission to rise. Kairos turned slowly and walked to his throne. He didn't sit or step up onto the dais. Just stood next to it.

"Speak."

He stood but kept his eyes cast to the elaborate stone floor. Gilded veins stretched from the throne outward to a circle. It reminded me a little bit of the god's symbol in the temple.

"King Kairos. We found Queen Nefali." He paused and glanced at us.

"Good. That will be all," Kairos dismissed him with a wave of his hand.

The sentinel didn't move.

"Why are you still standing there? You have been dismissed."

"I'm sorry, Sir..."

The king stepped up onto the dais. "Get on with it."

"Um... King Kairos..." The male was visibly trembling with fear.

Kairos stomped his foot and bellowed, "Speak!"

The male dropped to his knees and pressed his forehead to the floor in subjugation.

"Both the queen and prince have been found. It appears they were attacked during the night."

Katuri gasped.

"Excuse me?" King Kairos said through gritted teeth.

"Sir. The Queen and Prince are dead," the sentinel confirmed what Katuri had already assumed.

The other sentinel stepped into the throne room and gave the king a quick bow before speaking. "It appears they were trying to escape from the fire when they were, um, slain. Everyone has been accounted for—guards, servants. I assure you, King Kairos, we will find out who committed this atrocity."

King Kairos eyed me again but kept his thoughts to himself. His earlier outburst had now shifted to cold control. I much preferred his vocal outrage to this too-calm demeanor. He was less predictable when he was in this mood.

Someone snuck into the palace. Was the fire a distraction from the true target? Why would someone want Queen Nefali and the prince dead? Or maybe they just happen to be in the wrong place at the wrong time. There was no way the whole fiasco wasn't a planned affair.

"I understand. Leave us," Kairos said.

The guards looked at each other, the one rose from the floor, and they left as quickly as they'd come. Tense silence filled the throne room.

The king's nostrils flared with anger. "You *will* speak the truth. Your father threatened that if I didn't follow his instructions, something like this would happen."

I could see in his eyes he was going to force me to spill my secrets.

"I am speaking the truth. Why would I start a fire in the city? Why would I murder the queen and prince?"

"Desmund was with me. He couldn't have started the fire," Nyla came to my defense.

"There are other ways to start a forest fire than striking the match yourself." The king took another menacing step towards me. His hand was outstretched, ready to force me into submission and Powers Above knew what else with his compulsion. "Let's get on with it then."

"You will do no such thing," I replied.

I couldn't let him touch me. I knew of his power, his compulsion. There was no telling what he'd make me reveal.

Kairos stalked over to me like a prowling panther. His hands balled into fists and then he stretched his fingers out. It took every ounce of my strength not to turn and run. I prepared myself, prepared my magic. I released a breath, and I felt my astral projection shimmer into existence. It remained invisible to everyone but myself.

There was a subtle shift in the air and Nyla suddenly turned her head toward me, but she didn't look at me. She looked at my projection. I was amazed. Could she see it? No. There was no way. Her eyes looked glazed over and she was squinting a little. She wasn't focused on it, but rather the general area. Her hand reached out and hovered over my astral's face. Her fingers didn't contact my skin. I could feel like, though, like a tickling, feather light touch.

I was tired of hiding my power from Nyla. Each passing day I'd realized how much I cherished her and I had been lying to her. I'd waited long enough.

I felt my will slowly breaking. Breaking because Nyla, my Nyla, was looking at me like I was the center of her universe. It would all change at any moment. The second Kairos got his hands on me, my secret would be revealed. Nyla would abandon me, and I'd have no choice but to let her. I could choose to tell her, show her, myself, or I could allow Kairos to strip that right from me. Right now, I was trapped between a rock and a hard place.

As if he knew what I was thinking, King Kairos broke out into a contented, wicked smile.

"You have always had too many secrets," he sneered.

The astral projection I'd created suddenly appeared to everyone in a sparkle of light. It shimmered, transparent, but there.

"What's so secretive about an astral projection? We knew about that," Nazneen said.

She looked at me and I silently thanked her for standing with me.

I saw Garren lean towards Katuri. "We did?" he whispered.

She gave him a look that said, *not now*.

"There is more to you than that. There is no way your father would have kept you around if you only had a few parlor tricks," King Kairos sneered.

My astral projection solidified and became corporeal. It moved to stand on the other side of Nyla. At least now I could guard her from both sides.

King Kairos tucked his arms behind his back again and began to casually make his way closer. He came to stand before me.

"See. That wasn't so hard. Though I wonder..."

"Father, this isn't important right now. Mother and Logan have been murdered," Katuri sobbed. "Why are you so focused on blaming Desmund when there is clearly someone else out there with a price on our heads?"

Kairos still had a stupid smile on his face.

Suddenly, he lashed out, striking faster than a viper. He gripped my astral projection by the throat.

"Father!" Katuri cried. "What are you doing?"

"Shut up you insipid girl."

"Release him," Garren commanded.

He stepped toward Kairos but Katuri grabbed his hand. "Don't."

She was right. If Kairos touched Garren, he'd be able to make him do whatever twisted thing he could think of.

I always assumed my projection was safe but in its solid, corporeal form, it wasn't completely impervious to physical attacks.

I tried to pull the projection back to me but Kairos' grip prevented it. That was when I felt the compulsion. It wasn't instantaneous. It slithered like a snake around my throat and down my limbs. I forced my protection and power around myself but Kairos was strong. I gritted my teeth. How was he doing it? I looked around.

Realization smacked me in the face. It was the floor. I'd never noticed it before. The conduit he'd had built into his office. It was veined into the stone floor. Kairos' compulsion magic glinted in the veins as it moved from my astral and to my feet. The moment it touched my boots, I was glued to the spot. He'd only grabbed my astral to distract me. All of us were standing within the circle built around the throne. Deep, dark veins ran through the stone. I could see the compulsion magic pouring from Kairos where he stood and flowing to me. Why had he never done this before? Was he biding his time?

"Aha! See, I knew there was something else about you that you were hiding. I can feel your glamor. Interesting. Very interesting."

His compulsion caressed the glamor I'd firmly kept in place for the last several weeks. It shuddered under the king's power.

"Desmund, Desmund, Desmund," he tisked. "What have you been hiding from me?"

Terror flooded my lungs and I was drowning in the fact that my future was ruined. The circle of dark hells has come to be. The whole room went deathly silent. The king knew. How? There was nothing except the humming of my blood and panic in my head. Before my very eyes, my life was burning down.

I lifted Nyla's hand and pressed her fingertips to my lips. "I promise it's not what it seems. I'm so sorry."

She tipped her head in confusion. Powers Above, I wished somehow she'd been able to foresee this moment. It would have saved me in so many ways.

I didn't drop my eyes from Nyla as I released the hold on my glamor. The glamor I'd been wearing since the moment she first laid eyes on me. The glamor Corynne has so easily seen through. It melted away, revealing my true, monstrous self.

"Desmund?" I heard Nyla's trembling voice over the chaos inside my head. I couldn't tell if it was a plea or a reproach.

Kairos released the throat of my astral and it snapped back to me like a rubber band.

Nyla's petite hand was swallowed by mine and her chin tipped higher as she lifted her head to maintain eye contact. I didn't bother looking at everyone else's faces. I didn't want to see what they thought of my true, monstrous form.

I only had eyes for Nyla. I only cared about Nyla.

Shadows crept from the edges of the room toward me. Toward Nyla. I didn't move an inch as the dark tendrils wrapped Nyla with delicate ease and drew her backwards away from me. Her fingers slipped from mine. I almost broke when her touch disappeared.

King Kairos sneered nastily. "Don't you know who he really is? Desmund Allerick. Hadeon Allerick's son. Son of the seer. Demon."

PART FIVE

THIRTY-NINE
NYLA

Crimson eyes bracketed with sinister wrath. There was fire, choking smoke, and destruction. Pleas of mercy filled my ears. I felt concentrated betrayal, but then those eyes. They took up my entire field of view. Almost the same color eyes as the fiends had been. Villainous rage held me captive. The slitted pupils widened with recognition, and then mournfulness replaced the rage. I couldn't pull my attention from those eyes. They saw deep into my soul.

All my visions, all my nightmares, they had been *him*! It had been Desmund all along. Nightmares and visions of crimson eyes had been following me for centuries!

Strength and raw power radiated from Desmund. I studied him carefully. The ripple I'd seen so many times since meeting Desmund appeared. Rather than dissipating, though, the ripple swirled and then the male before us...changed.

Nobody in the room moved a muscle. The air was shifting as the tension grew. I couldn't tell if it was my power affecting the air or if it was the other way around.

What the actual fuck!

If I'd had my visions, my elemental power, and access to the wisps, I wouldn't have been so easily fooled. Or had I lost my visions so I wouldn't judge the male that was before me before I knew his heart? I wouldn't put it past the gods.

This is one of the reasons I'd isolated myself in the temple. Life was easier there. Ever since I left the temple, things have been unclear. My future had been shrouded in a haze.

"What are you?" Katuri whispered.

I didn't take my eyes off the male. He was still Desmund. I could see it—his strong arms, broad chest, and the same dark hair. But so, so different all at the same time.

Delrik's shadows, cool against my overheated skin, curled around my middle and edged me backwards away from the beast. I didn't fight against them. Each step I took away from Desmund left a gaping chasm in my heart. I kept my composure. If I spoke, I wasn't sure I'd be able to keep my reaction under control.

Curled horns that started a light near gray and darkened to black at the points protruded from his head. When he lifted his head, bright crimson eyes stared back at me, rimmed in black. They were depthless, yet gentle and pleading. He looked hopeless, broken, vulnerable. He'd grown over a foot and now towered well over both Garren and Delrik.

"Fiend," Delrik sneered.

Desmund blanched. The words were a slap in the face. I swallowed, but he didn't take his eyes from me. I fought to master my breathing. I didn't want to show any fear because I wasn't sure if I feared him the way I probably should.

A slow clapping came from my left. King Kairos had a wicked smirk on his face. He had known all along there was something different about Desmund. Based on the look on Katuri's face, she, however, did not.

"Desmund here has been an errand boy for his father over the last decade or so," Kairos sneered.

Desmund was Hadeon Allerick and Elenora's son. That's what he'd meant when he'd said he knew a seer. His mother. Not only was she one of the most powerful seers of our time, but with the Relika Stone she was near unstoppable. I say near because Katuri had ended her after she'd almost killed Garren. Katuri in her shifted wolf form had ripped her head clean off her neck and dropped it at Hadeon's feet.

That was why he was afraid of my visions.

At least, he hadn't been afraid of the visions themselves, more how I was consumed by them at first.

Had he been in Noirdan when we'd rescued Delrik? Had he taken part in torturing him? With his glamor, would Delrik have even recognized him?

No. Desmund didn't have a mean bone in his body. He was a healer. I knew him. The real him. His outer appearance may resemble a fiend, but he was not a demon.

The shadows still held me, my back to my friends. Desmund stood before me. From the corner of my eye, I saw movement and felt a stir of magic. Someone lashed out toward Desmund with their power. I didn't see who it was, and I didn't care. My elemental reacted before I could blink. A gust of air shoved Desmund out of the line of fire. I hadn't intended to use my magic to protect Desmund, but after 600 years of it, I trusted it without question. If my magic, a gift from the goddess of air Haizea herself, trusted this male, then so did I.

Primal rage and protection curled within me.

He. Was. Mine.

I shoved at the shadows, my hands going through them like a mist, but Delrik unwove them from around me. Nothing was going to stand between Desmund and me. And I wouldn't let any harm come to him. I moved myself between everyone else and Desmund. I didn't hesitate to turn my back on him and face off my friends. My family.

An angry hiss like a cornered, winged lynx escaped. I knew there was murder in my eyes for anyone willing to go against me to get to Desmund.

It was Garren who'd lashed out. His lips were pulled back, revealing vicious dragon teeth. He, too, was standing guard, mirroring me in his protection of Katuri.

Desmund took a microstep forward so his chest was against my back. I felt rather than heard a growl rumbling low in his chest.

I remained still as a statue, the seconds ticking by, with a beast of a male behind me. I heard a soft voice, her soft voice. Goddess Haizea.

Yes.

King Kairos looked back and forth between our divided group, happy as a clam, thriving on the discourse.

"Do you know what your father has done?" Garren asked.

"Of course he does. He's his right-hand man," Delrik answered. "I mean, look at him. He's practically one of them."

I felt Desmund shift on his feet behind me. He chose his words carefully. "I am no fiend."

"Could have fooled me," Delrik said under his breath.

Evren shot him a glare. "We should hear him out."

"Ashlyra," Delrik said through a clenched jaw.

"No," Evren said again. She wasn't backing down. "We should hear him out. If we had made assumptions about Alux's magic and not heard her story, everything leading us in this direction would be wrong. Everything about her shadows would have pointed to you as being evil as well. Nyla would've never found what she did. Katuri and Garren would never have learned to trust each other. I think Desmund at least deserves to be heard."

"Thank you, Evren," Desmund said. I quickly looked over my shoulder at him and smiled. Even his voice was deeper, darker.

I kept eye contact with my friends as I moved to stand side by side with Desmund. I reached my hand out toward him as another show of solidarity. I wouldn't turn on him just because he looked different or because he came from one of the most vile males I knew. There was a beat of silence. I stood frozen. Waiting. Then I felt Desmund move beside me with his hand in mine. I exhaled.

"King Kairos is right. I am Hadeon and Elenora's son. But I am not a fiend." I squeezed his hand, encouraging him to continue. I dragged my eyes from my friends' faces to look into his red ones. "This is my true form. I have been using glamor since we met. My appearance is the result of my mother using dark magic while she was pregnant with me. At least, that's what the healers had said when I questioned them."

I quickly glanced at the rest of my friends. There was shock and horror written on their faces. I squeezed his hand for encouragement. The jeering voice of the king brought me back to reality.

"Such a lovely, heartwarming story. Like father, like son," Kairos laughed. "Wicked to the core."

Desmund whipped his head, baring deadly teeth at the Forest Fae King. "I am nothing like my father."

"Could have fooled me," Kairos said.

"You are the wicked one," Desmund snapped at Kairos. His scarlet eyes flared. "You are the one turning a blind eye to the chaos my father has been creating all around Quinterre." Desmund turned to Katuri. "You have to believe me, Katuri. Your father may not be the bad guy, but he isn't good either," I plead.

"You're one to talk," Garren sneered.

"I haven't been the one turning a blind eye. Hadeon's been slowly poisoning the continent and leeching evil back into the realm. He's taken advantage of the tear between the worlds. He's practically undoing everything the gods had fixed way back during the rebellion."

"And you've been doing everything he's asked of you like a well-trained pup," Kairos chided."Transporting letters back and forth is nothing compared to..." King Kairos, with an overexaggerated flourish, reached into his chest pocket and withdrew an elegant scroll in smooth ink written on cream parchment. "Why don't we show your little lover how obedient you are?"

Faster than he was expecting, I ripped the letter from his hand. He hadn't been paying attention to me, so it had been easier than I thought to take Hadeon's letter.

Without hesitation, I began to read the letter out loud. "My ever faithful servant, King Kairos. By the time you receive this, the attack on Agni has been carried out. As planned, the fiends will arrive at Laeto Selva shortly after. I do hope Desmund is quick in his travels, otherwise you may fall prey to the plans. That would be a tragedy indeed."

Kairos lunged for me, but I expertly turned from his grip and tiptoed behind Desmund. He was a solid wall in front of me.

I continued. "As previously discussed, the fiends will pose a threat to your kingdom for you to save your people from. In return. I expect you to have the relic ready for retrieval."

"You were going to hand over the relic to Hadeon!?" Garren growled.

"Enough," Katuri snapped.

FORTY
DESMUND

My father knew of the relics. I knew this from what Nyla had told me the other night in the temple. What I hadn't expected was for him to take it from King Kairos. Nyla had said he wanted to collect them all, but to my knowledge, he had none of them. He'd never told me once about his plans for the tear between the void and Naśbar.

"Kat," Nyla said. "You can trust what he's saying is true."

Katuri looked back and forth between Nyla and me. Nyla was my only focus. She still had an unyielding grip on my hand. I looked down at her tiny hand, swallowed by mine. I'd had to hold myself back my whole life. My glamor only worked to cover my outer appearance. Moderating my strength, the quickness of my movements, and the texture of my skin. I was so used to hiding my true self from everyone that seeing Nyla willingly touch me uplifted me.

"How can I trust him?" Kat scowled. "His mother tortured Delrik by invading his mind," she said, gesturing to Delrik, who was standing with his arms crossed over his chest. "His father has murdered hundreds. Probably thousands."

The truth squeezed my insides. I knew all the things my parents had done. I'd tried my best to steer clear of their misdeeds, but I didn't have a choice the majority of the time. My father had forced his hand many times when it came to my compliance.

"You may not be able to trust him. Not yet. But I do. I trust him with my life. He is my life. He literally saved me from a painful death from the fiends and has done nothing to prove me wrong. Even Haizea has blessed him."

My heart broke and reformed as I heard her confess her love to her friends. She trusted me, and she trusted her friends. A wave of relief and unwavering love washed over me. The feeling was surreal. The emotion ebbed back and forth. I knew Nyla was feeling the same.

"You are going to trust a monster over your own flesh and blood?" Kairos spat.

"You lost our trust the day you forced your daughter into a blood-binding ritual against her will," Garren seethed, turning all his fury from me to his bonded's father.

"It looks like all turned out right to me," Kairos retorted.

Kairos turned on his heel and stomped toward the balcony. This whole damned palace had open-aired balconies and terraces. It made for easy dramatic exits for Kairos, though.

"And yet, Desmund," Kairos began from the balcony. "Did Katuri tell you *she* was the one who killed your mother?"

I turned to Katuri. For a moment, I saw the regret on her face. Not because she felt bad for killing my mother, but for the fact she hurt someone who'd become special to Nyla. The air was thick with tension. I didn't necessarily feel anger towards Katuri. Knowing her this short time, she wouldn't have done something so permanent without just cause. And knowing the terrible acts my mother committed, she most likely deserved it. I still had a small pang of hurt though. It didn't last long. A loud crack pierced the air, distracting me from any thoughts of my deceased mother. Kairos looked down at his feet and then back up to us all with wide eyes.

Suddenly, the stone gave way beneath him and he plummeted.

"No!" Katuri screamed.

Garren grabbed her around the waist before she could run to the edge, where the stones of the balcony were giving way. The stone all along the edge was crumbling into pieces, weakened by the heat of the blaze.

I ran forward and slid across the smooth stone floor on my stomach to the edge. I peered over and saw King Kairos hanging on by his fingertips, just out of reach. I inched forward and reached out toward him.

He strained with considerable effort, but managed to grab my wrist. I pulled with all my might. We are so close.

Kairos looked up at me. For the first time, I could see black rings around his irises. They were faint, but they were there. Then his lips curled. He leaned in close and whispered in my ear.

"Aw. Always the faithful servant. Your father was right about you. You are too soft for your own good."

My first instinct was to release him, to let him plummet to the ground and end all of this right now. I should let him drop to his fiery death. But something was holding me back. I refused to be like my father. I refused to murder simply because it was a convenient way out of the situation. I was a healer, despite everything my father had done to me and made me watch.

"I know everything you've done. Does your sweet Nyla? Her friends?"

"You know nothing," I sneered back.

My father had to be stopped, but for so many more reasons than my own. I took a breath. I couldn't let Kairos get away with sitting by while my father destroyed the realm. His daughter deserved the truth, just like Nyla deserved my truth. If I dropped him to his death now, they'd never know the truth. They'd only see me as the male who murdered the king.

I mustered all my strength and, with considerable effort, I lifted the Forest Fae King to safety.

FORTY-ONE
KATURI

By some miracle, Desmund, with all his otherworldly strength, lifted my father from certain death and deposited him in a heaping pile on the floor. They were both panting from the ordeal.

Suddenly, there was a glow from beside me. Nyla was having a vision. She sucked in a sharp breath. Desmund's red eyes flashed over to her. She suddenly gripped my hand, sweeping me into her vision with her.

A cascade of pictures flipped through my mind. My father had been meeting with Hadeon or Desmund over the last few years. The ones with Desmund were only him passing sealed letters. But the ones with Hadeon and my father were quite damning.

The pair sitting in my father's office, drinks in hand and laughing about Powers Above knew what.

Hadeon, clapping a hand on my father's shoulder.

King Kairos of Laeto Selva and the Forest Fae, looking out over the fighting pit in Noirdan where we'd fought Hadeon and Elenora, as they watch fiends rip each other to shreds.

The final vision was as if I was looking over my father's shoulder, reading a missive from Hadeon. The one Desmund had just delivered only days ago.

He'd known the fiends were coming to set the kingdom on fire. He'd known they were going to kill my mother if anything stood in their way. And he let it all happen.

"You knew," I said with resounding surety.

"It was the only way to get him to leave Laeto Selva alone. The sacrifice of one to save thousands. There was no choice." Though his face looked pitiful and full of remorse, his voice gave away his truth.

"And Logan?"

He flipped his hand casually. "He must have been in the way. Sad, I no longer have him, but he isn't needed. I have you."

"You don't *have* me," I snarled through gritted teeth at him. I felt my power and Garren's surge upward inside me.

Drake appeared at my side, taller than me, his presence sucked all the oxygen from the room. My bondmate's familiar came to me rather than standing by his master. Eleni boxed me in on the other side. My bondmate stood at my back.

"It's done. There isn't anything you can do about it now," my father said.

"You let my mother be murdered! And Logan!"

"He was a waste anyways. You will make a far better queen than he ever would've a king."

"You disgust me."

Delrik stepped forward. "We can't let the relic fall into Hadeon's hands. You don't know the chaos that he'll release. I've seen it. You don't want that in the realm."

"He's assured me nothing will come to Laeto Selva."

"And you believe him?" Delrik asked.

Delrik reached out with his shadows towards my father. "Katuri, I'm sorry, but he is a liability. We can't let him wander free. Especially knowing he has willingly helped Hadeon."

"I know," I said.

"We'll have Eleni and Drake guard him for now."

"You can't lock me away. I'm the King!"

"You are a liar and a killer," Delrik said. "And you will be handled as such."

Delrik took a step closer to the throne, closer to my father. When the shadows reached him, Delrik's whole body seized.

"You will not touch me. I am the King of Laeto Selva of the Forest Fae. You will bow to me."

Delrik's knees made a sickening crack as they collided with the floor. Evren rushed toward her bondmate. Kairos struck out at her, the conduit flowing from the floor into her feet and forcing her to bow at his unspoken command.

At first, her body relented to my father's compulsion. Her face was scrunched in agony.

Drake's wings pumped and he took off into the open rainforest, soaring higher and higher, away from the conduit-laced floor. He glided outside to the mezzanine attached to the throne room. I wasn't sure where he was going, but I knew he had a plan, a purpose. He wouldn't abandon us.

I wanted to reach for my friends, but there was nothing I could do. The memories of the pain of my father's compulsion flooded my senses. Even Eleni cowered away from my father, but she stood in front of Nyla, guarding her alongside Knox.

But then, I saw it. That telltale glimmer of a ruby. With great effort, Evren slid her palm along the floor, reaching her hand out in front of her. She spread her fingers along the conduit on the floor. Then she lifted her head and smiled. The shadows shared between her and Delrik leaped from Delrik to her. Delrik's incredible speed must have gone through the bond too with how quickly they moved. Her eyes shifted to the deepest onyx. In the blink of an eye, she was standing next to my father with the Ring of Teris glowing brightly.

"You shouldn't have attempted to over power me. Your compulsion is nothing compared to my strength. And now, it's mine." Evren's voice shook the walls with its power.

Delrik was released from the compulsion and he collapsed forward on their hands, panting heavily.

It was as if Evren was draining the life from him. Kairos slowly slunk down to the dais, a hand pressed to his head.

"What have you done?" he asked in a strained rasp.

"I've only taken what you've so generously given me. And now, I'm going to give it to your daughter, because she has been and will always be more worthy than you to possess such extraordinary magic."

Drake reappeared. His hefty body landed on the crumbled edge of the balcony. Rocks fragmented beneath his talons. He filled the entire throne room. Drake's tail started in one corner and his elongated body wrapped around the perimeter. His colossal head hoovered above Garren and me, glaring down at my father. The whole room vibrated with his fury.

My father was surrounded by raw power and an imposing sea dragon. To my father's credit, he looked terrified at the beast my bondmate's familiar had become.

Drake lunged forward, his teeth clamping down on my father's leg. He howled in pain.

"Do you want me to end him, Little Flower?" Garren asked through our bond. I looked to my left. *"I'm leaving it up to you. I will do whatever you ask."*

"I have a better idea."

I looked to Evren—my friend and my sister. She smiled affectionately at me, those black eyes gleaming. Then she slipped the Ring of

Teris off her finger. She held it out to me. It was an offering. It was the best gift she could have ever given me. My father's power had held me down in fear for so long. And now she was handing it to me on a silver platter. He'd never have control over me ever again.

When she dropped the jewel into my waiting palm, the strength thrummed as it made contact with my skin. The ring moved on its own accord and slipped onto the middle finger of my right hand.

Drake lifted my father and dropped him in front of me.

"Your stupid lizard bit me!" he yelled, examining his rather shallow wounds.

"Well, you shouldn't have tortured my friends. Or called him a lizard. He doesn't like that."

Drake bumped my shoulder with his elongated snout.

"I can do whatever I want. I am the *king*!"

He gathered himself up and brushed off his royal attire. He was leaning heavily to one side.

"You are no longer the king. I am relieving you of that duty starting now," I said.

"You have no power to do so."

"*I* have no power?"

I opened the bond back to Garren and before I could even ask, my bondmate surrendered it all back to me. All *our* power. All *our* strength. The draw down the bond between us was intense, seeking more and more power from him. Garren gave every ounce of power he possessed as he poured it into my soul. A cyclone of water and thorns swirled overhead, darkening the throne room. Holding both the water and earth elemental power, a power gifted to us from the Powers Above, and the powers captured within the Ring of Teris, I had never felt stronger.

My once moss-green eyes flashed teal and Garren's scaled trailed down my fingers that formed talons. Wolf fangs elongated.

"*I* have no power?" I repeated to my father. "No, Father. It is you who are powerless this time." I swear he smiled a deadly smile. With my father's compulsion powers in my veins, I forced him back to his knees, bowing at the queen of Laeto Selva and the Forest Fae.

"I love you so much, Little Flower," Garren said into my ear. He was pressed against my back, waiting for what I needed of him.

"Did you want to finish him?" I asked over my shoulder.

"Of course not. I surrender all my powers to you forever and always. You use them as you wish."

He pressed his lips to my neck.

I turned my slitted gaze to Drake. "Drake, would you do the honor?"

Drake grabbed the king by the bloody leg and tossed his body into the air. Kairos screamed in agony and fear. Then, my bondmate's faithful, handsome, powerful familiar swallowed him down in a single gulp.

FORTY-TWO
NYLA

I mastered my breathing and kept my face neutral as I pulled Desmund through the maze of hallways back to his bedchamber. We had to go the long way due to the fire damage. I needed to talk to him alone. We'd left everyone back in the throne room to deal with the aftermath of Drake eating King Kairos whole. I wasn't going to lie, I was happy he was gone. Though, I'm sure Drake's stomach would be upset later on. Nazneen pushed Desmund and me to the door and whispered that she and Evren would take care of Katuri for the night.

I led Desmund through the door and closed it behind us. The lock sounded with a resigned click. I pressed my forehead to the cool wood. I could feel him waiting behind me. He was less than three feet away. His essence filled the room. I silently thanked him for his patience. I wasn't sure what to say yet. I'd poured my heart out in confession to Katuri rather than saying it directly to Desmund. Memories swam in my mind—his caring touch, his gentle words, his calming strength. He wasn't a killer like his father. I knew it deep in my bones, and I'd defended him. I would *always* defend him.

I turned to see Desmund watching me with raw openness on his face. A face I knew but didn't know at the same time. I'd held him at arm's length for the longest time when we'd first met. I didn't want to make the same mistake again.

I let my eyes wander over his true form. He was taller, broader, bigger in every sense of the word. I quickly diverted my dirty mind. He literally just revealed the biggest secret ever, and all I can think about is how badly I want to jump him.

A half-hearted laugh spilled from my lips, and I covered my mouth with the back of my hand. Those deep red eyes were steady on my face. The tips of my pointed High Fae ears burned with the intensity of his gaze. I wasn't afraid. I was aroused. Powers Above. I rolled my eyes.

The corner of his mouth tilted up into a half-grin.

I knew, at this precise point in time, I was exactly where I was supposed to be. And so was Desmund. Our paths were fated to cross. My heart began to beat faster.

"I think I've been waiting for you," I said.

Vortex of his crimson eyes.

"What?"

"My whole life, I've been in limbo, waiting. I just didn't realize it. And for the first time ever, my future has been unclear until now. Or so I thought. I've been seeing you in my visions for years. With your glamor gone, it's obvious. I've been waiting for *you*, Desmund."

I had wild, primal, and fierce feelings for him. I loved it. Every part of it. And I loved him. There was no one else in this realm or the next. There had never been and there never would be again. Desmund was mine, and I was his.

"But you know nothing of my past," he said, his face clouded.

"But I know your future. I can see it. Ever since you removed your glamor. I see you. The true you. Nothing from your past matters now."

I pressed my palm to his chest and flashed a vision into his mind. Desmund, in his true form and a smile on his handsome face, holding my hand as we faced the future together.

His mouth tipped into a sexy smirk.

The need to touch him everywhere overwhelmed me, and I stepped into his arms, where he enveloped me in an embrace. With his new height, I barely came up to his chest. I brushed my lips against the coarse fabric of his shirt, frustrated that I couldn't touch his skin. His hand ran up my arm and around to the front of my throat possessively. He cupped my chin and lowered himself to my level. Then he crashed his mouth ravenously into mine. Abruptly ending the kiss, he pulled back to look down at me.

"You don't deserve someone like me dragging you down."

He tried to back away, but I reached up and bracketed his face with my hands. "I don't care what you have gone through. You are my future. We are the future."

He closed his eyes and rested his forehead against mine. After several deep breaths, he said, "Good. I'm glad you feel that way. Because

I don't think there is really anything that's strong enough to stop me."

He kissed me with all his heart. He's kissed me before, but not like this. Not like I was his every breath. It was frantic and pleading. It was consuming and giving all at the same time. It was begging for forgiveness and asking for acceptance of who he really was. He ran his hands from my shoulders down to my waist like he was committing every part of me to memory in case I decided to turn and run.

"Unless you tell me to stop," he said.

"No." I shook my head side to side. I would never tell him to stop. I pull his mouth back down to mine.

"What if I hurt you?"

"You couldn't, even if you tried."

FORTY-THREE

NYLA

"Tell me to stop," he said.

I pulled the ties of my dress and let it drop to the floor, leaving me in only a breast band and underwear. "No."

"I don't want to hurt you."

"You couldn't, even if you tried." He kissed me again. "Wait!"

He immediately stepped back, with a dejected look on his face. "I knew it."

I laughed again. I wrapped my arms around his waist. "We should probably shower."

I ran a finger across his cheek and showed him the soot and ash.

"Good point. Yes, definitely a shower."

I stood on my toes and kissed the corner of his mouth. My breasts pressed high in my breast band as my breaths grew heavy. I couldn't help it. He was making me feel everything and we hadn't even done anything yet.

"Are you going to yell at me?"

Was he referring to lying to me this whole time? Honestly, I wasn't mad at all. I understand why he hid his true identity. I probably would have eventually looked past his appearance since he'd saved my life. But if I had known he was Hadeon's son, I don't think I would've given him a chance to prove himself.

"Would you like me to yell at you?" I asked.

My heart began to race in my chest blocking out everything else. I only focused on Desmund.

"Maybe later," he said.

The smile that I knew from weeks of looking at his handsome face came to his perfect mouth, but it was punctuated with sharp teeth. Oh dear. Those could get dangerous.

I'd been going slow with him, at his pace. But tonight, I wanted all of him. I pressed my hands to his hard stomach and slowly pushed him backwards until we were both standing in the bathroom.

In one swift movement, he stripped his shirt over his head, revealing a chiseled chest and abdomen. I beckoned him closer with a curl of my finger.

Powers Above. My throat went dry. His body wasn't the only thing larger. I'd felt his cock before pressed against me during our many kisses. But now I wanted to hold it, and not only in my hands. A thick vein ran up the underside of him. A line of hair trailed from his navel down to the base. I licked my lips. I couldn't help it. He literally made me salivate.

Apparently I wasn't moving fast enough for his liking. Desmund took hold of my hips and guided me to the shower.

It wasn't an ordinary shower. No. This shower took up the majority of the wash room. Just as in the bedroom, there was a missing wall so that the rainforest was practically inside with us. Sleek teak wood lined the walls and floors. There was no door. Above our heads were several shower heads.

When Desmund turned the faucet on, freezing cold water drenched the two of us as if we were suddenly caught in a thunderstorm. I squealed and laughed. Thankfully, it didn't take long for the water to warm. Desmund curled his body down over me, his lips met mine, and he stole my breath. His considerable muscles were even larger in this form as he loomed over me. I didn't know where to look. Everything about him was beautiful. Especially his thick and heavy erection that was standing at attention, glistening with arousal.

There was a bar of soap sitting on a small shelf nearby. I brought it to Desmund's chest and began to lather him in suds.

"It's a shame you're so dirty," I said.

"Hmm. Terrible, terrible shame."

His cock jumped between us as my soapy hands roved his delicious body, wiping away all the soot from the day.

"Fuck. Do you know how amazing you look?"

"I do?"

"I hate that you felt you ever had to hide yourself from me?"

He didn't answer. I could feel him tensing.

"You never—ever—have to hide yourself from me. Ever again. Do you hear me?"

His hands went to either side of my face and he lowered his head to mine. His lips ghosted over mine.

"I promise, I will never hide myself from you ever again."

Powers Above, my damned knees buckled.

"Now, let me wash you so you can teach me some new things," he said.

He gave me a quick peck on the lips then turned me. He began massaging soap into my hair, being sure that every last bit of dirt and debris was gone. He scrubbed at my shoulders, and back, then lower, making sure I was clean all the way down to my ankles. Then he tapped my hip, silently asking me to turn around to face him. He worked his way back up. His mouth followed his hands.

Once he was finished, he nudged me backwards. There was a low bench that spanned the length of the wall. I sat in the middle with my hands behind me. I pushed my chest forward. When Desmund's eyes flared, I parted my legs for him, showing him how much I wanted him.

"Can I put my mouth on you?" he asked. "I've been dying to know what you taste like."

"You don't have to ask permission. I already told you, you can have any part of me."

I let my knees fall a little further open. Desmund dropped to his knees so fast, I felt the wood splint beneath them. Then he dragged his tongue from my center up to my clit. I dropped my head back.

"I thought you said you'd never done this before."

His response was to suck, hard, on my clit, making my hips jump off the bench. He grabbed my hips and pushed me back down. He held me there, feasting on me relentlessly until a climax clawed out of me.

He stood, pulling me with him so that we were chest to chest. With our size difference the shower probably wasn't the safest place to have sex for the first time. Proving my point, he turned us so my back was to the wall and my feet slipped from beneath me. Thank the Powers he caught me.

I couldn't help the laugh that burst from me. "We should probably do this in bed."

He smiled and nipped at my jaw. "It's probably for the best."

"I'd hate to break you on your very first time."

"You can break me into a million pieces anytime you please."

He reached behind me and turned the water off before gathering a fluff towel and wrapping it around my body. I snuggled into the plush material and patted my skin dry.

I took his hand and led him to the bedroom again. I stood and put my hands on my hips, looking him up and down.

"What?" he asked.

"Lose this," I said, tugging the towel he'd draped over his hips. I was greedy for him. I wanted all his weight on top of me. "I need to touch you again."

"Nyla..."

"Now," I demanded.

He dropped the towel with a dramatic gesture, sending it flying across the room. The back of his knees hit the bed, and he sat.

I refused to tear my gaze from him. My lips still tingled from his smooth skin.

He scooted back and I climbed over him, so I was sitting on his lap. His hands found my ass and his fingers dug into the flesh. Even sitting in his lap, I had to look up at him.

In a fluid movement, he flipped us so that I was on my back splayed across his bed and he was hovering above me. There would be no going slow, no teasing touches and kisses like before.

"Are you sure about this?" he asked.

A shiver rippled down my spine. "Yes," I whispered.

"I don't want to hurt you, Nyla."

"You won't hurt me. You could never hurt me."

A muscle twitched in his jaw. Anticipation hung thick in the air. Panting, he held himself off my body with his powerful arms. He lifted his hips, and I guided his cock to my entrance. The head of his cock pressed at my entrance.

"Like this?"

"That's perfect, Desmund." I dropped my head back as his thick head pushed into me. He paused when just the head of his cock was nestled inside my walls.

"Powers Above," he said reverently. "Nyla. It's so tight."

"We haven't even gotten to the good part yet."

"Fuck, I don't know how long I will last if you feel even better than this."

I swiveled my hips so that he sank in a little deeper.

He groaned as he closed his eyes and dropped his head into the crook of my shoulder. Steadily, he pushed into me, inch by glorious inch. I lifted my knees closer to my chest.

"Oh fuck," I cried.

He stopped, giving me a moment (or five) to adjust to his size. I looked down at where we were joined and Powers Above, he was only halfway inside me. I let out a choked laugh and forced myself to relax. My knees dropped as I gripped his ass and urged him deeper. I was beyond full. The pressure was incredible. I'd never felt anything better in my life. He was seated inside me to the hilt. His body shook with the effort of holding back. His breaths were coming sharply through his nose.

"So perfect," he sighed.

He was. He stretched and filled me. I was so fucking full, and it was incredible. He dropped his forehead to mine and I brushed his damp hair from his forehead, careful to not touch his horns.

"These have potential for some fun," I teased.

He growled low. "Nyla, the thought of you riding me, taking exactly what you want like that is about to send me over the edge."

He looked as if he was about to explode right then and there.

"Take a deep breath," I told him.

"Nyla, you just feel so good," he moaned.

I swiveled my hips, and his eyes rolled to the back of his head. "If you keep doing that, I'm not going to last longer than a few minutes."

"That's alright. I'm sure I can have you ready for round two in no time at all."

His intuition took over and he began to move. It took several minutes to learn each other's rhythm. We moved together, our bodies working together as one.

My climax was building. Starting from the warmth in my toes, it curled up, up, up. A wall holding back. Then my orgasm exploded, ripping through my body like hurricane force winds. I clung to him as my whole body writhed around him.

The moment I clenched around him, Desmund exploded inside of me. His whole body went taut as he came and a roar ripped from deep within him.

My nails dung into his shoulders and back. Waves and waves pulsed through me in aftershocks. Desmund worshipped my body with kisses as the best orgasm I'd ever had shifted my entire view of the world.

"You're a fast learner." I remembered the first time I said those words to him. It seemed ages ago.

He smiled. "I have a great teacher."

His breathing steadied and deepened as his powerful body drifted to sleep as he was still inside of me.

FORTY-FOUR
DESMUND

I woke with my arms wrapped around Nyla's waist, my head resting on her lower abdomen. I tipped my chin up slightly to look at her. She looked so peaceful. I'd never slept so soundly before. Knox was curled up between my feet. I didn't want to wake her. Not yet. She needed the sleep. It was still dark outside. I could feel my sore muscles from all the physical labor of cleaning up after the fire yesterday. Even my mind was drained from being outed by King Kairos and then him being eaten by Drake.

Nyla didn't want to miss the chance to offer her condolences to Katuri, despite the discomfort of my background hanging over us all. I knew we had to be up before the sun this morning, but I reveled in Nyla's presence a bit longer.

I'd replaced my glamor before we left my room. While we all knew who I was now, I didn't want all the staff thinking there was a fiend walking amongst them. The last thing we needed was more chaos to ensue. If I stood side by side with a fiend, it would be obvious I wasn't one, but without that reference, people would assume.

As the sun rose, the burial service for Katuri's mother and brother took place. Nyla and I hadn't seen anyone on our walk to where the ceremony was being held.

Marselina stood apart from the group. Her head was solemnly bowed as Queen Nefali and Prince Logan were wrapped in woven palm fronds and lowered into the ground. She'd hardly spoken a word yesterday, but she also hadn't hesitated in jumping in to assist. I couldn't imagine how she was feeling. I knew nothing of her relationship with Logan. He was haughty and obnoxious, but I'd never seen him act cruel to Marselina or any of the staff. He may have pretended to follow in his father's footsteps, but based on how Marselina was mourning, he appeared to not be as ruthless behind closed doors.

The head priestess from the temple was mumbling prayers over the bodies and preparing them for their final trip into Evermere. Flowers and ferns surrounded their linen-wrapped bodies. I knew the priestesses spent the majority of the night making sure everything was in order. People from all over the city had come and gone, too, leaving behind small tokens of their love for their queen and prince. Bronze coins to hand sewn dolls lay all around them.

"The goddess earth blessed us with this life, and now we will return the gesture. Allow the bodies of our great prince and queen to replenish the earth and heal our kingdom from the tragedy of the fires," the head priestess intoned.

That was all. No long speeches or eulogies. I preferred it that way, honestly. We would all wind up in Evermere in the end. Or at least, they all would. Me, I wasn't so sure.

Every dark remnant of my soul, if I even had a soul. Did demons have souls? I didn't think so. I'd been around fiends my whole life. There was no way they had souls. And I looked closer to a fiend than fae. Did that mean I wouldn't be in Evermere in the afterlife, but rather in the Void?

My arms encircled Nyla's waist, my chin resting on her shoulder. Her fingers curled into my hands. I'd never experienced the loss of a parent. I'd wanted nothing to do with my parents. And Nyla's parents left her at the temple. But to have someone you loved, even if you weren't on the best of terms, ripped away from you. It would hurt. I felt empathy for Katuri. In a matter of hours, her entire family was gone and she'd been thrust into queendom.

Nyla and I stood there, our bodies pressed together. All the fear and mistrust and darkness from my past and my future were settled with her in my arms. She was a beacon, a lighthouse in this dangerous world. I had relied on myself, but now the fates had given me Nyla. Together. Forever. And even if that forever wasn't meant to be in Evermere, I'd go to the Void knowing that I'd had a chance to love her for as long as I could.

Using her earth magic, Katuri erected a large stone from the ground, surrounded by vines and leaves. A burial site worthy of a queen and her son. I watched the bodies one last time as Katuri's magic covered them in the earth tomb.

"So much death," Evren said with heavy sadness.

"It's only the beginning," Nyla said.

I nodded. "War is coming."

"It's already here," Delrik said.

Garren and Katuri were seated on the dais. Garren had his head in Katuri's lap, staring up at the ceiling, and one foot hung off the edge. Katuri mindlessly ran her fingers through his blond hair. The juxtaposition of their air of casualness amidst the crumbled ruins of the balcony and charred trees was oddly comforting.

"So, are we just going to ignore the fact that there is literally a demon in our presence?" Garren quipped, breaking the silence.

His eyes darted to find me. I was sitting on the floor with my knees bent. Nyla was nestled between my legs. Knox, who was sitting sentry at my back, released a grumble. In return, Eleni's hackles rose. Knox swiped a paw out, knocking Eleni off balance. He was already bigger than her again. It hadn't taken long for him to resume his enormous size. Nyla had told me that the stronger her powers were, the stronger her familiar was.

"I have a feeling you've already made a few assumptions. I doubt anything I say will change your mind," I said.

Garren and Delrik were quiet, watching each other with unspoken conversation. The best friend pair had a unique connection, more as if they were brothers than anything.

It was Delrik who spoke first. "Why don't you start by telling us who you are. Then we will go from there."

"You already know who I am. Kairos wasn't lying. I am Hadeon and Elenora's son."

"Speaking from experience, you aren't always who people say you are. Just because you came from Hadeon and Elenora doesn't mean you are a copy of them. Or are you? Is that why you're here? As a spy? Are you here for the relic?" Delrik asked, but there wasn't any anger or blame in his voice.

Nyla had told me Delrik knew what it was like having strangers decide they knew exactly who you were before you even showed your face. I'd even assumed, upon seeing him that first time in all his darkness, that he was someone I didn't trust.

"No, but yes at the same time? I don't really know. I was never asked to relay information back to my father. I'm basically an errand boy. Kairos and my father had a working relationship, but I don't know any details other than the cryptic messages in the letters I carry. And I had no knowledge of the relics and how they were a part of my father's plan."

"How many times have you been here in Laeto Selva?"

"Five or six, maybe?"

Nyla lifted her chin to look at me up over her shoulder. "That's how you knew Logan."

I nodded. "Yes. Logan and I spent time together in the past. I don't think that means I knew him per se."

"Did you know Nyla was a seer when you took her?" Delrik asked.

"I didn't. I saw you guys fighting the fiends in the valley in Baxmar. I knew you were powerful, maybe even elementals, but I didn't know about her being a seer."

"Desmund saved my life. That is all you need to know about my time before we arrived," Nyla said. "You can pepper him with all the questions you want, but in the end, he is here to stay. If you want me to be part of this family you've built, then you get Desmund too."

If I was Nyla's calm, then she was my controlled chaos. We were in perfect balance, and I didn't want to ever live without her.

Nazneen clapped her hands. "Well said. Desmund, welcome to the family."

FORTY-FIVE
KATURI

It's been three days since the forest fire ravaged my home. I'd wallowed in pity the day of my mother and brother's funeral. I hadn't had a wonderful relationship since I'd been parted from them at such a young age. I think I was mourning the possibility of what we could have had since we'd been reunited. I'd never know what the future would have held if my father hadn't sacrificed them in his idiotic idea of saving his kingdom. After a day, I picked myself up and began the task of learning the ins and outs of Laeto Selva.

Garren picked up a charred piece of metal and then dropped it back onto the waste pile. "We have so much to do. How are we going to get this all cleaned up?"

Thankfully, it appeared that most of the homes surrounding the palace were spared. Only the west side of the palace had been burned. The beautiful thing about the forest is the regrowth. Fire and wind could do their best to tear it down, but it always returned, brighter and better than before. Just like I would. I'd been knocked down and had my family ripped from me, but I would build my kingdom back up with Garren by my side. I was queen of the Forest Fae and Garren was my king.

We'd spent the morning focusing on cleaning up the western side of the palace and helping to relocate those displaced from their homes. Evren, Nyla, and even Marselina, had stepped up to catalogue injuries, losses, and who could help others. They made sure no one was left without a roof over their heads and food in their bellies.

I took Garren's hand and led him past the temple and toward the throne room. Nazneen had Nyla's arm looped with hers. We were heading to the 'war room' to begin planning our next steps in finding the remaining relics. The Relika Stone was in a pouch around Delrik's neck. Cattleya's Key was safely beneath the temple. We'd gone through so much in such a short period of time and I still felt we were nowhere closer to reaching our end goal.

I pushed the grand doors to my new throne room open and froze on the spot.

Arik Hanover sat sprawled on my throne, one leg slung over the arm, the other twirling a knife. The last time I'd seen him, he was knocking on Evermere's door, too close to death. He'd helped us rescue Delrik from Noirdan.

He stood and causally brushed non-existent dust off his clothes before he made his way down the dais. He bowed five feet away from me.

When he lifted his head, his face was bright with a smile. "Queen Katuri. Congratulations on your ascension."

GLOSSARY

ABERRATION - the ability to distort sound

AFFINITY CELEBRATION - a weeklong celebration marking the day the War Across the Sea ended and the legion returned home.

AMPLIFYING STONE - a rare stone that helps concentrate one's magic and magnifies it, typically used among healers and seers.

ASHLYRA (ash-lie-ra) - the physical, mental, and emotional tie between bondmates made even more powerful through the blood binding ritual. Also used as an endearment.

ASTRAL PROJECTION - the ability to project oneself from the physical body into a different space in varying degrees.

ATALA (at-a-la) - the elemental Fae's shifted form.

AVE SAL - Hello

BLINK - the ability to move from one location to another instantly.

BLOOD BINDING - a ritual performed between two magical beings to combine their lives, souls, and magic.

BLOODTHORN - a poisonous herb that can be used to suppress magical powers.

BONDMATES - two halves of one soul or spirit

BOTO ENCANTADO - also referred to as encantado; a mythical creature native to the rivers of the Forest Fae Territory. They shift between a river dolphin and a humanoid form. They prefer warm waters. They are known for protecting those they cared about and drowning those who double-crossed them by luring them to the water with their mesmerizing songs.

BRIGADEIRO - a dense chocolate ball similar to fudge, rolled in chocolate sprinkles.

CENTAUR - creature with the head, arms, and torso of a man and the body of a horse

CESSAN VOID - the space between realms, also referred to as the circle of dark hells

COMPULSION - the power to force someone to act or behave in a certain way, especially against one's conscious wishes, through touch.

DARKSTONE - one of the rarest materials in the realm, given to the mortals by the gods. The Sanctum in Aesira is built entirely of darkstone.

DOLOR (doe-lor) - an herb that grows in the wild across Illoterra and in parts of Quinterre. Used to make doloryum.

DOLORYUM (doe-lor-ee-um) - a powerful drug made from the dolor herb. If ingested, it has a deadly effect. If crushed and added to a carrier oil, the aroma temporarily paralyzes and sedates. It is commonly used among healers to treat patients with painful injuries.

DI-GARA (die-gar-a) **NEVE**(nee-v) **ROTH** (raw-th) **VAR** (var). **CONSORS** (con-sore-s) **PAR** (par) **RIKNI** (rik-nye). **KAJ-FAR** (ka-j-far) **ATO** (ah-tow) **UN ISLA** (oon-is-la) - the ancient chant done by the priestess to finalize the blood binding ritual. Your souls are bound as one. Bound to each other and bound to the gods. A bond not even broken by death.

DRIYAD - spirit of the forest.

ENERGY CHANNELING - the ability to channel energy from one person or object and transfer it to another.

ESSENCE SCROLLS - written by the gods and given to the mortals of Naśbar. Explains how the gods created the realm and all the creatures within it

EVERMERE - the final resting place of the mortals and gods, watched over by the god/goddess of spirits. The land of the mortal afterlife.

FAMILIAR - can be used as messengers.

THE FATES - the Powers Above or gods.

FIEND - a hellish creature created using dark magic. Originally created from Fae being transformed, but over time, the beasts gained the ability to breed on their own. They come in many shapes and sizes, including having wings.

GLAMOR - the ability to alter one's appearance to hide specific features. Example, pointed ears or an Ashlyra mark.

THE GREAT CHAOS - released by the guild during the Uprising and then banished by the gods.

KOSHMARA - demonic hell horses from the void.

LILURA STEEL - metal found in the mines under Mount Lendorr, lighter than any other metal

MIND MANIPULATION - the ability to cause pain to another with one's mind.

MIND PROJECTION - the ability to change or influence one's thoughts.

MIND SHIELDING - protecting one's mind from intrusion. A skill anyone, with any level of magic, can learn.

MIND WALKING - the ability to see into someone's memories and thoughts.

POWERS ABOVE - the five elemental gods: the god of fire, the god of earth, the goddess of water, the goddess of spirits, and the goddess of air.

QUINTERRE - another name for the Western Continent use by the native High Fae kingdoms.

THE RELICS - five magical objects created by the gods as keys to the veils that connect the Mortal Realm of Naśbar to Aesira. The relics were hidden after the Uprising and the release of the Great Chaos.

RELIKA STONE - the relic from the goddess of air.

RING OF TERIS - magical ring created by the gods to contain Aluxyeras by stripping her powers. It has the ability to steal any powers used against its wearer and can be wielded as desired. Teardrop shaped ruby on a lilura steel band.

SANA CONSO LENIRE - 'heal, stitch, soothe' in the ancient language

SANCTUM - the center-most part of Aesira where the thrones of the gods sit.

SEER - the ability to receive visions of the past, present, and future.

SENSORY DEPRIVATION - the ability to remove the senses of someone.

SHADOW WALK - the ability to move from one place to another through a portal created by Alux's shadow magic.

SHIELD WEILDER - the ability to create a shield of protection from physical attacks.

SUPREME ELEMENTALS - Elemental powers aren't always passed within bloodlines. Most of the time, the powers skip many generations or are given to another who has been found worthy by the gods

TELEKINESIS - the ability to move things with one's mind.

TELEPATHY - one that can see thoughts.

TELEPORT - the ability to move from one place to another.

THE UPRISING - 700 years ago

THE VEILS - portals from Aesira into the Mortal Realm of Naśbar used by the gods to cross back and forth between realms. Accessed either with the blood of a god or a relic. They were closed after the Uprising and the release of the Great Chaos.

WAR ACROSS THE SEA (Also known as The Great War)

WARBLADE OF SILVERLIGHT - made of Lilura steel and impregnated with the wisdom of the Powers Above. Mountain Fae believed it brought guidance to the one that wielded it.

WISPS - threads throughout the realm connected like a spider-web. They are all around the realm, connecting everything together like a giant web. Wisps can be used by those with the proper magic to gather information, perform tasks, and guide those they desire.

About the Author

Megan L. Adams is a stay-at-home mom and military wife from Washington DC. She earned a Bachelor's degree in Biology from North Georgia College and State University but has found a passion in writing over the last few years. She is a new indie author focusing on fantasy romance. Her books have been sold in the United States, Canada, and across the world. When she isn't writing, she's exploring local bookstores and historic libraries while sipping on a latte. She loves to take care of her many orchids and house plants, as well as spend time outside. Her best writing buddy, Toma, is a two-year-old golden retriever-husky mix. She also enjoys a good glass of wine and reading to her heart's content.

You can keep up with Megan on her social media and website.

Instagram @author_meganladams
TikTok @meganladams
www.meganladams.com

www.ingramcontent.com/pod-product-compliance
Lightning Source LLC
Chambersburg PA
CBHW060545310726
48982CB00009B/1377/J

* 9 7 9 8 9 8 9 9 3 2 7 2 6 *